Time to
Check Out

Also by Grant Michaels

A Body to Dye For
Love You to Death
Dead on Your Feet
Mask for a Diva

Grant Michaels

Time to Check Out

St. Martin's Press
New York

TIME TO CHECK OUT. Copyright © 1996 by Grant Michaels. All rights reserved. Printed in the United States of America. No part of this book may be used or reproduced in any manner whatsoever without written permission except in the case of brief quotations embodied in critical articles or reviews. For information, address St. Martin's Press, 175 Fifth Avenue, New York, N.Y. 10010.

Library of Congress Cataloging-in-Publication Data

Michaels, Grant.
    Time to check out: a Stan Kraychik mystery / by Grant Michaels.
        p.   cm.
    ISBN 0-312-14434-2
    I. Title.
PS3563.I2715T56   1996
813'.54—dc20   96-6870
                                                        CIP

First Edition: August 1996

10   9   8   7   6   5   4   3   2   1

For conchs and tourists, without whom
Key West would be just an island.

Every aspect of this book—from its origin, through the writing, through the many revisions, right up to the signed contract—every step seemed to present a new hurdle for me, and I owe thanks to many people for seeing me through an extremely challenging period.

First and foremost, to my friends, thanks from my heart and soul and bones. You continue to nourish me.

Thanks also to Carole Anne Meehan and the Boston Center for the Arts.

Thanks to Keith Kahla for a second look.

And special thanks to a group of people unique to this book. Like my hero, I had naïvely assumed Key West was a kind of lost tropical world, a place of retreat to a quieter, more sensible time. I hardly expected the fizzy, dizzy kaleidoscope of flora, fauna, and personality that awaited me there—enough to inspire a whole book! So here are my thanks to the "conchs":

To Paul Hause and Osmo Soljavirta, owners of Caroline Street Books, and the two people responsible for my first visit to Key West; to Walter Davenport and the Key West Gay Arts Festival for sponsoring that trip; to Mike Dively, who invited me to return to the island and write in his cottage; to Dale Kittle, who graced me with the same generosity for another visit there; to Bruce Peterson, who conducted my very first live radio interview, and where, uncensored, I casually uttered naughty nether words over the airwaves; to Serena Sorensen for her public enthusiasm for my work; to Vicki Roush for dubbing me her "new best friend" just hours after my first arrival in Key West; to Chuck Lamb for mixing the best 'tinis on the reef; to Tom Luna for his mercurial appeal; to Richard Browner for his stimulating company (and to Walt DeMilly for introducing us); to Dennis Beaver for his hospitality at the Tropical Inn and for my very first poker game; to Kelly Moore, Gerri Louise Gates, Dannie Smith Joiner, Mary Falconer, and the other actors in Bruce Peterson's company for embracing me as their backstage mascot; to Bill Woolf for always nagging me to get back to work; and most especially to Jackie Ritke, conch emeritus, whose paintings of Key West venture far beyond pretty parrots and little fish.

—G. M.
Boston, 1996

Time to Check Out

1

Everyone out there wants somebody dead.

You can admit it. You've thought about it too. Yesterday, today, or tomorrow, however fleeting or enduring, however naked or veiled, the desire lurks in all of us.

I gazed down from my guest house window. Lines of people passed by on Duval Street, in couples and singly, locals and tourists, stray cats and geckos, all out for a morning stroll along Key West's commercial way. And I knew that every living creature on that sidewalk had at some time or other, in whatever language their killer instinct spoke, hurled the same fatal directive toward friend, neighbor, relative, spouse, mouse, boss, or bug: Time to check out, doll.

Despite the air-conditioning in my dim little room, sweat oozed from my heat-swollen brain and trickled past my eyes down the side of my face, creating a salty rivulet that got waylaid by the stubble of four days' growth of beard. October in Key West meant a last tidal wave of heat and humidity—stifling, oppressive weather that exhausted as much during sleep as in the so-called waking hours. And with my hypersensitive skin, avoiding the sun was an all-day preoccupation.

I had driven south from Boston to escape a dreamy life that had gone haywire. My lover had been killed the previous summer. Like all accidental deaths, it was senseless. He had been crossing a busy street while distracted by the sheer romantic beauty of his hometown, Paris. A changing traffic signal had combined with a faulty brake line on a UPS delivery van (pronounced "ooh-pay-ess" in France), and my man Rafik was alive no more. Defunct.

For whatever it was worth, there was a consolation prize. UPS had made a landmark decision and had settled generously with a domestic partner. That is, me. They took full responsibility for the accident and awarded me a zillion francs, which converted at the time to roughly three and a half million dollars. Rafik's own extravagant life insurance from the ballet company left me another million. So I was, at least from my working-class perspective, rich.

But was I smiling?

I shaved my head and mustache to remind myself that life could change without warning at any time. Then I packed my summer togs, threw the bags into my Alfa Spyder (that's another whole story), and set off as the Widow Kraychik for what I'd hoped would be sanctuary: a quiet guest house in a quiet off-season resort town, where I could regain some sense of equilibrium and find my new self.

Nothing turned out as planned. I found myself all right, smack on the southernmost latitude of the whole continental United States, at the last stop on U.S. Highway One, the end of the line, Key West, the asylum reef.

But that morning I had more pressing business than to fret about happiness or its loss, or even about sunshine and humidity. I had to change guest houses. I was staying at a place called the Crow's Nest, a restored Victorian mansion on Duval Street, at the east end of town. The manager, an old biddy named Augusta Willits, had taken an instant dislike to me. Maybe I reminded her of someone else, a nephew gone bad or something. Whatever the reason, I'd been asked with nary an apology to "vacate the premises" because of "emergency repairs" to the building. Mind you, the place was in flawless condition.

I had just returned from breakfast when I found a note tacked onto the door of my room. It was penciled in a nasty scrawl: CHECKOUT TIME IS 11:00! It was only a little past the hour, and I didn't see the reason for such urgency. Key West was a resort town after all. People were on vacation. Things were a little more relaxed—weren't they?—especially off-season. From what I'd seen at the Crow's Nest, the housekeeping staff didn't even show up until late in the afternoon. Why the fuss over a few minutes?

I reminded myself that nothing mattered anymore. Besides, my next abode, the Jared Bellamy House, was even nicer, *and* they had approved of the stubble on my head and face—very butch for me—when I'd gone that morning to arrange for a room. My hair was already glistening with its natural coppery sheen. But I saw silver too, which hadn't been there before. Another rite of passage, I guess.

So I repacked my bags back into the Alfa's tiny trunk, then headed to the Crow's Nest office to turn in my room key, hoping perhaps to irk Augusta Willits one last time and demand a refund for all the inconvenience. But the office was empty. I called out a few times without an answer. Then I heard the muffled chirping of an electronic alarm clock.

Beep-beep-beep. Beep-beep-beep.

I couldn't locate it at first, then realized it was coming from down behind the counter. I peeked over and heard myself mutter, "Aw, Jesus."

Augusta Willits was crumpled on the floor. Her tightly braided white hair was in disarray, and she looked cyanotic.

Beep-beep-beep, went the clock. *Beep-beep-beep.*

I ran behind the counter to help her. She wasn't breathing, and she had no pulse. A small electronic alarm clock had been jammed far into her mouth. It continued its discreet signal that the time for something had arrived.

As I started dialing the police, a man came charging into the office from outside. He looked around fifty years old, with frizzy gray hair receding high into his scalp. He smoked a pungent imported cigarette. From the looks of his clothes and his scrawny sunburnt legs, he was a tourist, and though his eyes were concealed by opaque sunglasses, he looked furious.

"My room is in squalor," he railed. "It shall be cleaned immediately or I will leave these premises!" He spoke with a German accent. "Do you hear me?" he yelled. "Put down that telephone and clean my room at once!"

"Achtung," I murmured.

Beep-beep-beep, went Augusta Willits's mouth.

The police answered my phone call. I identified myself, then told them what I'd discovered in the guest house office. One minute later I hung up the phone. The German tourist leaned over the counter and saw Augusta's body. He removed his sunglasses and stared.

"There is here a problem?" he said.

"That's right," I said. "A problem."

Beep-beep-beep.

"Should she some help be having?" said the German.

"They're coming," I said.

"But now?" He looked nervous.

"For now," I said, "we wait."

"Why are you not helping?" he said.

"She's dead."

The German's eyes bugged out. "So!" he said. "Now I am leaving."

"The police are on the way," I said. "They'll want to talk to everyone here."

"No," said the German with another glance toward the dead woman. "I have business now of extreme urgency."

"If you go now, they'll only chase you down faster."

That settled his eagerness to flee.

Meanwhile, Augusta continued *beep-beep-beep*ing.

The police arrived within minutes. The investigating officer was one Lieutenant Jesus Maria Sanfuentes. The name barely fit on his ID badge. He was a handsome tawny-skinned Cubano with sleek black hair and a tough chunky build. His hands were meticulously manicured, and he exuded the air of someone who kept his body squeaky clean. Yet he seemed overly serious, as though his name obligated him to fix everything wrong with the whole rotten world.

First thing he did was order the German to extinguish his cigarette. Meanwhile, his assisting sergeant spied Augusta's body and whistled softly. Then we all went through the usual routine. Yes, I'd found the body. Yes, I'd made the call. No, I hadn't touched anything. I suddenly felt self-conscious about how I looked. I hadn't shaved that morning because I didn't care much what people thought of me. But with the police taking their reports, appearances meant a lot, everything maybe. And there I was, looking like a displaced terrorist.

Beep-beep-beep, went Augusta.

I told the lieutenant I was on vacation from Boston and was going to be staying at the Jared Bellamy House, which seemed to impress him. When the cops questioned the German, his name, Adolf Dobermann, caused mild surprise with the lieutenant.

"So, Mr. Dobermann," he said. "Finally we meet."

"Do I know you?" said Dobermann.

"Your name's been getting around the island."

Adolf Dobermann smiled, as if the cop had intended a compliment.

From his shirt pocket Sanfuentes produced a small metal tin. He slid open the top and sprinkled a few black granules into the palm of his hand, then popped them into his mouth. Within seconds the air around him filled with the combined scent of licorice and violets. Then the cop said to Dobermann, "You're the one who's been buying up property all over the island."

"My money is good," replied the German.

"Your money's fine," said the cop. "But we'd also like to keep Key West in American hands."

"How provincial," said Dobermann. "Are you a real estate agent?"

"No," said Sanfuentes.

"Then I do not understand why this matter we are discussing," said Dobermann. "Now, please, I have urgent business, just as you have business of your own, Herr Lieutenant." He made a sour face toward Augusta's body. "What a squalid situation!"

He went to leave, but Sanfuentes stopped him.

"You'll go when I say so," said the cop. "Tell me where you're staying."

Dobermann replied haughtily, "I am staying here, but my room is squalid."

Sanfuentes said, "Why aren't you in one of your own guest houses? I hear you bought up quite a few."

Dobermann said, "They are all squalid now." He seemed to like the word. "But when they are fit for habitation, they will provide an extravagant income. And what will your sarcasm earn for you, Herr Lieutenant?"

"That's a good question," said Sanfuentes. "I never thought of it."

The German twisted his mouth slyly. "Perhaps you should." He began to light another cigarette, but Lieutenant Sanfuentes stopped him.

Meanwhile I glanced around the office for signs of foul play, and I did notice something missing. Until that morning, a large painting had hung on the wall behind the counter, done by a local artist named Jeri Tiker. The work had struck me as fresh and original and amusing. I had even intended to find her studio and spend some of my blood money. But the painting was gone, and the wall was bare. I mentioned it to the lieutenant, who noted it in his report.

Adolf Dobermann remarked, "It is rare for Americans to appreciate good art."

"You remember the painting then?" I said.

"Yes," replied Dobermann. "I recall it well."

The cop said, "When did you see it last?"

"Early this morning," answered the German. "I departed for my breakfast at eight o'clock, and the painting was there on the wall."

"Are you sure about that?" said Lieutenant Sanfuentes with new interest.

"Oh, yes," said Dobermann. "I paid it much attention because the painting would soon belong to me."

"Ah," said Sanfuentes. "So you have it now?"

"No," said Dobermann.

"What happened to it?" said the cop.

"I should hardly know that!" said Dobermann, punctuating his words with a little snort.

The cop asked, "Did you also see Augusta Willits this morning?"

"Yes," said Dobermann. "And she was quite alive."

Beep-beep-beep, said the object of our discussion.

The lieutenant made another note in his report, served himself another helping of breath mints, then said offhandedly, "Maybe that painting is connected to this . . ." His eyes moved toward Augusta's body.

"My dear sir," said Dobermann, "that painting was art, while this woman, you will forgive me please, was wasting oxygen on the planet."

The cop answered quickly, almost defensively. "Augusta Willits was a true islander. She never left the reef."

"And how it showed!" said Dobermann with a derisive little bark—*Hei!*—like a jackal.

Beep-beep-beep! said the body, sounding more irate.

For their part, the cops really didn't seem overly troubled that Augusta Willits, their beloved old townie, was lying there dead, *beep-beep-beep*ing away behind the counter.

The medical examiner arrived, a local doctor who went about his business leisurely. He determined the cause of death to be asphyxiation by a foreign object caught in the victim's throat. Then, finally, he extricated the alarm clock from the dead woman's mouth and silenced its infernal beeping.

Adolf Dobermann said, "And now, please, I demand that you shall release me. I will confer with my attorney."

"Attorney?" said Sanfuentes. "Did I accuse you of anything?"

"I assure you, sir," replied the German, "the business with my attorney is of another matter entirely."

"In that case you can go," said the lieutenant. "Just don't leave town without telling me."

Then he released us both. Outside, Adolf Dobermann lit one of his strong cigarettes. He smoked it like a nervous little bird, puffing furiously but not inhaling. Then he pulled out a small cellular phone and made a call.

I got into my Alfa and drove to the Jared Bellamy House. The desk clerk there seemed delighted to see me, though he didn't recall meeting me earlier. Perhaps he was hallucinating. It wouldn't have surprised me. I'd been on Key West only twenty-four hours, and already I sensed that many islanders stumbled through the day assisted by some kind of perception-enhancer. Some stuck to basics, like vodka, while the more intrepid souls pioneered the psychopharmaceutical frontiers, braving the latest FDA-approved miracles in capsule, tablet, or ampule form.

My new room was spacious and comfortable and cool. If my cat Sugar Baby had been traveling with me, she would have shown her approval by springing onto the bed and affixing herself spread-eagle to the chenille bedspread, all four sets of claws seeking hospitality among the puffy cotton tufts. My lover Rafik would have sought a different kind of hospitality between the sheets. But Sugar Baby was back in New Jersey with my two nieces, enjoying exalted attentions I could never quite render. And Rafik was dead, wherever that was. Buck up, I told myself. You got money. You got your health. Keep going forward.

So I unpacked my bags, then lay down for a bit and tried to read a book I'd brought with me. It was a runaway best-seller, *Only the Dead Know*, by a writer named Edsel Shamb. I had missed its meteoric rise while I was shuttling back and forth to Paris, settling Rafik's estate and burying his remains. I'd hoped to read the book in Key West, on my so-called vacation. But it was no use that morning. The recent trauma with the dead woman had left me too restless to read, so I went out. Considering what I had witnessed an hour earlier, I was ready for some chemical assistance of my own.

2

On my walk down Fleming Street I passed an old storefront. On the upper façade, lettering from a previous enterprise seeped wraithlike through the recent coat of paint, indicating the place had once been a commercial laundromat called Sudsomania. But a new wooden shingle above the entrance advertised the current business as a travel agency called the FLEMING LEMMING. Had they intended the allusion to suicidal rodents high-diving off the White Cliffs of Dover? A sign in the window read: FREE TOURIST INFO. Maybe they could direct me to a good martini.

I opened the door and felt a wave of blessedly frigid if smoke-laden air. The interior was severely cramped by rows of towering shelves, as though the place was really a small warehouse in disguise. The tall shelving created long narrow passages running from the front to the back of the space. A woman was arranging things in the far back, along one of the passages.

Out front an old metal desk and a low filing cabinet created a barricade to the shelves and the rest of the space. Behind the desk a man sprawled lazily in a chair, smoking. His eyes were concealed by mirrored aviator sunglasses. He was tall and big-boned, powerful too, though a bit fleshy, with dark features that created an intense though somewhat dissipated masculinity. His face seemed fixed with an insolent pout, as though brooding was his favorite sport. He looked about thirty. He turned his head toward me as I entered, but went on addressing the woman in back.

"And what if we don't get the place, Laura?" he said. "What do we do then?"

"Whatever you want, Josh," she replied from within the rows of shelving.

"That's nice," said the man. Then he lowered the mirrored shades and winked at me. "Best damn wife a guy could hope for."

Laura called out, muffled by the storage racks. "What did you say?"

Josh called back, "We got a customer. Imagine that?" Then he lifted his sunglasses back up over his eyes.

Seconds later Laura emerged. Like Josh, she looked about thirty. She saw me and smiled quickly, a nervous insincere gesture. A pale blue satin ribbon kept her long blonde hair pulled back off her face. She turned to Josh. "Let's hope for the best," she said. "Everything I have is yours."

Josh replied dryly, "A good thing to remember."

"I can call my broker," said Laura. "I'm sure there's something she can free up in my portfolio."

Josh grinned. "See how easy it is when you agree?"

Laura looked my way again. She was tall, with a broad sturdy frame. Maybe it was the sheer physicalness of her body, the big bones and firm muscles, that I found vaguely appealing. She'd be a generous handful for any man. She smiled at me again, this time more warmly, and with an odd hopeful look. Had she caught my appraisal of her physiquelike figure?

"Can I help you?" she asked, finally.

"Where's the closest bar?" I said.

Josh laughed. "Here I was, ready to sell him a first-class round-the-world tour, and all he wants is directions." Then he said to me, "Try the Lemonade Stand. All the tourists like it."

"Well that's exactly what I am," I said.

"You're not dressed like one," said Laura.

It was true. Since my skin tolerated neither sun nor sunscreen, I protected it with poplin slacks and a long-sleeved shirt of gauzy white cotton. It was another unanticipated drawback of choosing Key West for rest and recuperation: the tropical sun.

Joshua asked me where I was from, and I told him Boston. Neither of them was impressed. Laura then formally introduced herself and her partner. She was Laura Hope, he Joshua Aytem. They owned the business together and, Joshua was quick to point out, had known each other since college days. Laura then asked me where I was staying. I told her, and that *did* impress both of them. Joshua even took off his sunglasses.

"If you're staying at the Jared Bellamy House," he said, "you've got money to burn." He licked his lips lightly.

Laura said, "And if you want a good cocktail, you should go to the Tool Box. The bartender is gorgeous."

Joshua flared. "Hey!"

Laura said, "It's true, Josh. And this man looks like he might be interested." She turned to me. "We like to help out the gay tourists, tell them where to go, and what to avoid. You are gay, right?"

I said I was.

Joshua said, "Well, I'd still have a drink with you."

Laura said quickly, "It's too early, Josh. And we have inventory to do."

Joshua dismissed her with a wave of his hand. "Fuck the inventory."

I sensed the glowing embers of their squabble might ignite at any moment, so I tried to douse them with an offhand remark. "How did you came up with the name for your business?"

Joshua said, "You like it? I thought it was a good way to tell the customers to take a flying leap." Then he laughed riotously.

Laura said, "It's probably killing the business."

I said, "Is this some kind of store too?"

"Hardly," said Laura with a laugh, her turn for a private joke. "We assemble our own souvenir packages for the tour groups, things like aloe cosmetics, T-shirts, sun visors, hats, books, postcards—anything related to Key West."

"Looks like quite an inventory."

"Yes," said Laura. "Tourists expect a lot. And then there's my private collection of first editions."

"Her scriptures," muttered Joshua.

Laura ignored him. "Do you read?" she asked me.

"I try," I said.

She said, "Have you read Edsel Shamb?"

"I have that new one, *Only the Dead Know*—"

Joshua cut in, "That's old already."

Laura continued to me, "Mr. Shamb lives here."

"Half the year," corrected Joshua. "The other half he's in New York or L.A."

"But he *writes* here," argued Laura. She turned to me again. "Do you have any idea what an early first-edition autographed Edsel Shamb goes for?"

"No," I said. I had no idea, nor did I care.

Joshua said, "It would pay for one night at the Jared Bellamy House, where you're staying." Then he added for emphasis, "During season."

The chirp of a cellular phone interrupted our forced banter. Joshua answered the call, and once he recognized the party, put his sunglasses back on, then got up from behind the old metal desk and went outside to continue talking in privacy.

Meanwhile Laura smiled pleasantly as she gave me directions to the Tool Box, the bar she had mentioned earlier.

For my part, I was ready to leave. Their bickering reminded me of work, where from the styling chair I attended every nuanced variation of every battle ever fought in the arenas of domestic strife. Besides, the more mundane matter of my thirst needed attention—slaking—and soon. So I excused myself to Laura and headed toward the door. But I was interrupted by Joshua coming back in.

"Wait for me," he said, waggling a fresh cigarette in his lips, like a tough guy. "I'll have a drink with you. I want to celebrate." Then he tossed his pack of cigarettes onto the desk and said to Laura, "Guess who that was."

"Your boyfriend," she replied as she lit one for herself.

"Don't get funny. Something big is about to break." He glanced toward me, gave a smirk, then turned back to Laura and murmured

11

softly, "Don't call your broker yet. We're going to be fine."

Laura gazed at Joshua and he returned her look. Perhaps it was the reflection of herself in his mirrored shades, but that odd sense of hope appeared on her face again.

Joshua said to me, "Would you mind waiting outside?"

I answered him breezily, "Let's do that drink another time."

Joshua's mirrors were still locked on Laura's eyes, and their feet shuffled restlessly, as though resisting a throbbing urge to do a fandango. "Keep your drink," he said to me. "When this deal comes through, I won't need anything from anyone ever again."

Funny, I had all the money in the world and I still couldn't say a thing like that.

I left the Fleming Lemming and continued down Fleming Street. A few blocks later I passed an art gallery called the Echo Me. It was an old house that had been gutted to create a cavernous open space inside. By the artwork displayed on the porch I realized the Echo Me Gallery was the home of Jeri Tiker, the artist who'd painted the large canvas in the office of the Crow's Nest, the one that had disappeared in conjunction with Augusta Willits's death. The door was open, so I went in to meet the artist.

Jeri Tiker was a spare young woman, almost boyish in looks. Her red hair was clipped short, at most seven-eighths of an inch. She had green eyes and a big smile. In fact, she was almost an exact masculine female version of me, especially with my recent slimness. (I had always carried fifteen or so extra pounds on my rump. My former fanny was robust and solid—"splendid ass" my lover used to say—while the rest of me, especially with my strong long Slavic legs, was pretty much in proportion. It was a natural healthy look that some people like. My lover sure did, when he was alive. But after his death I lost every one of my appetites, including my beloved food. So by the time I got to Key West I was downright gaunt. Coupled with the graying stubble on my scalp and face, I probably looked terminally ill.)

Jeri was painting at a table in the center of the gallery. Four huge overhead fans created a pleasant breeze, despite the lack of air-conditioning in the place. She was applying an opaque azure blue to a sweater worn by one of the subjects in her painting.

"Kind of warm for a sweater," I said.

She looked up from the table, and immediately registered our mutual similarities, the outward ones. She smiled. "You look warm yourself, in those clothes."

"My skin can't take the sun."

"What about sunscreen?"

"I'm allergic."

"Me too," she said, then resumed her painting. "Too bad we came here, eh, with all this sun? I'm from Wisconsin. We wear a lot of sweaters there."

"Just looking at that painting makes me warm."

"That's good," she said. "A physical response."

I surveyed the gallery walls, which resembled the inside of a gigantic kaleidoscope. Every one of Jeri Tiker's color-saturated paintings depicted people relating to one another. There were no still lifes, no staid portraits, no scenes. All the work possessed that rare quality of showing the outer person, and also what was under the skin: the wary droop of an eyelid, the angry curl of a finger, the bemused tilt of a head, the sensual curve of a leg. Every detail reflected some inner aspect of the subjects. And then everything was painted over and over and over again with dense, deep, vibrant color, without shadows of any kind, allowing the layers of pigment to create their own third dimension. So in addition to their internal psychological messages, the surfaces of Jeri's paintings offered a visual smorgasbord for the rods and cones of an ordinary mortal's eyes.

I asked her how she'd come up with the gallery's name.

She explained simply, "My paintings are echoes of me."

"It sounds like the Italian word *eccomi.*"

Jeri smiled again and nodded. "Here I am."

"Here you are," I said. "You know Italian?"

"I was at the American Academy in Rome for a while."

So had Rafik been, once upon a time. Go forward, I told myself.

I said, "Wasn't one of your paintings hanging in the office of the Crow's Nest?"

Jeri nodded. "*Dinner of Uncertainty.* It's for sale, if you're interested."

"I would be," I said, "but I have some unpleasant news."

"For me? I don't even know you."

"I'm just the messenger," I said.

"Who sent you?"

"Fate."

Jeri rolled her eyes, dismissing yet another wacko tourist.

I explained, "Your painting isn't there anymore, at the Crow's Nest."

Jeri put down her brush. "Since when?" she said.

"Since this morning. I was, uh, checking out, and I noticed the painting was gone."

"Damn him," she muttered.

"Who?" I said.

"Nothing," she said quickly. "Never mind."

"It's not that Dobermann fellow, is it?"

"You know him?" she said.

"He was at the Crow's Nest too."

Jeri said, "He'd better pay for that painting before he takes it back to Germany."

"You think he has it?"

Jeri explained, "He wanted *Dinner of Uncertainty*, but he didn't want to pay for it. He was too busy throwing his money at the real estate brokers. But from me he wanted a deal. I told him I didn't sell my art that way."

"Good for you," I said.

Jeri fumed, "Then that old bitch Augusta wanted me to pay *her* for letting me hang the painting in the office."

"Well, she won't be collecting anything now."

"Oh, you don't know her," said Jeri.

"I know that she's dead."

The gallery went still except for the ceiling fans whirling quietly overhead.

Jeri spoke softly. "I didn't mean to call her an old bitch just now."

"Why not?" I said. "It's true, even if she is dead. That woman made my first twenty-four hours in Key West miserable."

"She does that to everybody," said Jeri. "Did, I mean. She used to pray for a tidal wave to come and cleanse the island of depravity and moral vermin. That's what she called us—moral vermin. You are gay, right?"

"Yes," I admitted easily for the second time that morning.

Jeri went on. "Augusta was always hoping we'd be washed away so she could live here on her cozy little reef with the few worthy people she approved of."

"How could she run a guest house on Key West and still hate gay people?"

"It was her son's place," said Jeri as she picked up her brush and resumed painting. "Peter Willits was her son. If you stay here long enough you'll hear about him. A legend in his own time was the great Peter Willits."

"In what way?"

Jeri sniggered. "He collected property. And people."

"Did you know him?"

"He was kind of two-faced," said Jeri. "I guess some people get so trapped in the closet it carries over into the rest of their life."

I said, "If his mother was any indication, the guy needed a double life."

"Well," said Jeri, "the battle continues. Augusta contested her son's will."

"Who won?"

Jeri paused before saying, "I don't know yet."

"Does it affect you?"

She put down her brush again. "If Augusta loses her case, I inherit this gallery."

"Just like that."

"Just like that," said Jeri.

"So Peter Willits wasn't so two-faced after all."

Jeri said, "Maybe he was feeling magnanimous when he made his will. Who knows? Peter hardly knew me, but he did know my work. Maybe that's why he left me this place. But now that Augusta's dead, I wonder what happens."

I told her the battle would continue in court even though both parties were dead.

"Really?"

"Nothing stops the law," I said. "Not even death."

Jeri's eyes changed from open and friendly to morbidly curious. She almost looked like one of the characters in her paintings. Then she said, "How did Augusta die?"

"She choked," I said. I didn't divulge the particulars of the death scene. I knew the police appreciated that, especially since a tiny detail could often expose a killer.

"Choked on what?" said Jeri.

"Uh, time will tell," I said evasively.

"Was she murdered?"

I nodded.

Jeri said bluntly, "Adolf did it and took the painting."

I advised her to talk to the police if she had evidence to support what she said.

"Who needs evidence?" said Jeri. "And who needs the police?"

"I need a drink," I said, changing the conversational tack. "And someone recommended a place called the Tool Box. Do you know it?"

"You'll do all right there," said Jeri. "Just make sure you spell it right."

"Spell it?" I said.

"Yes," said Jeri, then she spelled it: *tulle.*

"Like a ballerina's tutu," I said, and felt another twinge of loss for Rafik, only a twinge.

Jeri said, "The original owner was a dancer from New York."

I asked her, "Do you go there much?"

"Is that an invitation?"

"Sure," I said. I liked her already. She was spiky and direct.

Jeri said, "I don't usually go to bars, and definitely not this early in the day. I've got work to do."

"But you do drink?"

She guffawed. "You *have* to drink in this town. Otherwise you'll die of fright."

"Is it so bad here for you?" I said.

"It wasn't what I expected," she said. "I thought I was coming to a place that welcomed artists. A warm place, in weather and attitude. But the real local industry is tourism. If I could paint a hundred parrots a week, I'd sell them all."

"Instead you're painting sweaters."

Jeri said, "That's what I feel, so that's what I paint."

"Here?" I said, indicating the island reef at large, America's own tropical paradise. "You feel sweaters here?"

Jeri touched her temple. "I feel them here." Then she patted her delicate left breast. "And here."

I told her I'd come back another time. "I like your work," I said. "I have some money, and I don't like parrots."

"Then we agree on the important things."

I left the Echo Me Gallery and continued on my way to Duval Street where I did buy myself a frozen Bacardi lemonade and sipped it illegally while strolling along the sidewalk. It didn't quite hit me the way I needed, and I knew there was only one thing that would ease my jangled nerves from the stressful discovery of Augusta Willits's body. I needed a frosty cold martini, served up, with a twist. That would fix things just right. And what better place to find one than the Tulle Box?

3

The Tulle Box was part of an old but thoroughly modernized hotel on Duval Street, past the Crow's Nest, going toward the eastern horizon. The hotel itself was called La Diosa del Mar, Goddess of the Sea. The signboard out front listed its appealing amenities—central air-conditioning, private baths with Jacuzzi, wide-screen video, and full soundproofing—along with a concise history of the building for those interested in Key West architecture and anthropology, or whatever was left of it in the old building. At the very bottom of the signboard, like a secret postscript, were the words: UPSTAIRS AT THE TULLE BOX. You'd never find the place unless you already knew it was there.

I went into the hotel, sauntered through the plushly appointed

Victorian-style lobby, then headed upstairs. Raucous laughter and noisy chatter cascaded down the stairwell as I climbed up. The Tulle Box was certainly no secret to some folks. At the top of the stairs was a large open sunny area bordered by tall sash windows. Two sets of French doors opened onto a balcony. Occupying most of the floor was a huge circular bar, already busy with drinkers. The place was frigid with air-conditioning, and redolent of a familiar spice—clove, I think. The brittle glass surfaces of the windows and the French doors amplified the already unbridled cheeriness of an alcoholic oasis.

The bartender was a cowboy lover's dream, with a ruddy rugged face, sun-bleached eyebrows and mustache, and puppy brown eyes. He was wearing a high, wide-brimmed Stetson, and he greeted me with a welcoming smile, said hello as though he'd been expecting me all morning, even patted his big hand on an empty place at the end of the bar, a gesture that said, Sit right here, pardner. I had to obey. His eyes followed me to the barstool, along with that wide-open grin.

"You look like you need a martini," he said.

"How dry can you make it?" I asked.

"How tight can you pucker?"

"Depends on which lips."

The man sitting next to me overheard our exchange and said to the bartender, "Sounds like you got yourself some work, Ross."

"Nah," said the bartender. "We're just joshing." Then he set his big brown eyes back onto me and said in earnest, "Aren't we?"

"Sure," I said. Romance, sex, bah! Those parts of my life were in remission. I was in Key West to recover, to learn to grow beyond my emotions. Love too, bah!

Ross the bartender said, "You like your 'tinis dirty?"

"There's not much I like dirty," I said.

My next-door neighbor grumbled, "That's too bad."

I turned to him. "I meant literally."

"So did I," said the guy. Then he got up and moved to another place further down the bar. Maybe it was dirtier there. The stool he'd vacated had two big damp spots where his butt had been spread over it.

Ross glanced at me from where he was setting up my drink.

"Don't pay him no heed. He's been alone too long."

"I can see why," I said.

Then Ross said to me, "Olive or twist?"

Instinctively I replied, "Who was a Dickens hero?"

"Huh?" said Ross.

"*Jeopardy!*" I said cheerily.

Ross looked perplexed, but on the other side of the bar a big barrel-chested guy with a gray goatee and matching ponytail had overheard me, and he allowed a tiny smile. Turned out he was the one creating the spicy air with his clove cigarettes.

"Twist," I said flatly to Ross. Game shows were apparently not the way to test the waters in Key West.

Ross strained half the elixir into a small glass cruet nested in a bowl of crushed ice. The remainder he strained into a chilled martini glass. He twisted the lemon peel directly over the drink, not into the air as many bartenders mistakenly do. Then he placed the filled glass and the cruet in front of me.

"One 'tini up, double, clean, with a twist." He gave his slender hips one seductive gyration, then threw his arms upward and gave a sharp squeal, like a Vegas chorus girl. Exactly my kind of machismo.

Then he said huskily, "Go 'head," once again the cowboy dude. "You gotta put it in your mouth to taste it."

I took a sip.

"Good job," I said. In truth, I was in the hands of a master.

Ross grinned back. "Takes a 'tini lover to make 'em right."

Some faceless drinker at the bar muttered, "But you're not teeny, are you, Ross?"

"As if you would know!" Ross spat back at him, but he also seemed proud that his manhood was headline news. He turned back to me and said, "Where you from, anyway?"

"Boston," I said.

"No wonder you're dressed like that," he said. "Well, you just missed Poker Week."

"I don't play cards," I said.

"Not cards," said Ross. "Pokers! Hogs and chicks and that kind of stuff."

"Like a county fair?"

"Harleys!" said Ross. "Motorcycles. *Vroom-vroom.* You know? Real men and their babes."

From the other side of the bar came a penetrating woman's voice.

"Speaking of babes, Rossina, do you think we could get a little service over here, please?"

We both looked that way. A tall Junoesque woman with a massive pile of bleached-blonde hair stood with arms akimbo, looking impatient. She glared at us from behind jewel-crusted wraparound sunglasses that resembled a grotesque party mask. Her figure was exaggerated too, but it sagged just enough to be real. She looked like a real woman impersonating some eminent drag queen.

"Cozy!" said Ross. "When did you come in?"

"I could say half an hour ago, for all you noticed." She proclaimed everything she said. "Who's the new heartthrob?"

Was she referring to me?

Ross said, "This is . . . uh . . ." He turned to me. "What *is* your name, darlin'?"

"Stan," I said. "Stan Kraychik."

"We'll stick with Stan," said Ross. Then he called out to the woman, "This here is Stan, Cozy. Stan-the-Man from Boston. Stan, meet Miss Cozy Dinette. She's a singer, the best damn singer in town."

Miss Cozy Dinette took that as an invitation to join us. She came to our side of the bar and eased herself onto the barstool next to me. She was a voluptuous woman, full of sensual energy that seemed to snap, crackle, and pop from every part of her body. She slid her sunglasses up off her eyes and nested them into her high-fashion do. Her eyes were blue—a cool, clever diamond blue. Riotous makeup provided a first defense against the impending skirmish with middle age. She took my hand and squeezed it firmly.

"I can tell we're going to be best friends," she said. "You have what it takes to be a best friend of mine."

Ross gave me a dubious glance, then said to Cozy, "The usual?"

"Not today," said Cozy. "I need something extra strong and powerful. I just heard the most awful news." She raised her voice to force everyone in the bar to listen, which they did. "You all know Augusta, who runs the Crow's Nest?" she said.

Various grumblings traveled around the bar. "Killer crab." "Granny conch." "Tourist poison."

"That's her," said Cozy. "Well, she was murdered this morning."

Another wave of commentary swept around the bar. "Hallelujah." "A mercy killing." "Tell it to God, Augusta."

I said, "I guess she wasn't exactly the homecoming queen."

"Huh?" said Cozy.

Ross explained to her, "He's from Boston."

"Oh, I'm sorry," said Cozy with true sadness in her eyes. "That explains all those clothes you have on. Aren't you hot?"

Ross interrupted, "Just dish the dirt on Augusta, girl. You're the reporter."

"Once," said Cozy. "I was once. Just like Brenda Starr. But my property advisor told me this morning—"

"Your what?" I said.

"My property advisor," said Cozy.

"What's that?"

"Don't you own real estate?" said Cozy.

"No," I said.

"Neither do I," said Cozy, "but you still need a property advisor. You never know when you might get some real estate."

"Amen," sang various mixed voices around the bar, led by Ross.

"*Anyway*," said Cozy, "my property advisor has a client who found the body."

"Who?" I said.

"Some guy named Hitler," said Cozy.

"You mean Dobermann," I said. "Adolf Dobermann."

"That's it," said Cozy. "Dobermann, Hitler. What's the difference? But how do you know? This is hot off the press."

"I know because I'm the one who discovered the body, not Herr Dobermann."

"Oh, right. Sure," said Cozy. "Well, if you're so smart, Mr. Boston, how did she die?"

"She choked," I said.

"Go on," said Cozy.

"That's it," I said.

"There's more," said Cozy. "And if you don't say it, we know you're lying."

I hesitated. "The police asked me not to discuss any details of the crime scene."

"Whoah!" said Cozy. "Mr. Boston's working with the police."

I protested, "No I'm not."

Ross said, "Go easy on him, Cozy. He's just a tourist."

"A tourist who's got your blood moving again," she said, "after such a long, dry summer." Then she embraced me with her strong arms and said to the bartender, "He feels good, Rossina."

Ross smiled. Then Cozy stood up and addressed everybody in the room. "I'll tell you all how Augusta died. She choked on an alarm clock."

The Tulle Box exploded into laughter.

From across the bar the big guy with the gray goatee and pony-tail said flatly, "Some wakeup call, Augusta."

Again raucous laughter rang out.

Ross said to the man, "A little respect for the dead, please, Ed."

"As little as possible for that old corpse," replied Ed. He took a last heavy drag from his cigarette and filled the air around him with oily, spicy smoke, then extinguished the thing. Standing next to me, Cozy Dinette feigned a cough, then lit up a cigarette of her own, a slender pastel-colored shaft that my actual best friend Nicole would have approved of, except for the obvious presence of menthol.

Ross said to me, "Don't let them get to you."

"They don't," I said. "I know the truth. I was there. I found her body, and I made the call to the police. It's all in the reports."

The guy named Ed snorted cynically. "Looks like we got a junior PI visiting us here."

Cozy said to me, "You're serious, aren't you, Boston?"

"Sometimes," I said. "For occasions of life and death."

Cozy said, "I'm sorry. I wasn't trying to upstage you or anything like that."

Ed remarked, "You can't upstage someone you just knocked into the pit."

"That's enough, Ed!" she snapped. Then she turned to me and softened her voice. "I would never do that," she said as she snaked a long arm around my shoulder. "Not to a new friend of my old friend Ross."

"Right," said Ross. "Give her five minutes."

From across the bar Ed said, "All right. I admit the error of my ways, and to show my respect for our dearly departed Augusta Willits I'd like to buy a round of drinks for everyone, including yours, Boston."

"Thanks," I said, and lifted my glass toward him.

As Ross prepared drinks for the ten or so people there, he leaned toward me and said, "You know who that guy is, the one buying your drink?"

"I haven't had the dubious pleasure," I said.

"That's Edsel Shamb. He's a famous writer."

"What a coincidence," I said. "I brought his book with me to Key West."

"I'm sure he'll autograph it for you," said Ross. Then he turned to Edsel and said boldly, "Won't you, Ed?"

"Won't I what?" replied the gray-haired man as he lit another clove-scented cigarette.

Another voice answered quickly, "Sell out to Hollywood."

Ross said, "Autograph your book for Stan-the-Man here."

"I'll do more than that," said Edsel Shamb. "I'll inscribe it. Unless, of course, Mr. Stan-the-Man from Boston is a collector, in which case he'd want only my autograph on the title page. Are you a collector?" he said to me directly.

"Not of books," I said.

"Of what then?"

"Facts, details, experience."

"Whoah!" said Cozy Dinette again. "This is getting too intellectual for me. Where's that free drink?"

At that moment another person arrived at the top of the stairs. It was Joshua Aytem, from the Fleming Lemming, complete with mirrored shades. "Did someone say 'free drink'?"

"Come on in," said Ross. "You might as well join the party."

"Does my breath smell bad or something?" said Joshua.

Ross said, "Take it easy, okay? It's early in the day."

"I've got money," said Josh defensively. "Or I will soon."

"Sure you will," said Ross. He handed him a vodka-tonic like an off-the-rack T-shirt.

Joshua looked around the bar and said hello to nearly everyone. They all nodded or waved back coolly. When his mirrored eyes got to me he said, "Didn't take you long to make friends here."

Then Cozy Dinette began to tell him about Augusta Willits's death that morning, but Joshua stopped her.

"I already heard," he said.

"You too?" said Cozy. "How did news get out so fast?"

Joshua shrugged. "Small town."

"Exactly what kind of clock was it?" said Edsel Shamb.

Cozy said, "One of those small digital things."

Her report was inaccurate, for the clock had had hands, but I didn't say so.

Edsel chuckled and said, "Sounds like something on prime-time television."

"And don't you wish you'd thought of it, Ed?" insinuated another nameless voice somewhere around the bar.

"I would never have used a digital clock," replied the writer. "One with hands would show up better on the screen. And I'd also wonder if the time on the clock was important." He looked straight at me. "You said you collect details, Stan. And you were there, right? So what time did the clock say?"

I hesitated.

Ross said to me, "Don't say anything you don't want to."

"Oh, Ross," said Cozy, "you should encourage him. I can tell already, he'll do anything for you."

I said flatly, "The police asked me not to discuss it."

"What police?" said Joshua Aytem.

Cozy explained to him that I'd found Augusta's body and had called the police.

"You didn't mention that to me," said Joshua. He almost looked annoyed.

"Like I said, the police asked me not to discuss it."

Edsel said, "How could you see the clock anyway?"

"I looked inside her mouth," I said.

"*Aaaaag*," went Cozy.

Joshua said, "So you did find her body."

"Yeah," I said.

"You sure keep your lips tight."

"When I have to," I said.

I glanced toward Ross, who winked at me. Cozy noticed.

Cozy said, "Well, my friend Nancy got the whole story from Adolf Hitler, and he was there too."

Edsel said, "Why did Nancy tell you anything?"

"You know exactly why," Cozy said sharply.

"Oh, that's right," said Edsel. "You're supposed to inherit the Crow's Nest."

"What, you just discovered America?" said Cozy. "If someone was killed at the Gulf Coast Playhouse, you'd be notified for the same reason I was."

"Except I get only half of the playhouse," said Edsel.

"Maybe that's because you were only half a friend," said Cozy.

Joshua mumbled, "Maybe you're both talking too much."

"Too late," said Ross from behind the bar. "If Cozy knows anything, it's national news."

"Whose will?" I asked.

All chatter ceased and a momentary silence hung over the Tulle Box. It was interrupted by the chirp of a cellular phone.

"That's mine!" said Edsel Shamb as he quickly and nervously unfolded his phone to take the call.

Ross said to me, "He's waiting for Hollywood."

Cozy said, "Aren't we all?"

I repeated my question to Cozy directly. "Whose will?"

"What, dear?" she replied, as if answering a two-year-old.

"Whose will were you talking about just now? Peter Willits's?"

Cozy and Ross answered together, "Good guess."

Cozy said, "Peter left all his property to his friends."

I saw Ross's face contort briefly, then the cowboy smile returned as he said, "But Augusta contested the will."

"His mother, right?" I said.

"Right," said Cozy and Ross together again.

"And now she's dead," Joshua piped in.

Cozy said to me, "How do you know all this? Who have you been talking to?"

I shrugged. "Just the people I've been meeting."

Meanwhile Edsel ended his brief call. "False alarm," he said with a chuckle. "That was the poolboy."

"Who else was in Peter's will?" I said.

Nervous glances passed among everyone at the bar, as though the answer to my question was common knowledge, and the mere asking of it proved I was an outsider, an alien, a *tourist*, undeserving of the true dirt.

"Why does that matter?" said Cozy.

"It's obvious," I said. "Motive for killing Augusta."

Joshua said, "Next thing you'll be saying someone in here did it."

"Why not?" I said.

Edsel Shamb chuckled. "I think Stan watches too much TV."

"Au contraire," I said. "I'm reading your book."

I slugged down the rest of my martini and slid off the barstool.

"Leaving already?" said Ross.

"I've got sightseeing to do."

Edsel and Joshua laughed simultaneously.

"This is as good as it gets," said Joshua, indicating the interior of the Tulle Box.

Cozy Dinette came up close to me and leaned her tall body into mine. "Boston, dear," she said, "I'm singing tonight at the O-Side. If you want, I'll leave your name at the door. Just say 'Boston' and they'll let you in."

"Sure," I said. "I'd like to see some local culture."

Edsel and Joshua laughed again. I was causing a regular riot with them.

I waved good-bye to the bar in general. Various sluggish waves came back from people I'd just met but would probably never know. Edsel Shamb advised me to loosen up and have a little fun. Cozy Dinette reminded me to go and hear her sing that night. Joshua Aytem was hitting up another patron for a free drink. And Ross said earnestly, "Come back soon, darlin'."

I left the Tulle Box a little bothered, for I had just seen first-hand what could become of me if I surrendered to the life of a deadbeat. With my recent windfalls, there was no need for me to work ever again during my natural life. I could easily move to Key

West, buy a cottage, renovate it, and then sit back and dissipate myself into oblivion. I felt aimless enough that it almost sounded appealing. But I imagined myself five years hence and shuddered. I could be any one of those folks sitting around that bar midday. My old New England values would never tolerate such a capricious waste of capital. Then again, where exactly had the work ethic got me?

4

I returned to the Jared Bellamy House via Whitehead Street, which ran parallel one block south of Duval. Whitehead offered vastly different sights and sounds, for where Duval was almost pure commerce, Whitehead was more residential, with more trees, more geckos, more renovated mansions, and yes, along one brief stretch, more derelicts too. In that rundown segment even the trees and ground cover thinned out, leaving the area barren and dusty, almost desertlike. If your business acumen was so inclined, it was shrieking for development.

Further down the street, back in the protective shade of luxuriant foliage, sat a small group of houses that had been rezoned for commercial use, and on the porch of one house sat a woman poised like royalty. She wore a close-fitting turban of exotically patterned silk. With one hand she languorously fanned herself while with the other she held a cellular telephone to her ear. That hand also held a long black cigarette holder with a slender white cigarette at its end, wisely unlit, or she might have set her fancy turban on fire. Even from where I stood, I estimated she was in her mid-fifties, but well maintained, with a pale smooth complexion that nearly glowed even in the shade. She wore oversized tinted glasses only half as dark as real sunglasses.

Above her storefront hung a gargantuan T-shirt, waving softly like a banner in the zephyrs from the west. The T-shirt was blazoned with colorful graphics that read: ART TO A TEE.

The woman noticed me and I smiled toward her. Then she ended her phone call and moaned faintly.

"Are you all right?" I asked.

"I am at the mercy of wolves."

Uh-oh, I thought, and began to move on.

"Please," she said, "talk to me. I am so alone."

I wondered whether to spend a moment cheering her up. At least our exchange would be one-on-one, unlike the bullying gang of drinkers at the Tulle Box, or the sparring couple at the Fleming Lemming.

She said, "It is six months since Peter has died, and I am in hell, hell on earth, during all that time."

"Peter?" I said, though I guessed who she meant.

"A true prince." She eyed my long pants and cotton shirt, then faked a drag on her unlit cigarette. "You are a tourist, yes?" she said with mild contempt, then added quickly, "I am sorry. I should not say such things. You show modesty in your attire. You may be a prince yourself. One never knows when one is addressing true royalty nowadays. You see, even I have forgotten my own breeding. It has been so long. Here there is no propriety, no majesty."

"Yes," I said. "I'm sure you're right. Have a nice day."

I'm inane, you're inane.

I headed onward, but she called out to me.

"Did you know Peter?"

I kept walking but turned my head back to answer her. "No."

It was then, not watching my step, that I felt something soft under the sole of my sneaker, something liquidy and alive. I pulled back with a start and saw that I had stepped on a gecko. Miraculously I hadn't squashed the thing completely. It crouched there down on the sidewalk, as if caught in a freeze-frame. Was it startled, or dead? Its tail had broken off. Then the gecko twisted its head and looked up at me with angry reptilian eyes, as if to say, "You big stupid slob! Now look what you've done!" It flicked out its forked tongue once, twice, testing the air for predatory energy. Sensing none, it scurried off into the grass, leaving its tail on the sidewalk to wriggle and twist and distract its attacker—me—from chasing the more succulent body, with head and viscera intact. There was not a drop of blood anywhere.

"If it runs away," said the woman, "it is good luck."

"For whom?" I said, retaining my one grammatical tic, even in crisis.

"For both of you!" she said with forced laughter.

I turned to continue my walk home and almost collided head-on with a tall, handsome man. He was around forty, lean and tan, and he had, as much as anyone can, given the ravages of time and gravity, maintained the chiseled looks of youth. In silver-screen days he might have been a matinee idol. More recently that face and body would easily land him on television. He smiled and showed off the sumptuous results of modern dental technology, while sunglasses concealed any real message carried by his eyes.

"Kenneth!" called the woman from the porch.

"Stassya!" responded the man. Then he thrust out a big square hand to me. "I'm Ken Kimble," he said.

"Stan Kraychik," I said and shook his hand.

The guy must have worked out a lot. His whole body undulated in a slinky smooth contraction that finally ended up in his hand.

I said, "You look like a movie star."

"Do I?" he said with unconvincing modesty. "Where are you from?"

I told him. He wasn't impressed.

"How long have you been in town?"

"About twenty-four hours," I said.

"Having much fun?"

"I'm here to recover from—"

"Good!" he cut in. "Key West is the best place for that. You'll find good community spirit here. I can give you some names."

"I'm in mourning," I said bluntly.

"That's even better," Ken said brightly. "We have special work-shops for personal loss and re-entry into the world."

It sounded like a NASA space program. And from what I'd seen so far, lost in space was pretty much part of the local culture.

He said, "I'd like to welcome you personally to Key West." He handed me his personal card. It was a classy engraved job done on expensive stock. But what was that little blob over the "i" in his last name? A smiley face?

Meanwhile Ken was eying me up and down, as if to evaluate me in terms of desirability—or something else—as though I was concealing the stark truth, however good or bad, under my long sleeves and pants.

"How's your health?" he said.

"Fine," I said defensively.

"You look a little thin, and you're all covered up. I just wondered, maybe . . ."

"I'm fine!" I said.

Ken softened his gaze and tried to speak directly to my heart, or to some other part of me that didn't want to hear his spiel. "If you've come to Key West to die, you've made the best decision of your life."

"Thanks for sharing," I said bitterly.

"My pleasure," he replied. Then he shook my hand once more and put his muscles through another full-body wave. There was an odd sense of orgasm about it.

The woman sitting on the porch must have tired of our sidewalk gavotte, because she called out again, *"Kenneth!"* and waved her prop—the long cigarette holder—impatiently. "Are you coming or not?"

Ken took me up to the porch and introduced me to her.

"The Countess Anastasia Rulalenska," he said.

The name conjured a time when cosmetics were marketed with the cachet of Euroglamour instead of raw sex.

"Quite a title," I said.

Ken said, "You'll find a lot of that here in Key West. People don't stand on ceremony. A countess can run a T-shirt store and nobody questions it. It's personal fulfillment that's most important here."

T-shirts equal fulfillment?

Ken told the countess that I'd come to Key West to die.

"You poor boy," she said to me. "I had no idea."

"I'm not dying," I said. "Not yet anyway. It was my lover who died."

"Oh," said the woman.

Ken Kimble apologized for his mistake, then added, "I'm afraid we're not giving you a very warm welcome. Even if you're mourning, you should try to enjoy yourself here, have some fun."

"I'm not looking for fun," I said. "I'm looking for answers."

"Answers to what?"

Good question. Did I even know myself? "Well," I said, "for example, who killed Augusta Willits."

"Ohhhh!" howled the countess. "Did you hear? They did horrible things to her with a telephone."

I corrected her. "It was a clock."

Ken said, "How do you know that?"

"I, uh, overheard some people at the Tulle Box."

"Already?" said Ken.

I nodded. "And a painting was missing too."

Ken said, "Did you hear that at the Tulle Box too?"

I was about to reply when the countess pulled herself up sharply, as though she had lost her balance for a moment. Then she laughed nervously and said, "Oh-lo-lo. Do not tease him, Kenneth."

I said, "Either of you know about the will?"

"What will?" said Ken.

"Augusta's son Peter had a will, and she was contesting it."

"Oh!" yelped the countess. "How dare you talk like that! You are a stranger! You never knew Peter!"

Ken Kimble put one of his manly arms around her and cooed, "Easy, Stassya. He can't help it." Then he turned his eyes to me and said, "In the future you might question the veracity of things you hear in a cocktail lounge."

"Why?" I said. "People can lie or tell the truth anywhere, including me. For example, here's some real truth: I found Augusta's body."

"You?" said Ken and the countess together.

"Yes, and I called the police."

They looked at me as though I was selling snake oil.

"It's true," I said.

"What does your truth matter?" said the countess. "It is not important who found her body, but who killed her."

For the first time I agreed with the woman.

She went on. "And I think it was that young Tiker girl, the artist.

She went in to steal the painting, and when Augusta caught her, she killed her."

"Then you did know about the painting?" I said.

Neither person answered me.

I said, "Did you also know that Adolf Dobermann wanted it?"

"*Akh!*" went the countess. "You know Herr Dobermann too! Young man, are you with the FIB?"

"FBI," corrected Ken.

"No," I said. "I'm on vacation, such as it is."

"Whatever," said Ken cheerily. "Let's drop this morbid topic." He turned his square-jawed face to me and smiled. "Stan," he said, "we seem to have got off to a bad start, but I have a really good feeling about you." I could almost see smiley-faced bubbles popping out of his mouth. "Life can be good here if you know the right people, and I can introduce you. I hope you'll drop by my place sometime soon. I have a nice pool."

"Thanks, but I don't swim."

"Then sun yourself."

"My skin is too sensitive."

"Use sunscreen," he insisted.

"I'm allergic."

"You'll never get a tan that way."

"I don't want one," I said.

"Then why on earth have you come to Key West?" he said with his big expensive smile.

"I've tried to tell you," I said.

"Well, the invitation is open, if you change your mind."

The countess interrupted us again. "Come, Kenneth. We have matters to discuss." She got up from the chair and grasped Ken's manly forearm, then she tenderly stroked the smooth tan skin.

Ken made polite excuses then he bade me a fond farewell. Literally. He actually said, "I bid you fond farewell."

As they walked inside, I felt the porch shake under the countess's footsteps. So petite, yet so clomping. She may have had a title, but little regal deportment. Perhaps it was her only way of laying claim to the turf beneath her feet.

After that dose of quasi-southern hospitality I had an urge to return to my room and hide under the blankets. I walked quickly down Whitehead Street toward Fleming. The intersection of those two streets was also the official end of Route One, the great and infinite connector of the entire East Coast of the United States. The fact was stated blandly on a standard highway marker: END U.S. 1. It might as well have said: END OF THE WORLD. Anyone who's ever traveled along the eastern seaboard knows that Route One never ends.

Back at the guest house, the desk clerk gave me a message to call the local police. I went up to my room to make the call. Lieutenant Sanfuentes had run a verification on me up in Boston, and wanted to discuss what he called "a very private matter." Then he added, "The sooner the better."

We agreed to meet first thing the next morning at the police station. It couldn't have been too urgent, or he would have come and got me then and there.

After that I telephoned my best friend Nicole, the manicurist at Snips Salon, where I worked back in Boston. I knew she'd still be at the shop. The receptionist transferred my call right away, and Nicole came on the line with a question.

"Any decision yet?"

"You mean when am I coming home, doll?"

"First that," she said. "And then are you going to be reasonable and organize your life around a good day's work?"

"As if you should know."

"You may be rich, Stanley, but you still need daily structure."

"And you need a master colorist. But Nikki, everyone is coloring their hair from the drugstore these days."

"And they all need *you* to fix the results."

"So I'm to become a hair-maintenance engineer?"

"You're to put in a good day's work."

"Still, doll, there are plenty of good colorists in Boston. Hire one of them. The change would be good for the shop too, new blood and all."

"Darling, no one else could possibly work at your station. You know that. Even when I promoted you to manager, I didn't reassign your chair."

"Maybe you should put up a small plaque in my memory."

"Don't talk like that!" she snapped. "Rafik may be gone but you're still alive."

"Sometimes I wonder, doll."

"Don't be ridiculous. You said so yourself, you have to keep going forward."

"For what? Old age? Loneliness?"

"What's the alternative, Stanley?"

"Suicide."

"You're being operatic."

"I wouldn't expect you to understand, Nikki. No one can really understand suicide except those who've already done it."

"That's puerile and maudlin."

"Big words, doll. Have you been reading again?"

"If you must indulge in idle sentiment, Stanley, then make a date to kill yourself sometime in the future. Write it down in that nice calfskin appointment book I brought you from London. Pick a date and time, and write it in the book: KILL MYSELF TODAY. Then forget about it until the day arrives. *Then* see how you feel."

"Nikki, that's the kind of advice I give to my clients. Have you been eavesdropping?"

"I have a right to, Stanley. I own the salon. Are you eating yet?"

"A little. It's too hot here."

"Try, darling. You're far too thin."

"The locals eye me like I'm hiding lesions under all the cotton."

"That's not funny."

"It's ironic, doll. I'm trying to keep from getting sick in the sun, and people think I'm dying. Part of me has."

"Stop being morbid."

"With death and depravity all around me, what else can I do? At least I'm not crying much anymore. Maybe I've finally run out of tears."

Nicole paused before saying, "It had to slow down sometime."

"You were right," I said. "And I almost forgot. There's been a murder here."

"How nice for you, darling."

"Nice?"

"What do you want me to say?" said Nicole. "Leave that place and come home immediately?"

"No, no," I protested. "It's not like those other times. No involvement, I promise."

"Good," she said. "Now, have you met anyone interesting?"

"I met a woman who smokes the same cigarettes you do, except menthol."

Nicole gasped. "Well, there's no competition there. But darling, I meant a man."

"Nikki, you meant sexual distraction."

"It might help, like when people lose a pet. Sometimes it's better to replace it right away."

"Rafik was not a pet."

A disquieting pause followed.

Then Nicole said, "All I meant was with a new lover you could focus on the future. Why wallow in unhappiness?"

"You're right," I said blithely. "Why didn't I see that all along? From now on it's only happy faces for me."

"You don't have to go overboard," said Nicole.

"But I'm *in extremis*, doll."

"Yes, darling, you are an extremist, and I love you for it. Call me tomorrow and tell me about all the interesting men you've met."

Then, as usual, Nicole hung up without saying good-bye.

I tried once more to start Edsel Shamb's book, but I couldn't get beyond the language. Instead of projecting images from another world, he lulled me into torpor. I crawled off the bed and took another shower, then headed out for an evening's diversion to hear Cozy Dinette at the O-Side.

All happy faces.

5

The O-Side was a huge waterfront resort on the east, that is, the O-for-ocean side of town. After sunset on certain evenings the massive elevated deck surrounding the O-Side's swimming pool became an outdoor nightclub. Motel guests who wanted to swim during those times had to use the filtered lagoon on the property's beachfront. Yes, I said filtered.

As I approached the club I felt its music pulsing through the pavement. I followed the sound and vibration through a winding alleyway that provided parking for VIPs, judging by the cars parked there. The ground-shaking throbs intensified at each new turn of the alley, and finally, at the end, I came upon the broad wooden stairway that led up to the deck. A sign at the foot of the stairs read: COZY DINETTE AND THE FAMILY STYLE MEALS SING THEIR LOCAL HIT "CAN'T REMEMBER SHIT."

At the top of the stairs I viewed a writhing mass of bodies around the open pool, all moving to deafening sounds from a PA system that would have toppled the Colossus at Rhodes. Again I wondered, if this was off-season, who were all these people?

A young woman with a four-inch bone through her nose was collecting the hefty cover charge. The shallow arc of the bone paralleled the upper rim of the wire-framed sunglasses she wore, even though old Sol had long since plunged into the Gulf of Mexico. I had to yell to be heard above the insistent clamor of the music. I told her I was on the guest list, that my name was Boston, just as Cozy Dinette had told me to do that afternoon.

"But what's your *name*?" the woman screeched irritably, causing the bone in her nose to twitch and slant from side to side.

"Boston," I repeated.

"I don't care where you're from," she said, as though I was just another parcel of the tourist scourge she obviously detested. I suppose I was. But then, who was she with that bone in her nose? "I need your name," she said, "or else get out of line. You're holding everyone up."

"Try Stan!" I yelled.

She pored over the guest list like a beady-eyed accountant, eager to find nothing, so she could then thrust her empty hand at me and collect the cash.

"Stan the Man?" she muttered with a frown. "From Boston?"

"C'est moi."

"Go ahead," she said with enough acid to corrode galvanized zinc.

To think Rafik was dead, while that woman was bestowing her special kind of hospitality on the world.

My next challenge was to get a drink. I scanned the crowd and saw that four separate bars were open and busy, ensuring none of the patrons went thirsty. I snaked my way into the swarm around the nearest bar. Along the way I heard snatches of various conversations, most of which centered on the scandalous death of Augusta Willits at the Crow's Nest that morning. News traveled fast on the island reef. I tried to stand tall and remain calm above the fray, hoping that one of the bartenders might sense my peaceful energy through the noisy riot around me. It didn't work. But someone did nudge me from behind with a potent grab at my butt.

"While you're at it, get me a vodka-tonic."

I turned to see myself reflected in the mirrored lenses of Joshua Aytem, who ran the Fleming Lemming with Laura Hope.

"I'll pay you later," he said, then dissolved back into the crowd.

I finally got the drinks, then dodged my way back through the crowd like a two-fisted drunk. Suddenly I felt stupid and alone, for I'd been set up, charmed to fetch Joshua's drink. And like a mindless lackey, I'd done so, only to wander the hostile throng to find him. It was a familiar situation to anyone who's ever been too submissive. In my emotionally vulnerable state, I'd lapsed back into it, doing good things for others without regard for myself. I had the urge to fling Joshua's drink high over the crowd and beyond the wooden fence that enclosed the deck. Let the bastard go fetch for himself. But the crowd pressed against me too closely. And besides, I can't throw for shit.

I squirmed my way to the fence and found a little nook to nestle into, where the music was somewhat baffled by the sheer body count around me. I sipped my own drink and looked out over the mass of people. Everyone seemed blissfully engaged in the frenzy of a party, while I was somehow removed from it. It was never my idea of fun anyway, being crushed by a huge anonymous crowd with deafening noise all around. At least at the O-Side, I could enjoy the night sky overhead, so that's where I put my eyes for the next few minutes.

Like special effects to accompany the music, lightning flashes leaped among the banks of clouds that were gathering offshore. I was gazing skyward when I heard someone say, "Mother Nature's light show." It was Joshua again. "No wonder you got lost, you've been stargazing."

"I wasn't lost," I said.

Joshua grabbed the vodka-tonic from my hand. A few gulps later order was restored. He flung the empty glass over the fence, then pulled two crumpled dollar bills from his back pocket. He regarded them mournfully. "Are you getting another drink?"

"Not yet," I said.

He jammed the money back in his pocket, then lit a cigarette and let it dangle from his lips. He lifted his mirrored sunglasses and rested them in his thick wavy black hair. The night air and the wild music seemed to complement his brutal charm.

I asked him, "Where's your partner tonight?"

"Laura? She never gets out to these things."

"So you're here alone?" I said.

Joshua smirked. "Not quite." He patted the small cellular phone attached to his belt. "I'm connected to the whole world." Then he whimpered, "I need another drink. Do you want one?"

"Nah," I said. But when he left me I grabbed my chance to escape the clutches of his charm. I wrestled my way through the crowd to another part of the deck. On the way I did get myself another drink from one of the other bars, and also asked the barmaid if there was anywhere less crowded on the deck. She aimed me toward a thicket of young palm trees and elephant plants, what looked like part of the motel's landscaping but was actually a secluded portion of the deck.

By some miraculous aberration of architecture and acoustics, the area was almost completely out of earshot of the monstrous PA system that was shaking the rest of the deck. I peeked into the quiet little grove, where a few patio tables and chairs had been set up. At one of the tables were seated Edsel Shamb, Adolf Dobermann, and a woman I hadn't seen before. I concealed myself within the shrubbery surrounding the quiet little area. All three people were putting away their cellular phones, as though concluding a round of Flash Gordon with their walkie-talkies.

The woman stood up and prepared to leave the table. Her garment was a billowy expanse of gossamer silk voile, printed with large soft-edged splotches of lavender, blue, and aqua—all muted tones—then accented with areas of gold and bright raspberry. The yards of soft fabric somewhat concealed her ampleness, and despite her size and mass, the woman moved with quiet grace, neither rustling the air around her, nor shaking the deck beneath her feet. As she passed she glanced at me, and I tried to look like any other loiterer on the premises, but I could tell she had registered my face.

Left alone, Edsel and Adolf lit cigarettes and smoked as if consummating a secret ritual. Edsel smoked deliberately, trying to absorb every molecule of tar and nicotine contained in the heavy drag, while Adolf puffed and exhaled skittishly, barely letting the smoke touch the back of his tongue.

Still trying to conceal myself in the darkness and the foliage, I moved close enough to hear Dobermann say, ". . . my business is complete, so to Germany I will soon return."

That's when Edsel noticed me and said loudly, "Hey, there! Stan! You look lost."

Dobermann turned toward me too and said, "Hello there, my partner in crime." He laughed as though he'd made a joke.

"Come and join us," said Edsel.

"I don't want to interrupt anything," I said.

"We've just finished," he said.

As I pulled out a chair to sit, Adolf Dobermann extinguished his cigarette and stood up. He said to Edsel, "I shall tomorrow confirm with you the arrangements we have tonight made here."

Edsel replied, "I'll be home all morning, working on the pilot for that new series."

Then Dobermann turned to me and said, "I do not know when our paths again shall cross, so I will say now *auf Wiedersehen*."

He shook my hand, then Edsel's, and left us quickly. But through the same greenery that hadn't quite concealed me, I saw Adolf Dobermann stop and make a call from his cell phone.

Next thing I knew Edsel was offering me a cigarette, which I refused. (Never could manage the act without coughing.) Then he said, "I hope you're enjoying my book."

"It's . . . interesting," I lied.

He laughed. "The critics didn't like it either. But the public did. Even my publisher couldn't hide the sales figures on that one. *Only the Dead Know* just put a brand-new swimming pool in my back yard. Do you swim, Stan?"

"I'm a sinker," I said.

"Well, mine is a lap pool, only four and a half feet deep. You ought to come by sometime."

"I've heard you can drown in a bathtub."

"Only if you're not careful," he said.

"I keep a rubber ducky close by."

"That's a wise precaution for some people." Edsel extinguished his cigarette with meticulous care, a gesture Nicole would have appreciated. "Looks as though the rain's about to break," he said. "I'd offer you a lift, but I don't drive."

"That's okay," I said. "I came to hear Cozy Dinette."

Edsel made a contemptuous little sound. "She'll probably be rained out. Have you ever been in a tropical downpour?"

I told him no and he laughed.

"Well, if you get caught in it," he said, "just surrender. There's no use trying to stay dry."

Then he departed and left me sitting alone. I stayed like that awhile: alone, not thinking of anything, just being. The music was almost distant enough to become a mantra of its own. Then, just about the time I started getting bored with "being," the first heavy droplets of rain began to plop here and there on the wooden deck. Then came a roll of thunder that outwitted even the O-Side's behemoth sound system. As the rain gradually increased, the music faded quickly, followed by an announcement that Cozy Dinette's show would be postponed. And to all a good night.

Suddenly people were running for their cars or for taxicabs. There was absolutely no shelter from the rain on the pool deck. I watched the crowd, which seemed to know exactly where it was going, and I quickly realized that its synchronized flight was a conditioned response I hadn't yet learned. I stood observing instead of participating in the panic to escape the imminent downpour. I recalled Edsel Shamb's advice, which mirrored one of my own private mantras when nothing else would do. Surrender, I told myself. Surrender to the rain.

The crowd quickly vacated the pier and the pool deck, while I walked with a deliberate but relaxed stride. The rain was heavy, but my saturation had just begun, and the wetness was refreshing. Joshua Aytem stood under an awning at the end of the convoluted alleyway, where it met the street. A damp unlit cigarette hung from his lips.

"Do you have any money?" he said. "I forgot to charge my phone battery, and my ride left without me."

I don't know why I did it. Maybe it was those mirrored sunglasses and the heavy rain and his dark wet hair. (So what if he was straight? Sexy is sexy.) I reached into my pocket almost reflexively and gave him whatever bills were there. The steady rushing sound of the rain had put me in some kind of trance. Or else my surrendering mantra had. Or Joshua had. But I didn't care about anything anymore, least of all the paper change in my pockets.

He hailed the last free taxicab on Key West that night, while I surrendered to walking all the way back to the Jared Bellamy House. It took only a few more minutes of exposure for the pelting water to drench my clothes, then stream down my legs and fill my sneakers. After that it was easy, because I just couldn't get any wetter. Even when cars and taxicabs drove by and splashed me, none of it mattered. I was in another world where everything was simply wet, wetter, wettest.

Meanwhile the lightning glared so harshly, so blue-white that I had to squint. And then the thunder followed, dwarfing my memory of the O-Side's PA system to the tinny buzz of a transistor radio. The ground shook violently, and my whole body bounced upward, like a pea on a drumhead. It was man against the raging elements—wind and rain and lightning and thunder. I suppressed an urge to cry out, *"Heathcliff!"* Anyway I had no audience.

By the time I waded to Fleming Street, the crisis of the storm had passed, and the sound and fury had diminished somewhat, though the rain was still falling steadily. On the last soggy stretch of my walk home I sensed a car trailing slightly behind me. It followed for half a block before I turned back and glanced at it. It was a taxicab, and a brief flash of lightning showed it to be one of those big pink ones endemic to Key West. In all the rain perhaps driver and passenger were having trouble finding their destination. But midway up the next block it was still following me. I stopped and turned and faced the cab again. It stopped too, but the glare of headlights and the densely tinted windows prevented me from seeing inside. Even the lightning flashes gave no clue to the cab's occupants. We stayed like that awhile, me and a big pink taxicab at a peculiar impasse, its windshield wipers going *flup . . . flup . . . flup* like an unwavering automotive heartbeat. Then the driver punched the pedal and the car squalled off into the black night rain.

At the Jared Bellamy House, I stopped on the porch and let most of the water run off me. Then I got up to my room, stripped down, dried off, and went to bed.

6

The next morning I awoke hungry for the first time since Rafik's death. Perhaps my old appetite was finally returning. Maybe I was, as they say in the vernacular of psychopablum, *healing.* Maybe I would regain the many lost pounds of avoirdupois and return to my former essence, the down-home heartiness of a Slavic dumpling. I showered, and though I was eager for breakfast, I set out directly for the police station. Lieutenant Sanfuentes had wanted to discuss that mysterious "personal" matter with me, and I figured my long-lost focus on food could wait a little longer until after that meeting.

On the way to the station I saw that the previous night's storm had left much debris along the sidewalks and streets. Mostly it was palm fronds and other green leafy things, which made me feel like some kind of homecoming Jesus. But occasionally a huge branch blocked the way, torn from a palm tree's trunk, all brown and broken, with the gauzy underbark exposed like a tattered camisole.

The Key West police station was an austere brick building near the intersection of Simonton and Angela streets. It shared little of the tropical charm of Old Town surrounding it.

In his office Lieutenant Sanfuentes was cordial but direct.

"I ran a very thorough check on you up in Boston," he said, "and I got a lot more than I bargained for."

"Is there a problem?"

"Actually," he said, "it's good news. You got a big shot up in Boston who likes you."

"Branco," I said.

"Guy gave you a glowing commendation," said the cop. "They must've got a lot more liberal in Boston."

"Is this the personal matter you wanted to discuss?"

"Hold your horses," said Sanfuentes. "I'm getting to that." He took out his tin of black mints and tossed a few into his mouth. Licorice and violets filled the air. "See," he said, "we don't get too many murders around here, which is certainly good for tourism. I mean, who wants to visit a place where people are getting killed on a regular basis? You catch my drift?"

"Sure," I said, "but—"

"And Lieutenant Branco up in Boston told me that you have in the past supplied him with some helpful leads. His exact words were 'good help.' "

Good help. That was good news coming from someone like Branco, with his big strong feet planted in terra firma back in Boston. Branco had said something good and reasonable and true about me.

Sanfuentes went on. "And he suggested it might be to my benefit to keep the communication between you and myself open."

"So you want my help."

Sanfuentes spoke sharply. "Did I say that?"

"Not those words."

"That's right," said the cop. "Not those words. Just so long as we understand each other. I'm telling you again though, just to make sure. I didn't ask for your help. I got plenty of people on this case already, believe me. You won't see them, but they'll see you, every move. All I'm saying is if you happen to come across anything that seems, well, irregular—something you hear, something you see—then I hope you'll come by and shoot the breeze with me."

"I think I understand, Lieutenant. Will the rest of your staff know about me?"

"The people who should know will know," he said.

"Sounds easy enough then," I said. "I sniff around, then tell you what I find."

"Kinda like that," he said. Once more he fished out the small tin and popped a few more tiny black granules into his mouth. Once again the air was scented with spice and flowers. Then Sanfuentes said, "Y'know, now that I think about it, I'd like you report back here daily—say between four and six P.M.—whether or not you find anything. How's that sound?"

"I can manage that."

"We—I—just want to make sure you're okay."

It was a gentle reminder that despite all the good doobee jousting between us, I was still helping track down a killer. Sanfuentes handed me a card with his name and number. There was no smiley face above the *i* in *his* name.

"That number rings directly through to me," he said. "If I'm not here, my beeper goes off. If I don't hear from you in any twenty-four-hour period, and my contacts don't see you, I'm going to assume it's bad news, and we're going to come looking for you."

"So I've got to report in."

"You've got to report in," he echoed. "This is serious work." He thumped his chest with his middle finger. "And I'm responsible for you."

Most straight men don't have the guts to say something like that to someone like me.

"You can go now," he said.

And that's how the Key West police engaged my unofficial help in their investigation of Augusta Willits's murder. In his own way Lieutenant Sanfuentes had been friendly toward me, not quite what I'd expect from a cop in the southernmost part of the deep south. Then again, as a Cubano, he'd probably had to work extra hard to prove himself worthy of his position. Maybe our common struggle for acceptance made the guy sympathetic to me.

I was absolutely ravenous when I left the station. On the way to breakfast I passed the Echo Me Gallery, which was open. I went in to say hello, maybe even invite Jeri Tiker to breakfast. We could have a civilized talk about art and life over coffee and omelettes. It was unlikely that she'd have any customers at that early hour. But I was wrong. Through the open door I saw that Adolf Dobermann was in the gallery, and he was arguing with Jeri. His back was toward the door and Jeri was out of my sight line, but I heard them both clearly.

"My dear young girl," said Adolf, "I simply want to take some of your work back to Germany. You should be delighted."

"There's nothing simple about you," Jeri said angrily. "You already stole that one from the Crow's Nest."

Dobermann laughed. "Silly girl! Why should I steal your painting? What proof do you have?"

"Because I wouldn't give it to you," said Jeri.

"I offered to you a fair price, just as I am doing now for these . . . these illustrations."

"If you think they're so worthless, Mr. Dobermann, why don't you take your money somewhere else?"

Dobermann shook his head ruefully. "Too much temperament."

Then he cast his gaze around the gallery, as if appraising its true worth in net income per square foot. "I think perhaps I will buy this building and make a charming cafe. The tourists will come for Black Forest cake and *Mokka mit Schlag*. It will attract a high quality of people."

"Get out of here!" screamed Jeri. "Out, you filthy landowner pig!"

A gecko scurried across the wooden porch floor in front of me. Then I felt the springy slats move slightly under my feet. I turned to see Joshua Aytem standing behind me. His mirrored shades couldn't conceal his amusement.

Adolf Dobermann appeared in the doorway as he called back to Jeri Tiker inside. "We shall see who wins this little game of cat and mouse, Fräulein Tiker!"

A half-used tube of cadmium white paint came flying out the door and bounced along the porch. Adolf Dobermann laughed jovially and said, "You missed!" Then he lit a cigarette and puffed at it nervously. He passed us briskly. "Good morning, gentlemen," he said amiably, nodding at us with sunglass-covered eyes. Then he continued on his way, heading up Fleming Street, leaving little puffs of smoke in his wake.

Joshua chuckled and said to me, "Typical morning in Key West. Did you enjoy the fight?"

"I didn't hear much," I said.

"Funny, I was standing behind you, and I heard every word."

"It's nobody's business," I said.

He shrugged. "You live here awhile, you learn to enjoy other people's business."

The dark stubble on Joshua's face reminded me to shave soon. On him it was sexy. On me it was grubby.

Joshua talked on, his sunglasses concealing what his eyes were saying. "If you came by our place this morning, you could have watched Edsel Shamb signing books."

"You sell books?"

Joshua said, "It's part of a package tour we're doing on Key West writers."

I said, "Will you feature the famous author lounging by his new pool?"

"Fucking wading pond," muttered Joshua.

"It's a big deal to him."

"He likes to brag about it," said Joshua, "but size isn't everything. He may have the longest one on the island, but so what? Ken Kimble's has much better proportions, with good details up and down the whole thing, and then that beautifully sculpted bottom."

46

Jeri Tiker appeared in the doorway. "I thought I heard voices out here," she said. "It sounds like you two are talking about—"

"Swimming pools," I said quickly.

"Ken Kimble has the real showplace," continued Joshua. "All landscaped with flowers and ground cover, trees all around. Very private."

I said, "What is it with all the swimming pools here? It's an island surrounded by tropical waters, yet everyone has a pool."

"They think the water is poison," said Jeri. "No one who lives here goes in the water."

Joshua added, "The only safe place is the O-Side lagoon. They filter it. Imagine that? They filter the goddamned ocean."

I told him I already knew that, which only irked him more.

Jeri said to me, "Has Ken Kimble invited you to his place yet?"

"Kind of," I said.

"You should go," said Joshua, "especially if he's having one of his parties. Usually Ken lives like a monk, but then he flips out and goes the other extreme."

Jeri said, "Augusta Willits used to organize police raids to stop them."

"Raids?" I said. "Why?"

"Why do you think?" said Joshua with another shrug. "She wanted Peter all to herself."

"Peter?"

"Her son," said Jeri. "I told you about him yesterday."

"I know," I said. "But I don't get it. Police raids against Peter and Ken?"

Joshua said, "I thought you knew everything, Mr. Encyclopedia."

"Is Ken gay?" I said.

"He straddles," said Jeri.

Joshua added, "And sometimes he falls off."

"So," I said, "dead Augusta's dead son Peter was attracted to Ken Kimble, but neither man dared to act on it, but Augusta was still jealous, so she called the police about Ken's parties, trying to stop them so her son Peter wouldn't be tempted to explore his own sexual urges anymore."

"Wow," said Jeri. "Are you some kind of shrink?"

"I tried to be, once."

Joshua said, "I can see why you flopped."

"Well, boys," said Jeri, suddenly impatient, "you'll excuse me, but I've got work to do."

"We're not here together," I said quickly.

"Well, smell you," said Joshua. Then he said to Jeri, "Laura and I want to help you."

"You want to buy a painting?" said Jeri.

"No, but we heard about the one that was stolen from the Crow's Nest, and we thought maybe you'd like to hang a few pieces in our place. We get a lot of people buying boat tours and tickets to the conch trains, so your work would get a lot of exposure, maybe sell faster."

"But that's exactly how I got burnt," said Jeri, "by hanging a painting for the tourists to see, and then someone stole it."

Josh said, "Laura thought you'd be happy about it."

"Thanks anyway," said Jeri. "I'll manage on my own."

I offered her the consolation that usually only great art was stolen.

Joshua said to me, "If you don't want to have breakfast with me, do you have four-fifty I can borrow? I need cigarettes."

"I only have a twenty," I said.

"That's fine," he said. "I can pay you back."

"But I'm going to buy my breakfast."

"Go to Camille's," said Joshua. "You can charge it there, and there's a bank machine next door."

"Maybe you should try the bank machine," I said.

"I lost my card," whined Joshua.

Jeri said, "Can you two argue about cash somewhere else? I'd like to get back to work."

I took out my wallet and pulled out the twenty-dollar bill. As I handed it to Joshua I said, "Were you at the Crow's Nest anytime yesterday morning?"

Joshua snatched the bill from my fingers. "You think I did something?"

"Maybe."

"Like what?"

"I don't know," I said. "That's why I'm asking."

He sniggered. "You better be careful. You're showing signs of tropical fever."

Just then Joshua's cellular phone signaled an incoming call. He answered it, made some obscure monosyllabic sounds, then ended the call quickly. "Gotta run," he said to me and Jeri. "Thanks for the loan." Then he laughed and headed back up Fleming Street.

For her part, Jeri Tiker declined my invitation to breakfast. She wanted to paint. Now that was real discipline, putting art before food. So I headed down to Duval Street alone, to find Camille's and get some breakfast.

At one of the cross streets a pink taxicab passed by. It had dark, heavily tinted windows, just like the one that had trailed me the previous night. I got a quick make on the license plate: KEY–CAB.

At Duval Street I headed toward Camille's Cafe, which had been my destination even before Joshua had mentioned it. The desk clerk at the Jared Bellamy House had raved about the buckwheat waffles with fresh fruit. And their *café con leche*, the Cuban version of a *caffè latte*, was purported to be the best on the reef, bar none.

On my brief stroll along Duval Street the tourists were already crowding the sidewalks. Many of them comprised oddly mismatched honeymoon couples: Hunky, Adonis-like grooms craned their necks to cruise other musclemen passing by, while their brides looked on confounded, as if to say, "He never looked at other men before he joined that gym."

I paused on the sidewalk outside Camille's and took in a bit more of the tourist parade before going inside.

A voice behind me said, "See anything you like?"

It was Edsel Shamb.

"I see a lot that amuses me," I said. Gauging from his dark sunglasses I wondered if *he* could see anything at all. "I heard you were signing books at the Fleming Lemming."

"That took only a few minutes," said Edsel. "I put a pen in my hand, then turn on the autograph machine, and away it goes." He laughed.

I told him what I'd been speculating about the married couples walking along Duval Street.

He said, "I hope you're not one of those people who thinks everyone is secretly gay."

"No," I said. "Just the usual ten to twenty percent."

"That many?" he said with a chortle. "Well, I'm not."

"Then I guess you're in the other eighty to ninety percent."

"I like gay people, though," he said, without apology. "I use them in my books whenever I want to spice things up."

"Just like real life," I said. "The court jesters."

Edsel Shamb laughed uncertainly and said, "Can I take you to breakfast?"

"But, sir," I said coyly, "we hardly know each other."

"What better reason then?" he said. "Besides, haven't you ever depended on the kindness of strangers?" He spoke the words as if he had found their magical combination all by himself.

"Tennessee Williams," I said.

Edsel smiled self-consciously. "I sometimes tune into his residual energy here on the island. I've been quoting him a lot lately. And I'll confess, I'm lonely for stimulating talk down here. It's nothing like New York or L.A. And when I met you yesterday, you impressed me as being pretty smart. That's partly why I'm inviting you to breakfast. For myself."

"You want to walk your wits around the block with me."

"That's right," he said. "A new voice in the wilderness. Have you been to Camille's yet?"

"That's exactly where I was going," I said.

"Then you shall be my guest," said best-selling Edsel Shamb as he opened the door for me.

7

Inside Camille's, Edsel suggested we take a table by the window. "To enjoy the panorama of tourists," he said grandly.

"And other island life," I added.

He smiled to acknowledge my lame joke. We were both a barrel of laughs that morning. But that's what I was there for, after all, to amuse him, to help pass the leisure time of Key West's self-appointed literary giant in his moment of fulguration.

Seconds after we sat down, a perky waitress with dark curly hair and an ample bosom approached our table and took our order. When she left, Edsel asked me if I minded if he smoked. I told him no. He lit up one of the spicy fags, then asked what my last name was.

"Kraychik," I said.

"Ah," he said, "you're Czech. That explains your smooth, pale skin. I'll bet there's not a hair on your body, at least from what I can see of your wrists."

"You're right," I said. "Except for that fuzzy little patch down there, I'm slick as a porpoise when I'm wet."

Edsel seemed to like the image. In fact, for a straight guy he seemed awfully intrigued with my body. But then, he was a writer, supposedly observing life's excruciating details. That's how he smoked too, in excruciating detail. Each puff was choreographed, every voluminous inhalation, every pregnant pause, every languorous exhalation.

Edsel said, "Are you attached?"

"Even when my lover was alive, I never used that word to describe us."

"You had an open relationship then?"

"No," I said quickly. "At least not by choice."

Would I ever overcome the guilt that I, the plain Jane with the once-barren sex life, had been the one to break the spell of monogamy between us?

"Did he die recently?" said Edsel.

"Last summer."

"AIDS?"

"No," I said, getting defensive. Even in that special horror of gay life I hadn't quite earned first-class citizenship, for my lover had not died a tragic and heroic death in the front lines of battle. There had been no lingering, no chance for me to care for him, to make amends for all our petty strivings and misunderstandings, to hold him until the last flicker of energy left his body. Instead my lover had been extinguished like a hapless bug, a victim of impromptu and immutable physics: moving vehicle against live body equals death.

"No," I said again. "He had an accident."

"I'm sorry," said Edsel.

"Me too," I said. "Let's talk about more pleasant things. What's it like to be a famous writer?"

He made a self-deprecating little chuckle that he'd rehearsed to perfection. "I'm not so sure that's a pleasant topic either," he said. "Or that I'm so famous. Not yet. The momentum is building, that's for sure."

"You make enough to put in a new swimming pool," I said.

"Life is good," he said. "But everything has its down side too. That pool will cost a fortune to maintain, and I'm not sure where that money is going to come from."

"Royalties," I said.

"Eventually," he replied. "But my agent is often late with the checks, and the publisher's sales figures are always jimmied, in their favor of course, so by the time I see any money, I'm in such debt that it's all spent already."

Awwwwww. Poor little best-seller.

"But your books are everywhere," I said. "You've got to be doing all right."

Edsel smiled the smile of the knowing. "You have no idea," he said. "But what will really put me over the top is a movie deal. Or better, a TV series. I'm working on one now, a pilot that should put that woman on prime-time television to rest once and for all."

"I kind of like her," I said.

"You do?" said Edsel.

"She's amusing."

"Who needs amusing?" he said. "There's no grip to the shows. There's nothing to worry about. No one has anything to lose. It's like playing connect-the-dots. It's pap."

"And your stuff is stronger?" I said.

"My stuff, as you call it, is about life and death."

"Maybe network television isn't ready for life and death."

Edsel smiled. "You need to expand your vision, Stan. Get Boston out of your bones."

The waitress arrived with a heavily laden tray. My three waffles were arranged on the plate like a small teepee over a mound of fresh fruit, with more fruit arranged copiously around the edge. I poured the warm syrup over everything, and eagerly prepared my fork for its first crunchy plummet. Then I looked toward Edsel and saw before him a small bowl half-filled with yogurt sprinkled lightly with granola. It wasn't exactly a life-and-death breakfast for the life-and-death writer he claimed to be.

"Enjoy!" he said to me.

"You too," I said with feigned heartiness. His breakfast looked like punishment rations.

Then the chirp of a cellular phone came from within his satchel. He took the call, said yes he was at Camille's, and yes it was okay, and then he hung up. "We are about to have some company," he said to me. Then he tried eating a couple of spoonfuls from his bowl, but he seemed to have difficulty swallowing. Finally he said, "What do you do in Boston?"

"I'm a hairdresser."

Edsel grabbed for his water and took a hasty gulp. Perhaps I wasn't manly enough to be having breakfast with him after all, the famous author cum wildebeest hunter.

"Any hobbies?" he said quickly.

"Needlepoint," I said, hoping to nourish his worst fears.

He shuddered. "Really?"

"No," I said. "But I have done some amateur PI work."

"Really?" Edsel said again, but without a shudder.

"Yeah."

"With the police?"

"Uh-huh."

"Well, well," he said, sounding relieved that I had some vestigial testosterone in my blood. "What a coincidence that you found Augusta's body yesterday."

"It was a silly way to kill someone."

Edsel added, fairly singing, "Just like something on television." He toyed with his yogurt—he really didn't want to eat it—then continued. "Still, Augusta's death has generated some excitement around here, something different from the tired old routines of abuse and recovery. In our cloistered little world someone actually had the guts to kill another person. That's real life and death."

Outside the cafe, I saw Laura Hope parking a small motor scooter on the sidewalk. The little thing was quite dusty, but seemed to do its job well, for Laura had secured a box of books behind the driver's saddle. She hauled the box into her arms, then entered Camille's and scanned the place for Edsel, though with her dark sunglasses, she had difficulty seeing indoors. She finally saw him and came to our table. She glanced vaguely at me, and focused herself on the writer.

"You didn't tell me you were with someone," she said. "I didn't mean to interrupt your breakfast, but when I called just now it sounded as though it was all right, and I—"

Edsel Shamb put up his hand to silence Laura. Then he moved his yogurt aside and pulled out a pen. "Just lay them out," he said, patting the tabletop in front of him, "and I shall bestow my enchanted mark upon them."

Laura quickly set up a stack of books. Then she took one copy, opened it to the title page, and placed it before Edsel. While he signed it, she prepared another book. Having applied his money-making name to the page, Edsel lifted his pen. With one hand Laura removed the autographed book, snapped it closed, and returned it to the cardboard box, while with the other hand she placed a fresh open copy in front of Edsel to sign. She moved smoothly and efficiently, shifting the books with barely a pause.

I said, "You two have obviously done this before."

"We have," she said through her sunglasses. "And I've done this for other famous people too." Then her forehead creased. "I didn't know you knew Edsel."

Edsel answered for me. "We're just getting to know each other." He continued signing books as he spoke. "Stan is a very interesting person. He's even worked with the Boston police. Imagine that? And he's the one who found Augusta's body."

"Well, well," said Laura with forced enthusiasm. "Maybe you'll find her killer too."

"Maybe," I said. "Were you at the Crow's Nest anytime yesterday morning between eight and eleven?"

Laura froze, books mid-shift in each hand. "I most certainly was not," she said curtly.

"You have an alibi?"

"Who are you to ask me?" she said.

"It's just a simple question, Laura. You don't even have to answer it."

"That's right," said Laura. "I don't, and I won't."

Then she turned her more affectionate—or should I say fawning—attention back onto the local celebrity, which was just fine with me, since I wanted to enjoy my breakfast and coffee while they were fresh. When Edsel had signed the last of the books, Laura arranged them all neatly in the box, then stood up and said a cordial and sincere thank-you to him. To me she turned and fairly snarled, "Enjoy your breakfast!" She might as well have said, "Choke on it." Then she stormed out of the cafe with her boxful of valuable signed first editions.

"Another giveaway," said Edsel with a deep sigh. "She and Joshua are always organizing some 'famous authors tour' of Key West, and to promote the things they give away signed copies of books."

"You still get the royalties, don't you?"

"Of course," he said. "Autographs may be free, books are not."

I said, "I wonder why Laura was so curt with me."

"You did kind of lace into her, asking her whereabouts yesterday morning."

"If people want to joke about my being a sleuth, then I might as well play the fool to the hilt."

"Very clever," said Edsel. "I've used that tactic too."

"Where were you yesterday morning?" I said.

He smiled. "You like to provoke people, don't you?"

"Are you hiding something?"

He said, "I was on the phone with my agent."

"All morning?"

"You can check my telephone bill when it comes."

I said, "Maybe we won't have to wait that long."

"You're suddenly very serious."

"It's a mask," I said. "If I don't do that, I come off sounding like Nancy Drew."

Edsel laughed heartily at my remark, too much so. "That's very good," he said, then repeated the name, "Nancy Drew." Then he laughed some more, but it was forced, like a show for some absent audience.

I tried to ask him about the mysterious woman he'd been sitting with at the O-Side the previous night, along with Adolf Dobermann, but that only launched him further into the laughing jag started by my mention of Nancy Drew. When the joke finally passed, whatever it was, he put his spoon into the pasty muck before him and pushed it around some more.

He said, "Did you always want to be a hairdresser?"

"I tried being a shrink, but it didn't agree with me. So now—" Suddenly I felt self-conscious. I was about to share a personal truth with a stranger. I really was too lonely.

Fortunately we were distracted at that moment by another familiar figure approaching along the sidewalk in front of Camille's. It was the Countess Rulalenska, purveyor of artful T-shirts on Whitehead Street. She wore her usual half-tinted glasses, which partly concealed her eyes. That day she'd fashioned her snug-fitting turban from a silk scarf of magenta, orange, and turquoise geometrics. She was talking on her cellular phone while she sucked at her cigarette holder with its pristine unlit cigarette. Our gazes met through the plate-glass window. Then she quickly averted hers to a shop on the other side of the street. She allowed another brief glance toward our table, long enough to identify my breakfast partner. When I looked at Edsel, I caught him studying me, as though trying to get behind the mask I was wearing for him that morning.

"The countess," he said grandly.

"The deposed aristocracy," I replied.

"I wonder what she thinks," he said, "now that Augusta Willits is dead."

"Were they friends?"

Edsel smiled mischievously. "You might say they ran a three-legged race, with Augusta's son between them."

"Sounds a bit incestuous."

"You'll find a lot of that around here too," said Edsel. "You almost feel left out if your folks didn't diddle you."

That disquieting exchange was broken by the sudden high-voltage arrival of Miss Cozy Dinette in Camille's Cafe.

"Boston!" she yelled as she entered the place.

"Oh, no," grumbled Edsel.

Cozy came directly to our table and pulled a chair up next to me. Her sunglasses that morning were a mass of rhinestone "feathers" sweeping back off her face into her hair. "Hello, Ed," she said with exaggerated friendliness, then she turned her attention—heart, body, and soul—to me. "Boston, we got rained out last night."

"I know," I said.

"Are you coming to the bingo party tonight?"

"Bingo?"

"At the Tulle Box. You've got to come. It's a fund-raiser."

Edsel squirmed irritably in his chair.

I said, "Isn't that where we met yesterday?"

"Yes!" said Cozy, erupting with volcanic verve. "*Our* place! They have an outdoor cabaret upstairs. I'm singing there tonight."

"Unless it rains again," I said.

Edsel added, "We can only pray."

Cozy advised him to go fuck himself. Then she said to me, "I'll leave your name at the door. There's bingo until eight or so, then a warm-up act, and I go on around nine."

"I'll be there," I said.

A quiet chirp from inside Cozy's straw bag indicated a phone call for her. "I know who that is," she said. "I'm late."

"As usual," said Edsel.

Cozy replied, "I do just fine without a time clock, Ed."

Then without answering her phone Cozy got up to leave the cafe as abruptly as she'd arrived. At the door she performed a lavish Dior turn and yelled back into the kitchen. "Camille! Camille, honey!" Then she blew big air kisses and waved her arms in that direction. "Love you, girl!" And then she was gone, and we all quivered in her wake, all except Edsel.

"What a crock of shit," he said.

"You don't like her?"

"You spend any time with her, you'll see why."

"She seems so bright, so positive, so vivacious."

"She's got you dazzled already," he said.

"She's a ball of fire," I countered.

"Scratch the phosphorous, find a bitch."

"What did she do to you?" I said.

"Skip it," said Edsel.

"Well," I said cheerily, "there's one good thing about this place, I mean, besides the food. There's plenty of foot traffic passing by."

"That's exactly why I come here," he said. "It's like Fifth Avenue and Forty-second Street, or Hollywood and Vine."

"Or Sodom and Gomorrah," I added.

Edsel laughed, then asked me if he could use the line in one of his scripts. I said sure, but I felt kind of sorry for him, a best-selling author filching lines from a hairdresser.

We finished breakfast, I thanked him, and then we went our separate ways. The only trouble was, he seemed to have a clear direction for the remainder of his day, while I faced a long hot afternoon of aimless drifting.

8

I considered doing something an ordinary tourist might do, like taking a ride in a glass-bottomed boat and watching the pretty fishies swim about the coral reef. Perhaps spending time like that would help me sort out the loss of Rafik. When he was alive, I had balked over commitment. With him dead, I could embrace the void. But that grotesque alliance with my dead lover would probably thrive far into the future, while my unofficial duties with the Key West police had a daily deadline of six o'clock. With less than five hours to dig up something for Lieutenant Sanfuentes, grieving for Rafik would have to wait.

I set out for Whitehead Street to pay a call on the Countess Rulalenska. Though she had snubbed me earlier through the window at Camille's Cafe, I would confront her where she couldn't escape—in her T-shirt shop. When I arrived at the store, Adolf Dobermann was there too, completing a massive purchase. Both people saw me enter the shop, but neither one acknowledged me. The countess waved her cigarette holder about, unlit and smokeless as usual. Dobermann smoked one of his short, imported jobs. He insisted to the countess that everything he'd bought was to be gift-wrapped, then crated and shipped to him in Germany, and damn the cost.

"I spare no expense," he said, "when it is for friends."

"Ah, yes," said the countess. "I was once as fortunate as you, but all is lost now. All I have retained is my title."

For all it mattered in a T-shirt shop.

She went on. "And I continue my appreciation of art."

Dobermann said, "And I continue my appreciation of real estate." He laughed heartily.

The countess joined him with a mirthful trill, then asked, "How will you pay today, Herr Dobermann?"

Dobermann smiled. "How do you think?"

"Oh-lo-lo!" said the countess with a coy little laugh. "Are you flirting with me, Herr Dobermann?"

"No," he said flatly. "I am flirting with my credit. I am sure you know exactly what I mean. Now if you please, make a receipt and tend to this business."

"Very well," said the countess. Her playfulness vanished instantly. She slapped a form on the counter, and Dobermann scribbled a careless mark on it, something meant to be his distinctive signature. Then he strode past me on his way out of the shop.

"You are everywhere," he snarled.

"It's a small island," I said.

"Yes," said Dobermann. "Perhaps too small."

Then he left.

The countess's face brightened with the German's departure. Then she clenched her cigarette holder with her teeth and began the task of wrapping each of the T-shirts he had purchased. She ignored me, probably hoping I'd vanish, like an unwelcome apparition.

I said, "Who does the art for your T-shirts?"

She cut and folded and taped the wrapping paper without looking up. "I use many local artists," she said.

"Some of the work looks exactly like Jeri Tiker's."

The countess replied blandly, "If anything is similar, it is she who has copied my merchandise."

"But Jeri Tiker was painting back in Wisconsin, probably before you were even in this country."

The countess raised her nose high in the air and said, "I know nothing of that. What is Wisconsin? Another country?"

"I suppose from your perspective, yes. How well did you know Augusta Willits, the woman who was killed yesterday?"

The countess stopped her infernal gift-wrapping and looked me straight in the eye. "What is your intention, young man?"

"I'm curious who might have had sufficient motive to kill her."

"That is a matter for the police, not for a tourist."

"What about her son, Peter? How well did you know him?"

There was the chink in the countess's armor.

"No one knew him as I did," she said. She fussed with her prop—discarded the old unlit cigarette and installed a fresh one—then continued talking, but with even more imposing airs. "Peter was a prince," she said. "He understood the meaning and importance of good breeding and a great family name. He was the only one on the island with refinement. I don't understand how that disease could dare to kill him."

"AIDS doesn't reason," I said.

"Do you know what Peter was going to do for me?" Then she caught herself. "Of course not," she said. "How could you? Tourist." Then she related Peter's great personal promise to her, the one he had been unable to consummate before succumbing so unjustly. "He promised me he would give me a new air conditioner, a real one, put into the ceiling, not in the windows like the commoners have. It was for my complexion. Peter always said my skin was the proof of my royal blood." She lifted her chin slightly and turned her head back and forth to tighten any slackness over the jawbone. "You see even now how clear and smooth it is?"

Thanks to cosmetics and a tuck or two.

She continued. "Peter wrote it in his will for me, the air conditioner. But his mother stopped everything. Augusta would not pay for it."

"And now she's dead."

"Yes. What a pity," said the countess, pitilessly. "But now I have hope that Peter's will can be executed properly."

"There's always hope," I said inanely. "But only if Augusta's contest is lost."

"What do you mean?" she said, suddenly worried.

"If the court awards Peter's estate to her, it doesn't matter that she's dead. *Her* will will be executed, including everything she won from her son."

The countess looked alarmed. "Are you saying that Peter's property will not go back according to his original intention?"

"Not if the court decides for Augusta."

"*Akh!*" went the countess. I half expected a solemn drum roll to accompany her. Instead, the telephone rang. She crossed the floor to answer it, clomping heavily, like an animal with cloven hooves.

Again I wondered how such a small body made such ponderous sounds. She answered the phone, recognized the caller, and listened to the message. Occasionally she replied with a quiet yet anxious "Yes" or "I see." But as the message continued, her alarm grew, and her voice became hoarser, almost gravelly as it said, "Is there nothing more we can do?" Then it returned to a more submissive "I see." Finally she hung up and cried out disconsolately, "All is lost! Everything!"

"What happened?"

"Peter's mother has taken everything from the rest of us and left it all to her church. The church! Damn her heathen soul! Now what am I to do?"

"You can appeal the decision," I said.

"But there are so many of us involved."

"All the more chance of reversing the decision."

"No," said the countess. "It is not possible."

"Why not?"

"You cannot understand. And now please," she said coolly, "you will excuse me, but I must prepare these things for Herr Dobermann. He is a very difficult client. And I must close the shop now. Good day."

Her message was clear: Get out.

I headed up Fleming Street and stopped in at Jeri Tiker's gallery. She was sitting at her worktable in the center of the gallery's floor, and was staring at a cat perched on a nearby stool. The animal returned her intent gaze. Then, finally bored with the moment, the cat jumped down and pretended to explore the gallery. Jeri continued following it with her eyes, and also mimicked the cat's gestures with little movements of her own. I asked her what she was doing.

"I'm psycholoading," she explained. "It's how I study my subjects. I open the windows on my subconscious and let all the energies register there. Then when the psychosponge is full, I close the window and paint."

Jeri must have caught my dubious gaze.

"I'm not crazy," she said. "It works. That cat will probably show up as a human in some future painting."

"Lucky human," I said.

"Yeah," said Jeri. "I kind of feel bad for the animals when I paint them as humans, but it's my way of trying to elevate us. In art school they always told us that good art should elevate and challenge. The challenge part is easy for me," she said as she indicated the whole gallery, as if her work was challenging. I found it exhilarating. "But as far as elevating, well, sometimes I think being a cat would be just fine."

Our kitty klatsch was interrupted by the arrival of Ken Kimble, soap star manqué, replete with sunglasses, muscles, teeth, and a stylish over-the-shoulder kidskin purse for his cellular telephone. He glanced quickly around the gallery, then addressed Jeri directly, dispensing with the social niceties.

"I can see now why you're causing such a buzz."

"A buzz?" said Jeri.

"There's a buzz going around about your paintings."

Jeri said, "What buzz?"

Ken said, "I hear it everywhere."

"Funny I don't," said Jeri.

"Buzz, buzz," I murmured.

"Sometimes the artist is the last to find out," said Ken.

"Like Norman Mailer," I said. "Supposedly he didn't know he'd written a best-seller until he read about it in the Sunday paper."

"That's ridiculous," said Ken. Then he said to Jeri, "I'm willing to help the buzz and buy some of your work. People on this island tend to emulate my taste."

"Really?" said Jeri. "Too bad we're not in Manhattan."

"Why?" said Ken.

"That's the island I'd like to win over. Maybe if you bought that big painting I'd have the money to go."

Ken glanced at the painting Jeri had pointed to. Then he went closer for a scrutinizing assessment. It portrayed two young women, one pale and naked, the other ebony and clothed, both reclined in a passionate embrace beneath a "family portrait" whose members were also racially diverse.

As he studied the work Ken said, "I don't know why, but some of your characters look familiar, but I can't exactly place them."

"Everyone I paint comes out in some other form, even myself," said Jeri.

"You mean altered and distorted?" said Ken.

"Not to me," said Jeri.

"Well, it's certainly a clever way to express yourself without risk of slander."

"You mean libel," I said.

Ken turned to me. "Do I?"

"Slander is verbal, libel is graphic."

Jeri said to me, "Let him say what he wants."

Ken said, "I'd like to take this one on approval. What are your terms?"

Jeri suddenly became all business. "You pay for it, it's yours."

"Do you deliver?" he interrupted.

"For a charge," she said.

"That's certainly no concern for me," he said, as if rich people never cared about money, and only artists groveled for it and padded their prices with things like delivery charges. "My only concern," said Ken Kimble, "is if I don't like it, will you take it back?"

"If you think you might not like it," said Jeri, "then don't buy it."

"But it might grow on me," he said. "How long would I be able to keep it?"

"Until it doubles in value," said Jeri.

He paused, then said, "Are you being impertinent?"

Jeri replied, "Are you being an asshole?"

"How dare you!"

"Don't patronize me," said Jeri. "I changed my mind. That painting isn't for sale."

"What!" said Ken.

"*While the Family Watches* is not for sale. It just went off the market."

"How can you do that?" spluttered Ken.

"It's my work," said Jeri. "And I don't want to sell it to you. I can change my mind too, just the way you want to if you hung it in your living room and decided it didn't match your color scheme."

"I came in here wanting to buy a painting," said Ken Kimble, "and now you refuse to sell me one. Don't you realize how lucky you are that someone like me is even interested in your work?"

"I've been painting in this studio for a whole year, Mr. Kimble, and I've never seen you in here until now. So I can't help wondering, what is it that you really want, and who put you up to it?"

"Well!" said Ken, now fuming with rage. "It's no wonder you have financial problems. You act like a prima donna and you're not even a chorus girl."

Jeri cocked her head and studied Ken Kimble from various angles, psycholoading her subconscious just the way she'd done earlier with the stray cat. How would she reincarnate Ken in some future work?

Ken blathered on. "With your attitude, you'll be lucky to be painting T-shirts."

"Go tell it to the countess," said Jeri. "I said no to her sleazy offer too."

Ken Kimble left the gallery in a rage.

When the air had quieted down, I said to Jeri, "Why did you do that? He really wanted that painting. You would have had some cash."

"I couldn't bear to have it hanging in his house like it was in a bank vault appreciating in value. That's not why I paint."

"But you need money, Jeri."

"I know, but does that mean my paintings have to become investments for other people?"

"On this planet, yes."

Jeri went to her worktable and sat down. She pulled out a clean sheaf of art paper, then she jammed her brush into an awful ochre-colored clump of excess pigments at the edge of her palette. With that she slashed out a big ugly dollar sign on the paper. She even signed it in the lower right-hand corner.

"There!" she said. "That's my latest portrait. A priceless work of art. It's called *Ken Kimble*."

I chuckled. "At least he can't sue you for libel."

"Why not?" said Jeri.

"Because the resemblance is undeniably accurate, even for a court of law."

"Someone like Ken Kimble would sue me just to make trouble."

"Notoriety will make you famous," I said.

"I don't want notoriety," said Jeri. "Or fame. I just want to paint."

"What about Manhattan?" I said. "Didn't you say you wanted to win those folks over?"

"Yeah," said Jeri.

"So maybe a little fame isn't bad."

Jeri Tiker's eyes became wistful. "Sometimes," she said, "I wish I could just skip the difficult part of becoming an artist—the struggle, like what's happening now—and just get to the secure phase of my life, when every brush stroke carries the weight of all those years of experience. Then I won't care anymore about people like Ken Kimble coming in and buzzing around me like an irritating bug."

"Sorry to break the news," I said, "but the chance for some security is about to get a little harder for you." I told Jeri to expect a phone call soon, bearing the unpleasant news that Augusta Willits had won the contest for her son's estate.

"I guess we'll have to appeal then," said Jeri.

"It's going to be a Sisyphean task."

"A what?" said Jeri.

"A big problem. Augusta left everything to her church."

Jeri sighed heavily. "It figures," she said. Then she sighed again. "Well, until I get to that comfortable, purely expressive phase of my life, I guess I'll just keep working."

I headed toward the door. "Thanks for the lesson," I said.

"Lesson in what?"

"Psycholoading the psychosponge," I replied. "I may use it in my dissertation if I ever go back to school, with your permission, of course."

"It's yours," said Jeri Tiker.

I left her studio and continued up Fleming Street, which took me past the Fleming Lemming. Laura Hope was sitting outside on the sidewalk, having a cigarette and coffee and reading a book, though with her dark sunglasses, seeing anything on the page must have been a challenge. She glanced up and, to my surprise, waved me over.

"I apologize for my behavior this morning at Camille's," she said. "I've been under a lot of pressure."

She sounded sincere, yet she blew smoke at me.

I said, "That authors' tour must be keeping you busy."

"Among other things," she replied with a sideways glance, as if she wanted to view me without the dark lenses, or else tell me something that she dared not.

Inside the Fleming Lemming the telephone rang, but Laura made no move to answer it. "That's either something unimportant or a problem," she said. "And I'm on break."

"Joshua can get it," I said.

Another elusive glance from Laura. "He's not here." Her voice sounded almost relieved, liberated, and I sensed she might talk to me.

"Did you know Peter Willits?" I said.

Laura smiled. She put out her cigarette and closed her book. Then she removed her sunglasses and aimed her bright blue eyes directly into mine. Without the shades, Laura's big square facial bones were even more apparent. "I might as well tell you now," she said, "so you don't stumble around trying to guess what the truth is. No, I hardly knew Peter Willits, but, yes, he named me in his will."

"Really? For what?"

Laura pressed her lips together. "I was to inherit this place."

"The Fleming Lemming?"

"Yes," she said.

"Why would he leave you such valuable property if you hardly knew him?"

"Because Peter Willits loved books, just like me. And he knew that my real dream was to have a bookstore."

"Is that what Joshua wants too?"

"Not quite," said Laura.

"What happens if you get the place?"

"I'll cross that bridge then," she said. "For now, I'll just wait."

"For what?" I said.

"To find out who wins Peter's property—the ones he intended to have it, or the mother who intruded. It's between us and Augusta now—or her estate, since she's dead."

"You mean her church."

Laura's face blanched. "What?"

"Augusta willed her entire estate to her church."

"How do you know?" she said.

I told her the news she apparently hadn't heard yet, that from the netherworld Augusta had won her son's estate, which meant the church had won everything too.

"You certainly get around," said Laura. "And we're all in worse trouble than I thought. This whole mess was bad enough with Augusta alive. But now, facing her church, it's going to be a monstrous fight."

"You'll appeal it, won't you?" I said.

"We'll really have to join together for that," said Laura.

At that moment Joshua Aytem bounded out the front door of the Fleming Lemming. "Coffee al fresco today?" he said to Laura. His sexy stubble reminded me once again to shave.

Laura replied, "Josh! Did you come in the back way?"

"Well, I didn't use the front door, did I?"

"No," came Laura's meek reply. "You finished early then."

Joshua said, "I called here a few minutes ago. Why didn't you answer?"

"I was having a conversation," she said. "Remember those?"

There was an awkward silence as Joshua finally acknowledged my presence. Despite his mirror-hidden eyes, he was clearly annoyed that I was outside his storefront talking to his wife.

"How did the meeting go?" Laura said to him.

"We'll talk about it later," he muttered.

"Just tell me if I have to call my broker, Josh."

He aimed his mirrored eyes at me and said, "Would you excuse us?"

"I was just on my way," I said.

Then he said to Laura, "Inside." And in they went. He locked the door behind them. Then he closed the blinds on the door to keep anyone from looking in. Only then did I hear their muffled voices assaulting each other, probably the standard preamble to an afternoon frolic.

As I continued my walk up Fleming Street, a pink taxi with heavily tinted windows passed by slowly, as if trailing me. The license plate KEY–CAB confirmed that it was the same vehicle as those other times. I found a pay phone and called the pink cab company to find out who the driver was. They answered almost immediately, and I told them I wanted to file a complaint. The dispatcher said she'd take the report, but she couldn't tell me who the driver was.

"For security reasons," she said. "I'm sure you understand. We can't give out the identities of our drivers. You never know what kind of crazy people are out there."

I told her that was exactly my point.

She said brusquely, "Tell me what happened."

I told her.

She said, "Is that what you want me to write in the report, sir? That one of our cabs slowed down to see if you wanted a ride?"

"It was *following* me," I said sharply.

But when I identified the cab's license plate for her, she replied quickly, "That's not one of our vehicles."

"It sure looks like one," I said.

"We have no vehicle with a plate that says KEY–CAB."

"Are you sure?"

"I ought to know," she said, now thoroughly irritated with me. "I own the company and I've registered every car in my fleet."

I thanked her for no help and hung up. It was almost five o'clock, so I headed to the police station to make my first official report to Lieutenant Sanfuentes.

9

Five o'clock," said Sanfuentes as he led me to his office. "You got a whole hour to spare."

I recounted everything I'd seen and heard that day, however indirectly it reflected on the death of Augusta Willits. Sanfuentes took few notes, as though he already knew everything I told him.

Then I mentioned the bothersome pink taxicab.

"Maybe the driver thinks you need a lift," he said, brushing it off. "Last night it was raining pretty hard, and today, I don't know, maybe you went shopping and had a load of bundles."

"I didn't go shopping, Lieutenant."

"Okay, okay," said Sanfuentes. "All I'm saying is maybe that cab was just trying to give you a chance to hail him."

"It's not a real cab."

"How do you know?" said the cop.

"I called the cab company, and they don't have a car with that plate."

"Is that so?" Then he shrugged. "We got a lot of independent cabbies around here. Maybe one of them painted his car pink."

"Wouldn't the cab company protest something like that?"

"What are they gonna do?" he said. "Sue the guy for having a pink car?"

"It looks like a pink *cab*, Lieutenant. That's different. It's almost a trademark."

Sanfuentes wouldn't buy my argument. "Did you ever think maybe the guy driving that cab likes you?"

I ignored his taunt and asked if I could see copies of Peter and Augusta Willits's wills.

"No way," said the cop. "That's private stuff."

"I thought a will was public information when it's in probate."

"Is that so?" said Sanfuentes again. "Then if you can get your hands on a copy, be my guest."

"What about yours?"

He paused, then said flatly, "I think I mislaid it."

"But the motives are all there."

"Oh, really?" he said. "Tell me about these motives."

His voice held more challenge than interest. Still, I explained the obvious, how everyone who stood to inherit property from Peter's estate had a good reason to stop Augusta from contesting the will—that is, kill her. Sanfuentes agreed, and asked me what else I expected to find in the two wills.

"I don't know," I said. "That's why I want to see them."

"Nah," said the cop with a stubborn shake of his head. "I think we have a little misunderstanding here. Your job—correction, your small favor to me—is to look and listen and then come and talk to me. It is not to advise me how to run my case. Are we clear on that?"

I told him if I knew what he was doing on the case, I wouldn't have to duplicate his efforts.

His reply?

"Go ahead and duplicate them—if you think you can."

Then he suggested I was taking my assignment too seriously, at the expense of enjoying my vacation. As if to placate him, I told him I was going to a bingo party that night.

"Don't lose your shirt," he said.

"I can keep my clothes on for bingo," I said.

"That's a good start," said the cop.

Duly slapped on the wrist, I left the station and headed back to my guest house. I stripped and lay down on the bed and let the air conditioner blow cool air over me. I tried one more time to get into Edsel Shamb's book, especially since I'd spent some time with him at breakfast that day. I thought it might give me a window into his writing but it didn't help. It was like watching television from the printed page. I closed the book and rolled over onto my front side. The wavy patterns of raised cotton chenille scrubbed softly against my chest and belly and thighs, much the way my lover's body hair used to stimulate me. I drifted off pleasantly for a short nap.

When I woke up I called Nicole and told her about my unofficial job assisting the Key West police. She was hardly pleased.

"You treat these things like a puzzle, Stanley—an innocent game—and you seem to forget that somewhere along the string of events, there's a killer."

"Nikki, what I'm about to say might sound a bit exalted."

"Then don't say it."

"I have to. It's like a cosmic joke on me. You know how I always dreamed of being rich, but never really believed it would happen? And so instead I dreamed and hoped for love. And I got that, finally, for a little while anyway."

"What is your point?" said Nicole, already impatient.

"The point is, I lost my love and found myself rich. And I don't even care now."

"You will in a few years, darling."

"Nikki, right now I don't care if I live or die."

"Stanley—"

"Let me finish. If I don't care about anything—I mean generally—I mean, you're still important, and the cat is important, and I love you both—"

"I suppose that's something," she said testily.

"But I need a reason to get me through the day. Even you said I need structure."

"I meant something practical, not finding killers."

"Branco does it."

"Stop calling him that!" said Nicole. "You are not Branco. I mean Vito!"

"But maybe I can work for him, Nikki. He said he'd help me get into the police academy. That would be a major coup for someone like me."

"Ah," said Nicole. "So this is really a quest to prove that a hairdresser is as worthy as a police officer."

"What's wrong with that?"

"Stanley, you have a life already, a good life. You have satisfied clients, you have creative freedom, and you have me."

"And I need a change."

"Am I so horrible to work for?"

"No, Nikki. We'll always be best friends. But this has nothing to do with you. It's me. Part of me is dead, and I'm trying to revive the piece that's still breathing. I just want to try this sleuthing bit awhile."

"And that's exactly what it is," said Nicole. "A bit, like on the stage. Don't discard your past so easily, Stanley. And don't forget that your clients at the shop can't kill you."

"They can cause psychic death."

"Well," said Nicole with a big sigh, "at least we're arguing again. Perhaps there's hope."

"Bitter hope."

"Stop it," said Nicole. "Are you going to call Vito?"

"I want to prove myself first."

Nicole roared her boisterous laugh, and I had to pull the phone from my ear. When she quieted down she said, "You sound like a prince who must slay a dragon to win a damsel's heart."

"Branco is hardly a damsel."

"Yes, Stanley, and you're hardly a prince. Now just be reasonable and call the man if you need his help. Vito and I are both on your side. And in the meantime, try to eat something."

"Yes, ma'am."

"And call me."

"Yes again."

Then Nicole hung up.

She had unwittingly bruised my ego, telling me I wasn't a prince. Who knew that fact better than I? But it was still unnerving to hear it stated so flatly from my beloved, trusted, unconditional friend. I gazed into a nearby mirror.

"You are not a prince," I said.

How would I console my wounded ego with such bitter truth? My inner child was no use, since I'd aborted her long ago. And that recent brigade of cosmic healers, the angels, had somehow overlooked me in their circumnavigations of the globe.

So instead I took a shower—you can't shower too often in the sticky heat of Key West—and I finally lathered up and shaved the many days of stubble from my face. I did retain the short mustache whiskers for an illusion of toughness. Then I picked out a bright little ensemble for the evening's outing: pink shorts and a gray polo jersey. The sun was down so my skin was safe. Besides, under cover of night my pale, pale Czech complexion would appear less glaring than it would in the direct tropical sunlight.

I checked myself in the mirror. For someone who was trying to bid adieu to the past and embark on a new life, the picture wasn't bad. The most obvious change was that the dumpling had become a breadstick. My face was gaunt, with cheekbones protruding, and the skin around my eyes was darkened with grief and trouble. With my smooth slenderness I almost looked like a boy—a boy who stayed up too late and did naughty things—a boy with strong sturdy legs and gray and copper bristles coming out of his head. I still didn't know quite who I was.

As I passed the front desk downstairs, the receptionist whistled at me and said, "Get a load of those gams!"

I glanced at him over my shoulder and gave a little back-kick with one leg. "You should see me *en travesti,*" I said, "when I play a real man."

"You mean with a harness and titclamps?" said the clerk.

If he could perceive that side of me so easily, I was a cliché after all.

When I arrived at the Tulle Box, Cozy Dinette was at the upstairs bar, sitting alone and lubricating her vocal cords with a preshow cocktail. She saw me and called out, "Boston!" and waved me over to her. She greeted me with a big hug, and ran the top of one hand tenderly over my clean-shaven jaw and cheek. "Nice," she said. "And I like the 'stache too."

In return I complimented her evening eyewear, faux emerald-studded frames with pale champagne lenses. "Boston," she said, "I have more shades than Imelda had shoes." And she laughed her raucous laugh.

I looked for Ross, my favorite cowboy bartender, but Cozy told me he was off duty that night, that he had other jobs. She must have seen the disappointment in my face, because she said, "I hope you're not getting hopeful ideas for him."

"Kind of, sort of," I said.

"Don't," said Cozy.

"I thought you two were friends."

"Boston, I love him, but even the people you love most have things about them you wouldn't tell your best friend. And since you're my newest best friend, I'm telling you to keep it strictly huggy-kissy with Ross."

"If I get that far."

"Oh, you will," said Cozy.

I ordered a martini from the Great One's runner-up. Though he did well, he was no match for Ross, the absent master.

Sitting on the other side of the circular bar were the Countess Rulalenska, wearing her semipermeable eyeglasses, and Ken Kimble, wearing his semipermeable muscles. Ken seemed to avoid my eyes. Perhaps he was embarrassed by the scene he'd made that afternoon in Jeri Tiker's gallery. The countess, meanwhile, oblivious to her self-appointed station, guzzled champagne and carelessly waved her unlit cigarette-in-holder around.

"Excuse me," I said to Cozy, "while I go raise the nap on some-one's velvet glove."

"Hers?" said Cozy, indicating the countess.

"And his," I said.

"Why? Ken's a nice guy."

"Too smooth to be true," I said.

I went and stood in front of Ken and the countess, who were facing each other on their barstools. They tried to ignore me, so I spoke up, friendly like.

"Nice to see you two here tonight."

Without missing a beat, Ken replied, "I'm always here for the bingo parties. They're fund-raisers, and I always make a generous donation."

"Cash?" I said. "Or something more tangible, like artwork?"

"Sometimes both," said Ken, cool and collected.

"I need a donation too," said the countess. Her speech was slightly slurred. "Or I shall never have my air-conditioning."

"Stassya," said Ken, "nothing is final yet." He spoke firmly, as though trying to shut her up. But with the help of too much champagne she would have her say.

"Whom shall we fight now?" she said, using good grammar, which may have been just one more regal affectation. "The woman is dead."

Ken said, "Augusta didn't get herself killed on purpose."

"Still," said the countess, "she *did* stop my air-conditioning." She turned and faced toward me. "You cannot imagine the discomfort I must endure."

I said, "If you don't like the weather, maybe you should go home." Sound advice from a sun-sensitive sissy in Key West.

The countess glared at me. "This is my home. But I need money. Perhaps *you* can help me."

I said, "What about your friends?" I glanced toward Ken, who defended himself quickly.

"I'm having fiscal issues."

The countess rotated the barstool so that her whole body faced me directly. "Did you not acquire a large sum of money recently? Surely you have more than you need."

There it was: royalty appealing to a hairburner for air-conditioning.

I said politely, "I'm sorry."

"Don't you have any cash?" she said, raising her voice.

Her directness flustered me. "Not really," I said. It was almost true, for I'd put most of the money into responsible investments until I decided what to do with it. I mean, besides blowing it.

The countess pressed on. "When will you have some?"

I hesitated. "I'm not sure."

Suddenly Cozy Dinette was standing between us. "Leave him alone, Countess! He's not a bank machine."

"But what am I to do?" said the countess.

"Figure it out yourself!" yelled Cozy. "You act like you're the only one who lost something. We all lost, Countess. Face it. It's time to join the human race."

But the countess just clucked her tongue. Then she rotated herself away from us and back toward Ken Kimble. She lowered her voice and murmured something to him. Then she glanced over her shoulder and tittered quietly at Cozy and me.

Cozy grabbed my arm. "Come on," she said. "Let's go play bingo."

On the way down I asked Cozy what she'd meant about everyone losing. "Who's everyone?" I said.

"Never mind," she said. "It doesn't concern you."

I stopped on the stairs and pouted. "Some best friend you are," I said, "keeping secrets."

"What secrets?" she said.

"Cozy, I already know Augusta won her case and got everything from Peter's estate."

"So . . . ?" she said.

"So who else was in Peter's will?"

"That's not important," she said.

"But everyone had a motive to kill Augusta."

"Not necessarily," said Cozy.

"But you'll all appeal the decision, right?"

"Actually, our lawyer has advised against that."

"Maybe you need a new lawyer."

"We already have the best one on the keys. Really, Boston, leave it alone."

"Are you hiding something?"

Cozy flashed her cold blue eyes at me. "Look, whoever killed Augusta was too late. She'd already won."

"Maybe you didn't know that at the time."

"Me!" said Cozy. "Jeez, Boston, when you turn, you really turn."

"I want to make sure my best friend isn't a criminal."

"It could be worse," she said.

"How?"

"I could be lying." Then Cozy laughed and said, "C'mon, let's go win piles of cash."

We entered the downstairs patio, where the bingo game was in high gear, crackling with the desperate energy of gamblers. Most of the donated prizes had been claimed already, but the huge cash pot had not been played for yet. To add spice to the game, the cost of the cards had been raised every round as the value of the offered prizes went up. Half of all the money taken during the evening went to support a local hospice. The other went into the cash pot. Cozy and I entered the game just in time to play for that big prize, when the price of a single bingo card was twenty dollars. She looked at me and said, "What do you think? Too high?"

"These days, doll, it's all or nothing for me."

Cozy bought one card, I bought five.

When I handed the guy a hundred-dollar bill, he complimented my legs. Within five minutes Cozy proved herself a latent prophet: I won the cash pot. It contained almost five thousand dollars, which was a far better return on the hundred bucks than anything a legitimate broker had got me so far with Rafik's blood money. Still, I knew other people needed that bingo loot a lot more than rich little me did. And the countess wasn't among them. So I donated it all to the hospice fund. Then I wrote an IOU for roughly five thousand more, just to round the total up to a nice even ten. I had too much for myself anyway.

One of the young guys who'd been playing the game exclaimed hotly, "Are you crazy? You don't give the cash pot away."

"I do," I said.

He grumbled, while another stranger, an older guy, came up to me and said, "I like impetuous men. And I like your fuzzcut too."

"It was self-inflicted," I said. Then I complimented him on his hair, which was suitably youthful for his far-from-boyish age.

"Oh, Kitty," he said, turning playful, "don't flirt with this old thing. It's called all-day-at-work-and-it-fell." Then he laughed and tottered off.

With the bingo party over, the upstairs cabaret was officially opened, so Cozy and I went back up. She dashed backstage to get ready, while I took a seat near the door. Meanwhile the audience had to endure the preternatural wailings of the warm-up singer, a rank novice who caused me to wonder if humans really were the only primates who sang.

Two more cocktails and three-quarters of an hour later came the announcement for the evening's featured event, Miss Cozy Dinette and her band, the Family Style Meals. They opened the set with their local hit single, "Can't Remember Shit," and finally I got to hear it. The song began as a quiet blues ballad about a woman who'd lost her one man and then sank to the bottom of existence with a bottle in her hand. Cozy reinforced the message of her performance by imbibing a large cocktail onstage. But then, broken and downhearted, the heroine of the song finds her inner strength, and empowers herself and rises victorious over a wasted life of addiction and abuse. It was a paean to recovery, and by the end of the song Cozy Dinette and the Family Style Meals were rocking the timbers of the Tulle Box. Despite the irony that Cozy Dinette was thoroughly intoxicated while singing about the triumph of recovery, the audience went wild.

That's when I realized I'd had all the fun I was going to have that night, and it was time to leave. I headed back downstairs. As I passed a tiny lounge off the main lobby, I noticed three people sitting around a table in a faraway corner. They were Edsel Shamb, Adolf Dobermann, and the mysterious woman in voluminous silk. Their tête-à-tête was a déjà vu, for I had seen the same trio at the O-Side the previous night. And Dobermann was supposed to have left town already.

I approached their small table. The corner location had confined the dense smoke from Adolf's and Edsel's cigarettes, creating a private Alhambra around the three of them. But the trio had also left their sunglasses at home, so I got to see everyone's eyes, albeit in the protective gloaming of a crowded, noisy, smoky cocktail lounge.

Edsel saw me and called out my name. My legs got an appraising glance from him as he said, "Did I hear right? You won the cash pot tonight, then turned it all back in."

"News travels fast," I said.

"Something like that, sure," he replied.

I shrugged. "It's only money."

"We could all use more of that." Then he gestured toward Adolf. "You two have met already."

I nodded a greeting to the German, who didn't return it.

Then Edsel introduced the woman in silk. Her name was Nancy Drew. No sooner had Edsel said it than she corrected him.

"Nancy *L.* Drew," she said, emphasizing the initial. "I'm the attorney, not the other one." Perhaps it was her idea of a joke, but there was certainly no mistaking the two women. A single garment from this one's wardrobe—the cost of materials alone, considering the yardage required and the going rate for silk voile or crêpe de chine—would exhaust any advance on royalties, perhaps even a movie deal, that the lesser, literary Nancy Drew might have garnered.

"I'm Stan Kraychik," I said. "What's your specialty?"

A professional to the marrow, Attorney Nancy L. Drew answered reflexively, "Real estate, probate, and corporate law."

"The clean stuff," I said. "Are you by any chance Cozy Dinette's attorney?"

My question caused a moment of suspended animation at the table. Even the clouds of smoke stopped moving.

Then Nancy L. Drew said, "Whatever makes you ask that?"

I replied, "Cozy Dinette just told me she's got the best lawyer in Florida. And with a name like yours, you almost have an obligation to be the best."

Nancy L. Drew said, "A reputation is based on more than a name."

"That's hardly a direct answer," I said.

"And it's hardly any of your business," said Nancy L. Drew.

Adolf Dobermann gave me a rodentlike glare, then said to the others, "My good friends, should we our business elsewhere continue?"

Edsel said, "What business? Have another beer, Adolf."

"No, no," said the German. "Enough."

Nancy L. Drew said, "It's late for me too. I have an early day tomorrow."

I held up my hand. "Stop the excuses, folks. You can continue your public forum in complete privacy, for I'm on my way." Half-hearted farewells followed as I left their table.

Once out of the Tulle Box, I turned up a narrow alley that led to Simonton Street. Someone called to me from behind, and I turned. It was Ken Kimble. He walked toward me, all the while staring at my pale but naturally muscular thighs and calves.

Ken said, "I want to apologize for the countess."

"It doesn't matter," I said. "I hardly know her."

"Stassya didn't realize your money came from someone's death."

"Most inheritances do," I said.

"Yes," he said quickly, "but there's something else, just between you and me." Ken paused then, suddenly awkward. For a moment the spiritual enthusiast went away, and he was just another pile of well-honed muscles. "I'm hosting a little party tomorrow evening, very private. I'd like you to come."

I guess exposing my legs and arms had dispelled any concern about symptoms I might have been hiding.

Ken went on. "There'll be a lot of interesting men there."

"Didn't you say earlier you were having money problems?"

"I keep a special account for leisure," he said.

What else did he do but leisure?

Then Ken added suggestively, "I enjoy blowing a big wad on parties."

"I'd better bring my wet suit."

Ken Kimble scowled.

I said it was a joke.

He said, "Do you have issues about sex?"

"My lover is dead."

"How long are you going to mourn for him?"

"Until I'm done," I said.

"Don't wait so long that you miss all the fun."

"I live for more than that."

"You have guilt issues too."

"Not guilt, Ken. And not issues. Just plain old sadness."

"I understand," he said. "You're in denial. You have all the classic signs. But take it from someone who has been through the dark forest, until you can address those issues and accept what really happened to you, and *own* all the things you've done to bury the truth and keep it hidden, until you can forgive yourself and those who violated you, you'll never truly heal and realize yourself. And I can help you."

"You can start by using plain English."

He shook his head sadly. "You're exactly how I was—so, so stubborn."

"Thanks for the advice, Ken. And for the invitation."

"I hope you'll come."

"No promises," I said.

He shook his head again. "Unable to commit," he said.

I took a roundabout route back to the Jared Bellamy House. I wasn't quite ready to encapsulate myself in my room again. And I wondered if there was any plain old-fashioned fun on the island, the kind that didn't require you to excavate repressed memories first. I took a detour down Windsor Lane, one of the narrow and less traveled streets. It became extremely dark where the road passed the cemetery. The streetlights had gone out too, probably from the previous night's rainstorm. Then I heard the sound of a car motor behind me, trailing along with me. I turned. Though the headlights blinded me, I knew it was the same pink taxicab as before. I raised my hand to hail it, as if I needed a lift, but the cab raced its engine and zoomed off.

So much for Lieutenant Sanfuentes's friendship theory.

10

On my way to breakfast early the next morning I met Laura Hope on her motor scooter coming up Fleming Street. She seemed bright and cheerful, and so did her motor scooter, all shiny clean and sparkling in the sunshine. She invited me to the Fleming Lemming for coffee. Once inside she scurried around opening up the place. She was late, she said, so the coffee would take a little while.

From deep within the storage shelves she called out, "I just sold a rare first edition this morning. Oh, do we ever need the money!"

"No wonder you're in such a good mood."

Laura reappeared out front, fairly chirping. "It feels like a holiday. First that sale, and now Adolf Dobermann is finally leaving the island this morning. It's such a relief, after all the delays. But Josh is taking him to the airport right now. Finally he'll be gone from here. I hope for good."

"You don't like him?"

"I don't really care," said Laura, "not for myself. It's Josh. He's too involved with him. It's almost like a spell, and it's only because Adolf has so much money to throw around."

"You know," I said, throwing a little fuel onto the fire, "twice I've seen Adolf meeting with Edsel Shamb and a woman named Nancy Drew. And both times Joshua wasn't there."

"That's exactly what I mean," said Laura. "They just use him, and they make important decisions without telling him."

"Is Joshua in business with them?"

"Not really," she said. "He just did errands and things." Then she looked at me with new eyes. "It's unnerving how easily you get people to talk to you."

"It's hereditary," I said. "My aunt Letta's the same way. She knows everybody's business, and nobody knows hers."

That's when Joshua rushed in from outside looking flushed and worried.

"Is he here?" he said breathlessly.

"Who?" said Laura.

" 'Who?' " said Joshua, mimicking her. "The Prince of Wales."

Laura said, "You mean Adolf?"

"Oh, you *are* awake," said Joshua.

"I thought you went to get him."

"I did, and he wasn't there. He left a message at the Crow's Nest saying he'd meet me here."

"That's odd," said Laura.

"What's going to be odd," said Joshua, "is if I don't find him soon Mr. Dobermann is going to miss his flight."

"Not again!" said Laura. "Where could he be?"

"I don't know," said Joshua.

"Call him," she said. "He has a cell phone, doesn't he?"

"Shit," said Joshua. "I'm not thinking straight. Thanks, Laura." He quickly dialed a number and waited, but there was no answer. "Something's wrong," he said. "Adolf always answers, even if he's on the crapper."

Laura said, "Did you check his appointment book?"

"I can't find the damn thing."

"It's right there," she said, pointing to the top of Joshua's desk.

"I must be losing my mind," said Joshua. "It wasn't there the last time I looked."

"Maybe you were blinded by love."

"Cut that out!" snapped Joshua.

"Or maybe it's Adolf who's in love with you?" she said. "Why else would he keep canceling his trips home?"

"Don't start, Laura. Not now."

"He can't bear to abandon you here in Key West with *me*."

Joshua managed to ignore her taunts while he flipped through the appointment book. "He's got to go back this time," he said. "He's got business to conduct in person."

"Or else what?" said Laura. "Another harebrained scheme will fall through?"

Joshua said, "I wonder if he went to the Twin Palms."

"Why would he go there?" she said. "That place has been closed for years."

"I don't know, but it says right here in his book, *'Twin Palms 8:30'*. But why didn't he have me drive him there?"

"Maybe he's seeing someone else," said Laura.

"I said cut that out!"

"Let's hope nothing happened to him."

"Was that a death wish, Laura?"

"Maybe that's what *you* want, Josh."

"We're real close, Laura, you and me, to a nice long ride on the gravy train. Just for your information, Adolf wants me to manage all his property here on the island. You know what that will mean for us, to have all those tourists in the palm of our hands?"

Laura said, "Tell me."

"We'll be Key West's one-stop tourist center. We'll handle theater tickets, rides on the conch trains, sailing trips, dinner groups, not to mention our cut of their tabs at Dobermann's guest houses. It's guaranteed revenue, Laura."

"Nothing is guaranteed, Josh."

"Oh, yeah? You know how much he's going to pay me? A hundred thousand a year for a part-time job."

"Do you have a contract?" said Laura.

"We have a gentleman's agreement," said Joshua. "Something you wouldn't understand."

"You're an idiot, Josh."

"Yeah, well, look who's my partner. Anyway, I'm driving out to the Twin Palms." Then he turned to me. "You want to come? You really ought to see this place. It's a fallen shrine to the party days on Key West."

Their conjugal typhoon had risen swiftly, and I wanted a speedy escape. "Sure," I said. "I like fallen shrines."

We rode in a big green sedan that had been rented by Adolf Dobermann during his lengthy stay in Key West. Joshua seemed anxious as he drove to the other end of the island.

"I hope he's okay," he said. "If anything happens to Adolf, I'll lose the biggest break of my life."

"What could happen?" I said.

Joshua clenched his jaw. "Who knows?"

We drove past the official Coast Guard marker for the southernmost point of the continental United States. Joshua said the giant buoy was also dubbed the world's biggest butt plug. Maybe he was trying to lessen his anxiety, or maybe he liked sounding sexually hip.

The Twin Palms was a derelict old place concealed behind a grove of palm trees and badly overgrown vegetation. Joshua pulled into the parking lot, not much more than a small field of red clay, muddy potholes, and tropical weeds. He sounded the horn long and loud, and then called out Adolf's name. There was no response.

"Something isn't right here," he said. His voice sounded dry. We got out of the car, and I noticed that a side door of the building was slightly ajar, so we went in that way.

We found Adolf Dobermann's body on the floor just inside the door. Around his neck was a rolled-up, tightly knotted T-shirt. It was hand-painted, exactly like something from the Countess Rulalenska's shop.

Joshua said, "Looks like the clock just struck thirteen for Mr. Dobermann. Good thing I deposited his check yesterday."

I said, "We'd better call the police."

"I think somebody already did," said Joshua.

Lieutenant Sanfuentes was just entering the abandoned guest house with a small army of cops behind him. He looked down at Dobermann's body and shook his head. "Everything that guy touched turned nasty," he said.

Joshua said, "Well, now he's *kaput.*" Then he laughed. "Hey, I learned some German before he checked out."

"Very funny," said the lieutenant. "You fellas mind telling me what you're doing here?"

Joshua explained how we'd ended up there, after a roundabout trip that began with his appointment to drive Adolf to the airport. Just then a turboprop airplane roared by overhead. We all looked up.

Sanfuentes said, "I guess he missed his flight." Then he turned to me. "And what are you doing here?"

"I came along for the ride." My voice sounded defensive. "Joshua, tell him."

Joshua said yes, he'd asked me along.

Sanfuentes said, "So you'd be sure to have a witness."

"What?" said Joshua.

"Funny how you got the urge to drive out here," said the cop.

"You can't blame this on me," said Joshua.

The cop shrugged. "Here you are with the body."

"Come on," said Josh. "I have no motive. We just happened to find the guy."

"And there's no love lost between you and him?" said the cop.

"It was business!" said Joshua. "Period. Don't make it more than it is."

"Okay, okay, cool it," said Sanfuentes. "Maybe I was a little out of line there, Josh. I'm a little edgy myself, y'know? We don't often get two bodies in a few days of each other, both of them in guest houses." He looked around the dilapidated place. "Although you can hardly call this dump a guest house. So as long as both you guys have alibis, I'm sure there's no problem."

I blurted, "But what about . . . ?" Then I stopped myself.

"Yes?" said Sanfuentes.

I was about to claim diplomatic immunity, since I was working for the Key West police, however unofficially. But Joshua didn't know about that, so I checked myself.

I said, "I'm not sure I have an ironclad alibi."

"Then you'd better get one," said Sanfuentes. "In fact, stainless steel is better. It doesn't rust." He chuckled quietly. "This salt air is a bitch."

The medical examiner arrived and after a few minutes conferred with Sanfuentes. He theorized that the victim had been strangled with the T-shirt, but he'd know for sure after an autopsy.

"Yeah," said Sanfuentes, "the body looks nice and clean." Then he turned to Joshua and asked, "So how'd you guys get in here again?"

"The door was open," said Joshua.

"You have keys?" said Sanfuentes.

"The door was ajar," I offered.

Sanfuentes snapped at me, "I heard what he said!" Then he turned back to Joshua. "Tell me again your connection to the victim."

"I'm his personal representative."

"Personal representative?" said the cop. "Since when?"

"Since yesterday," said Joshua. "Adolf had big plans to develop some properties here on the island."

"I heard about that," said Sanfuentes. "Lotta folks didn't care too much for the guy."

"They didn't complain about his money," said Joshua.

Sanfuentes glanced toward the body. "So much for his money. My crew will take your reports, then you two boys can go."

Had the lieutenant meant to conjoin us as "boys"?

We gave our reports separately to different cops. My version was simple: Joshua and I had found Adolf Dobermann's body just before the police arrived. For some reason though, the cops didn't appreciate the simplicity of the truth. Then again, I only knew the facts from my side of things. Joshua really could have invented the whole story of missing Adolf that morning, along with the message to meet him back at the Fleming Lemming. Maybe he'd gone to the Twin Palms and killed Adolf, then returned to the Fleming Lemming. But the big green car bore no traces of the red mud that was everywhere outside the Twin Palms. Still, it would all be easy enough for the cops to trace.

When I finished my report, I looked around for Joshua, but he'd already left the crime scene without me. That's also when I noticed a cigarette squashed into the mud by someone's footprint. From what I could see it was unfiltered and looked as thought it hadn't been lit. I hunkered down close enough for a telltale sniff, but Sanfuentes caught me before my nose did its work.

"What'cha got there?" he said.

I pointed to the cigarette. He had one of his staff photograph the thing from countless angles. Then, wielding tweezers with the deliberation of a neurosurgeon, Sanfuentes extricated the thing from the mud and put it in a plastic bag. He told another crew to make plaster casts of all the footprints in the area.

"Get all those tire tracks too," he said. "Bike and car."

Then in a quiet aside for my ears alone Sanfuentes said, "Don't worry too much about your alibi. Your pal in Boston warned me that you got some kind of weird magnet for finding bodies." Then he chuckled to himself. "He said maybe you got a Perry Mason complex."

So Branco had speculated about me with another cop. Well, well.

I used the moment of confidence to ask Sanfuentes again if I could see the two Willitses' wills. He told me he still hadn't found his copies. I told him I didn't believe him. He told me he didn't care what I thought. I told him what Cozy Dinette had mentioned the previous night, how "everyone" had lost, and I wanted to know who "everyone" was.

"Cozy Dinette, eh?" said Sanfuentes. "Maybe some people flap their hole a little too much."

"She has a right to say whatever she wants, Lieutenant."

"And you have a right to listen," said the cop.

"Then why can't I see the wills?"

"Tell you what," he said. "Since Miss Cozy Dinette is so eager to talk to you, why don't you ask her to show you her copy? That way I don't have to lie if we all end up on the witness stand."

"Lie about what?"

"You," said Sanfuentes. "This arrangement with you is highly irregular, and I'm not sure how much longer I want to continue it."

"You say you want my help, but all you do is slap my hand."

"That's right," said the cop. "You can go now. We'll talk later."

So I set out on foot back to town. I still hadn't had breakfast, but by that time, after finding Dobermann's pallid corpse, I'd lost my appetite again. I really didn't want to lose more weight. Contrary to that aphorism about wealth and waistline, you *can* be too thin.

I decided to pay a call at the Echo Me gallery. Maybe I'd eat better if Jeri Tiker came along with me. As I approached the place, I saw a bright red Range Rover pull out of the adjacent driveway, then head quickly up Fleming Street. It left thin trails of water, as if it had just been washed and not completely dried.

I went and knocked on the gallery's front door, but there was no answer. I called out Jeri's name a few times. Again no reply, which was odd, since someone had just been there. I went around back and discovered a door had been jimmied open. As I pushed it cautiously to let myself into the gallery, I heard a voice behind me.

"Can I help you?"

11

Jeri Tiker was straddling her bicycle.

"Well?" she said accusingly. "What are you doing here?"

Fact was, she'd caught me snooping. I lowered my head in shame, and then saw that her bike tires were crusty with mud. I said sheepishly, "I thought you needed help."

"Help?" said Jeri. "I'm standing right here and I'm just fine."

I told her I'd seen the red Range Rover pull out of the driveway, and when she didn't answer the door, I thought maybe something had gone wrong. Jeri seemed to want to believe me.

"I saw that red car too," she said. "We might as well go in and see what they took."

At first glance inside, things were moved out of place everywhere, but nothing appeared damaged. And from what Jeri could determine, nothing was missing.

"I wonder what they wanted," she said, but she appeared calm about the incident, almost as though she'd expected it. "There's certainly no money here. Only my art and materials."

I offered to call the police.

"Why bother?" said Jeri. "Nothing's taken."

"You should file a report anyway, in case you find something missing later on."

Jeri reluctantly agreed, so I called Lieutenant Sanfuentes and told him what had happened.

"Twice in one morning," he said on the phone. "Are you trying to make more work for me?" He sent his sergeant to take a report. He came and did his work. It was all matter-of-fact, especially since nothing was damaged or missing. The sergeant did advise Jeri to install a stronger lock on the back door.

"Sure," she said. "Like I have money for new locks."

When the police left I offered Jeri lunch at Camille's Cafe. She protested that she had work to do, but I insisted that she'd paint better on a full stomach.

"Why are you doing this?" she asked suspiciously.

"It's my way of supporting the arts in Key West."

To that Jeri submitted and said okay.

At Camille's Cafe I told her that Joshua Aytem and I had discovered Adolf Dobermann's body that morning.

"Good riddance," she said as she chowed into a buttery glazed mushroom-and-cheese omelette. The mention of Adolf's death seemed to fortify her appetite, though not mine.

I said, "He was strangled with one of the countess's T-shirts, those hand-painted jobs."

"Good again," said Jeri. "Maybe some poor artist finally got fed up with working for pennies. Do you know what the countess offered me to paint some T-shirts for her?"

I had no idea. Jeri told me.

"A buck a shirt," she said. "Hand-painted! She pays the Cubans even less. And you know what she sells those things for?"

"From what I saw, around eighty bucks a pop," I said.

"Painted on one side only. The other stuff is even higher. And for that she pays them a quarter a panel. It's robbery!"

"But they still do it," I said.

"What choice have they got? To the countess art is just another form of labor. Dobermann felt the same way, the slimy bastard. I'm glad to hear someone finally got him. As far I'm concerned, all those aristocratic types should be exterminated with art objects." She forked a big chunk of omelette into her mouth and chewed vigorously.

I noticed that other customers around us were eavesdropping as Jeri ranted on about the indignities suffered by artists, along with her unique final solution to the problem.

I said, "I didn't think you'd take Adolf's death so personally."

"It's a victory," she said. "You know how he's been harassing me to sell him, *give* him, some of my work? So last night I threw the *I Ching*, and my question was, 'When will Adolf Dobermann go away?' And the *I Ching* told me, 'The journey is in your hands.' So I said, 'Let him die.' And now he's dead."

"Chalk one up for the *I Ching*," I said.

"Yeah," said Jeri. "I think I'll throw it again tonight. There's a few other people I'd like to say bon voyage to."

A voice behind us asked, "Are you taking a trip?"

Jeri and I turned to see Edsel Shamb standing near our table.

"Hello, Ed," she said. "No, I'm not going anywhere. If I ever do, it'll be a one-way ticket out of this loony bin."

"But as an artist you should like Key West."

Jeri replied, "Easy for you to say. You're always traveling, while I'm stuck here painting parrots, and fish, and geckos for the tourists."

Edsel invited himself to join us. Jeri didn't seem to mind. She told him about the break-in.

He asked, "Was there much damage?"

"No," said Jeri. "And nothing was taken, as far as I can tell."

"Not even money?" said Edsel.

"There's no money in the studio." Jeri made a sad little laugh. "There's no money anywhere in my life."

Edsel said, "If you need help I'd be glad to lend you—"

"No, thanks," she said. "I'd rather sell a painting."

"I'm sure you will," said Edsel. "In fact, a clever thief would have taken some of your work. I predict it's going to be extremely valuable someday."

"So does Ken Kimble. So did Adolf Dobermann," said Jeri, then added, "that crook."

"Ah, yes. The itinerant German aristocrat," said Edsel. "He left for Germany this morning, didn't he?"

"He left for nowhere," I said. "Adolf Dobermann is dead."

"Dead!" Edsel seemed alarmed by the news.

I told him Joshua and I had found his body that morning.

Edsel slammed one of his hamlike fists on the table. His alarm had quickly transmuted to bravado. "How do you do it!" he said.

"Here I write mysteries for a living and I've never found a single body. And for you it's the second time in just a few days, isn't it?"

"Who's counting?" I said.

"You found Augusta Willits too, didn't you? If this keeps up I should think the police might suspect you of nefarious deeds."

I said, "Weren't you and Adolf involved in some kind of business together?"

"Business?" he said.

"I saw you twice with him, meeting with that lawyer Nancy Drew."

"That was purely social," said Edsel.

Jeri Tiker snorted. "Sociopathic maybe."

"Be kind to the dead," said Edsel.

"Why?" said Jeri.

Just then came a familiar muffled chirping from within his satchel. He dug his hand inside and pulled out the leather pouch that held his itty-bitty cellular telephone.

"Excuse me," he said politely, as he unfolded the device.

Propriety aside, getting a phone call in Camille's Cafe was giving Edsel Shamb a nice high-tech hard-on. He became increasingly animated by the call. It lasted about a minute, a real quickie, but when Edsel refolded the tiny telephone he was flushed with afterglow.

"I've got to go now. That was my Hollywood agent. They've just sent a fax." He took a deep breath, then spoke slowly and deliberately, as if to confirm the words for himself. "This is the big one."

No sooner had he departed than Cozy Dinette walked by Camille's and saw Jeri and me sitting in the window.

She dashed into the cafe. "Boston!"

I told her I had enjoyed her cabaret act the previous night, then I attempted to introduce her to Jeri, but they'd both met already.

Cozy then invited me to a fund-raiser that night.

"Another one?" I said.

"There's good community spirit here," she said.

Jeri said, "Except for artists."

I told Cozy I was invited to a pool party at Ken Kimble's.

"Really?" she said, raising one eyebrow. "He's long overdue."

Jeri said, "He's a creep."

Cozy quickly rebutted. "Ken Kimble contributes generously to every charity in this town."

"And he treats artists the same way," said Jeri. "Like charity."

"Sometimes that's what they need," said Cozy.

Which was not the way to Jeri's heart.

"At least I know whose side you're on," said Jeri.

Cozy blithely dismissed her and turned back to me. "Just watch out you're not the guest of honor tonight, Boston."

"Why?" I said.

"You may not be ready for that kind of attention," said Cozy.

Jeri said to me, "I told you the other day, they're orgies."

"They are not," said Cozy. "They're just, well, erotically liberating events. When Peter was alive, bless his fundamentalist little heart, he used to call the police to raid Ken's parties."

"I thought Peter and Ken were friends," I said.

"The best," said Cozy, "and the worst." Then she laughed boisterously. "Imagine calling the cops? Leave it to Peter."

I said, "I thought it was Peter's mother who sponsored those raids."

Cozy said, "First it was Peter, and after he died Augusta took up the banner. Difference is, Peter did it mostly as a practical joke, to provoke Ken. He really cared about him."

"Strange way to show it."

Cozy went on. "All the cops ever did was ask Ken to keep the noise down. It was Augusta who got serious. You'd see her picketing down by the buttplug, carrying a banner and crying out, 'No more orgies!' " Cozy laughed again, and added, "Poor thing."

"Well, they're both dead now," said Jeri.

Cozy said, "What are you, the voice of doom?"

Jeri shrugged. "At least Ken Kimble doesn't have to worry about the police anymore."

I asked Cozy how she knew so much about the parties.

She said, "Peter and I were very close. I thought I told you that. Back when Ken's wife was still living here, the parties used to be mixed events."

"Ken Kimble has a wife?"

"And two kids," said Cozy. "Close your mouth."

"Where are they now?" I said.

"In London. Six months of the year he packs them off to a flat in Kensington and he comes to Key West to read new scripts and build his art collection." Cozy leaned closer to me and said, "But Ken also comes here to, er, explore his other side, the part he used to keep hidden. In the old days the pool parties were mixed. Now they're specialized. Ken flies the boys in just for the weekend."

Jeri interjected, "Like imported delicacies."

Cozy scowled at her.

Jeri said, "Ken Kimble's got too much money and not enough problems."

Cozy turned to me again. "By the way, Boston, just in case you do get away from Ken's party with your pants on, my fund-raiser is at the Seven-Oh-Seven."

"What's that?" I said.

"Boston!" she said impatiently. "What have you been doing since you got here?"

"Finding bodies," said Jeri.

Cozy glowered at her, then said to me, "The Seven-Oh-Seven is a club. It was started by an airline pilot years ago. I'm surprised you haven't been there yet. It's the kind of place you'd like. Regular folks."

"I'll try to make it."

Cozy glanced at her watch and said, "Oh no, late again." Then she set off as swiftly as she'd arrived, pausing again at the door to turn and yell toward the kitchen, "Hey, Camille! Love you, girl!" And then she was off.

Jeri said, "Finally, the curtain comes down."

"Why don't you like her?"

"You know that line about still waters running deep?"

"Sure," I said. "But Cozy is hardly still."

Jeri said, "I rest my case." Then she shook her head dismally. "I don't know how much longer I can take this place."

"We can go, if you want," I said.

She replied, "I meant Key West. If I end up inheriting that gallery, I'll sell it and go to New York."

Her comment reminded me that she must have a copy of Peter Willits's will. I asked her if I could see it.

94

"Sure," she said. "But why?"

"I want to see what everyone was supposed to inherit."

"Then it won't help," she said. "No one got a copy of the whole will. The executor gave each beneficiary only the paragraphs that pertained to her or him, nothing more."

"I never heard of such a thing."

Jeri said, "You never dealt with Nancy Drew."

"Why would she do that, separate the will into pieces?"

"I guess she thought we'd be satisfied enough with whatever we got, and that would keep us from contesting the will. But instead everyone was running around trying to find out what everyone else got."

"Like secret test scores."

Jeri said, "Then Augusta contested the will anyway, and won."

"You'll appeal though, right?"

"Why bother?" said Jeri.

"Jeri, you just admitted that the gallery would give you some security." That was me, the recent heir and would-be securities expert advising an artist how to get some for herself.

"What am I supposed to do?" said Jeri. "Hire a lawyer?"

"What about the rest of them? Isn't anyone appealing the award to Augusta?"

"No," said Jeri. "Nancy Drew said it wouldn't help."

"But lawyers love to appeal unfair judgments. Why is Nancy Drew accepting it?"

Jeri shrugged and made no reply.

I said, "Something isn't right there."

"Maybe you can fix it," said Jeri.

I paid our bill and we left Camille's. Jeri seemed kind of glum, but who could blame her, after learning that she'd pretty much lost her chance to inherit the Echo Me, and then having a break-in that morning? I walked her back to the gallery.

A few blocks up Fleming Street we noticed two Key West police cruisers parked in front of the Echo Me Gallery. When we got there we found the cops waiting for us. Lieutenant Sanfuentes was leading the pack himself, so whatever had brought them there was apparently too important for his sergeant to handle alone. Sanfuentes introduced himself to Jeri, then turned to me and said, "For an amateur dick you sure take your work to heart. This is the second time today you've been one step ahead of me."

"It's completely unintentional," I said.

The cop half smiled. "Don't be so modest." Then he told Jeri he had a warrant to search the Echo Me Gallery.

"Why?" said Jeri.

Sanfuentes said, "We got a tip-off you might be concealing evidence on these premises—a painting that was stolen from a crime scene yesterday morning."

"Who told you that?" she said, suddenly vehement.

"I can't divulge my sources," said Sanfuentes.

Inside the gallery the cops were methodically going through all of Jeri's things: her completed work, her work in progress, her stored materials, and her personal things too. They seemed to be a lot more thorough than the intruder had been earlier that morning. Jeri reminded Lieutenant Sanfuentes that the gallery had been broken into just an hour or so ago.

"I know," said Sanfuentes. "That's why I'm here with the boys now. Something wasn't quite right about that report, so I wanted to see things for myself."

Two of his crew came out from the back part of the gallery balancing a large framed work of art between them.

"Oh, no!" said Jeri. "That's *Dinner of Uncertainty.*"

One of the cops told Sanfuentes they'd found it in a storage closet, behind some old broken-up frames.

"Yours?" said the cop to Jeri.

"I painted it," she said.

"And was this on display at the Crow's Nest?"

"Yes," said Jeri.

"And then it went missing, right?"

"That's what I heard," said Jeri.

"I wonder how it got back here," said Sanfuentes.

Jeri said, "Maybe the person who broke in here earlier brought it back."

"And why would someone do that?"

"Maybe to incriminate me."

"You?" said Sanfuentes. "Why you?"

"To deflect suspicion from themselves," said Jeri. "If the painting was stolen from the murder scene, and now I have it, it makes me look guilty."

"That's exactly what I was thinking," said the cop.

Jeri said, "But what about the break-in? I filed a police report, didn't I? Is that what a guilty person does, call the police?"

"I don't know," said Sanfuentes. "Sometimes they do. Let's say you had nothing to do with getting this painting back here. Okay? I'll buy that for now. So then, can you tell me who might want to make you look guilty, like you just said?"

Jeri became frustrated, and her eyes got teary. "No," she said.

"So," said Sanfuentes, "we're back where we started. See, I wonder if maybe you had this painting in here all along, since yesterday morning, when you took it from the Crow's Nest. And maybe you staged that break-in earlier today as a little hoax, just to distract me."

"You're wrong," said Jeri. "Someone *was* in here."

"Lieutenant," I said, "I saw the car too. It was a red Range Rover."

"Is that so?" said the cop. "That's an import, isn't it?"

I said it was.

Sanfuentes went on. "I pretty much know the cars around town, and I don't recall anyone owning any Range Rover."

"Maybe it's new," I said.

"Maybe," said Sanfuentes. Then he turned to Jeri. "Miss Tiker, I'd like you to come to the station with me."

"But I haven't done anything wrong," protested Jeri.

"I never said you did," replied Sanfuentes. "I just wanna ask some questions. That's my job. I'm not accusing you of anything . . ." He trailed off, implying what he didn't say: yet.

12

Jeri was taken for questioning by Lieutenant Sanfuentes, while part of his crew stayed on and continued their search, as though hoping to uncover more incriminating evidence.

For my part, having dealt with the police three times that day—once with a dead body—I decided to spend a little time trying to enjoy my vacation. So I headed toward Old Mallory Square on the gulf side of town. A sprawling luxury hotel, the Pier House, ran along the water for a good stretch of the shore there. Part of the hotel grounds was a network of boardwalks that interconnected numerous decks and outdoor bars, some of them built quite high for an unobstructed view of the gulf.

At the far end of one boardwalk I found an outdoor cafe overlooking the nearby marina. I sat under a small umbrella-shaded table near the railing, and then found myself staring directly down onto a couple lunching at an outdoor table below me. It was Ken Kimble and the Countess Rulalenska, whose turban that afternoon was jungle red silk. The odd thing was, both people were talking into cellular telephones while toying with their respective lunches. Perhaps they'd inadvertently phoned each other without realizing they were having lunch together. The distance and the breeze prevented me from hearing them, except for the few sibilant consonants that made their way up to where I was sitting. A few minutes later Ken put his phone away, while the countess continued her conversation. So they were separate calls after all. Neither person noticed me, not until someone on my level of the deck ran noisily across the wooden planks to my little table.

"Boston!" exclaimed Cozy Dinette, her face ablaze by giant orange sunglasses with reflective blue lenses. "Is this what you do all day, sit around and drink martinis?"

Her rowdiness caused Ken Kimble to look upward. I knew he recognized me, even through his sunglasses. I waved, but he didn't wave back. Cozy peered over the edge to see what had caught my attention. She quickly recognized the couple below.

"Ken!" she yelled. "Up here! Yoo-hoo!"

Once again he looked up, and that second time he waved a vague friendly gesture. Through it all the countess continued talking on her cellular phone and playing with her food. Without a free hand, she had retired the cigarette holder for the moment.

Cozy said to me, "I just came from an interview and an audition, and you'll never guess what happened. The Pier House offered me a regular weekend gig. Isn't that fantastic?"

"Sounds like cause for celebration," I said. I had heard that the Pier House was the most prestigious of the large hotels on Key West.

"Let's tie one on," said Cozy. "Drinking in the afternoon seems so right, especially since I'll be doing my recovery show the first four weeks. Isn't that a hoot?" Then Cozy released some of her trademark unbridled laughter.

I glanced back down at the lunching couple below us, but in the intervening moments they had vanished.

"Oh," said Cozy, with a sad mew. "They've gone."

"I didn't think you cared much for the countess."

"Live and let go!" she said. "Why hold a grudge?"

"A grudge for what?" I said.

"For her still being alive," replied Cozy, "while Peter Willits is dead."

"You can't blame her for that," I said.

"No?" said Cozy. "Oh, I miss him terribly." Her mouth drooped slightly, reflecting a sadness I had never seen on her face. "Peter was my best, best friend of all. No one knew him like me, Boston. You know, I took care of him in the hospital. I would have nursed him right up to the end and held his hand until he died. Except Augusta got a restraining order put on me and Ken and—" Cozy stopped herself. "Hey, Boston, let's get some champagne. I want to celebrate my new gig."

So we ordered a bottle of champagne and a gargantuan platter of grilled prawns. While we waited I told her I was still trying to get a copy of Peter Willits's will.

"Why?" said Cozy.

"It's obvious that the motives are there."

"Motives for what?"

"Killing Augusta," I said.

"Why do you care about that?" said Cozy. "Are you working for the cops or something?"

"Or something," I said quickly. "Let's just say I like to know what's going on in other people's lives. Maybe it's from being a hairdresser so long. All those fumes went to my head, and I got addicted to gossip."

"Jeez," said Cozy, "that's even flimsier than Dan White's Twinkie defense."

"And look what happened to him. But I'm a good guy, Cozy. Honest I am."

"I hope so," she said. "Well, if snooping around in other people's wills is your idea of vacation fun, I can tell you pretty much what everyone was supposed to get from Peter."

"You can?"

"Sure. I was on the laundry list along with the rest of them."

"Well then, start at the top," I said.

I recalled that Jeri Tiker had told me no one got a complete copy of the will. Perhaps Cozy had compiled her own, after coercing the pieces of information from everyone else.

"Number one," said Cozy, "would be me. And you already know I was supposed to get the Crow's Nest guest house."

"Right," I said. "And Jeri Tiker the Echo Me Gallery."

"I thought you didn't know anything," said Cozy.

"I know a few things."

Cozy slid her orange-framed sunglasses to the tip of her nose for a moment and aimed her pale blue eyes onto me. "Any others you already know? I don't want to waste my breath here."

"Laura Hope and Joshua Aytem were supposed to get the Fleming Lemming."

"You've been busy," said Cozy. "But your facts are slightly off,

Boston. The Fleming Lemming was for Laura alone, without Josh."

"Why was that?" I said.

"Ask them," said Cozy, and she lifted the shades back over her eyes.

"That's all I know," I said. "Now I'll listen to you."

But Cozy, despite her sunglasses, stared at me as if to discern how deeply entrenched my lying persona was. Apparently Jeri Tiker and I were not the only practitioners of psycholoading the psychosponge.

Unfortunately that's also when the food and champagne arrived. So the details of Peter's will were superseded by Cozy's raving about the grilled seafood. She drained her first glass of champagne like a cool summer beverage. I refilled it and then toasted to best friends and new lives. She drank up with me, then popped a fat shrimp into her mouth.

I prompted her to continue the list of Peter's legatees. "Was the countess getting anything?" I said. "I mean, besides the air-conditioning in her shop?"

"Try Blue Water Tours," said Cozy, noshing on another plump crustacean. "It's the biggest fleet with the biggest boats."

"She didn't get the shop?" I said.

"That shop never belonged to Peter." Then Cozy said, "You know, Boston, I'm not so sure I should be telling you this."

"Why not?" I said. "What can I do? It's only information, and I'm harmless." I refilled her glass.

"Still . . ." she said.

"Are you hiding something?"

"Aren't we all?" she said. Then she took a deep breath and told me that Ken Kimble and Edsel Shamb were to be joint owners of the Gulf Coast Playhouse. "It was Peter's only mistake," she said.

"Mistake?"

Cozy explained, "Those two guys would never be able to run a theater together. Ken would want to keep it a cozy little community playhouse, and Ed would go for Hollywood glitz."

"In Key West?"

Cozy said, "Mr. Shamb is a very ambitious man."

"You seem to know him well."

"That was *my* mistake," said Cozy. She emptied her third glass of champagne. "Well, that's the end of the laundry list."

"But what about the Twin Palms?" I said.

"The what?" she said.

"Wasn't the Twin Palms in Peter's will too?"

"Who told you that?" said Cozy.

"I guessed it," I said.

But Cozy remained silent as she gazed out over the gulf. And though her eyes were concealed by those opulent, outrageous sunglasses, I sensed a faraway look in them. The champagne had worked its magic. To get her attention again, I told her that I'd heard Nancy Drew had given all the legatees only a piece of the will, just the part with their name on it.

After hesitating, Cozy said, "Maybe whoever told you that is lying."

"Why would they?"

"To keep you guessing."

"What about you? Are you lying?"

"You'll have to figure that out yourself."

I pressed her further. "Do you know why Attorney Drew won't appeal that award to Augusta?"

"I'm sure she has her reasons."

"But why aren't all the people who were supposed to inherit from Peter doing anything about it? You, for example. You were supposed to inherit the Crow's Nest. Why aren't you fighting for it?"

Cozy said, "I'm going to tell you a secret, Boston. Can you keep a secret?"

"Depends."

"It doesn't matter anyway," she said, "so I'll tell you why I personally am not attempting to appeal the award to Augusta. It's because I think the whole thing was rigged."

"Rigged? By whom?"

Cozy answered, "The judge who made the award to Augusta was a deacon at her church. I think he convinced her to leave Peter's property to the church, where it would ultimately be in good hands, that is, his. Once she did that, he decided in her favor."

"Isn't that illegal?"

Cozy shrugged. "He's gone now anyway, nowhere to be found."

"Why aren't the police looking for him? How can he get away with what he did? Why isn't Nancy Drew throwing the book at him for a miscarriage of justice? He might have even killed Augusta just to get the property."

"Listen to you," said Cozy. "You know what, Boston? I don't know. And you know what else? I just reached the point where I don't care either."

With the food and drink consumed, Cozy stood up unsteadily, caught the edge of the table for balance, and said, "This has been swell, Boston. Thanks a pile. But now I'm going to finish this party off right and go find me a man."

And away she tottered. I stayed awhile and looked out over the gulf's placid waters. Drinking and eating to excess was a pleasant way to pass time, but I'd had my fill of so-called vacation fun. Boredom was the bane of any full-blooded Gemini like me, and I felt the need for stimulation. Unlike Cozy, though, I wasn't about to seek it in the flesh of another man. My diversion was more purposeful. I headed back to the Echo Me Gallery to find out how Jeri Tiker had fared with the Key West police.

13

It was around three o'clock when I arrived at the gallery. I found it locked up. In fact, it was worse than locked up. The place had been sealed by the police. I quickly reasoned if the gallery had been impounded, something had gone awry during the routine questioning of Jeri Tiker. I set off directly for the police station.

Inside the station, propped up on the floor behind the front desk was Jeri Tiker's painting, *Dinner of Uncertainty*. The police had seized it as evidence then left it on the floor. I felt bad for the painting. It belonged on a wall, where people could look at it.

I told the cop at the front desk I wanted to see Lieutenant Sanfuentes. The call went in, and Sanfuentes came out. He didn't invite me back into his office, and from his brusque manner I sensed he wanted me out of the station fast.

"Mr. Kraychik," he said. "You did such good work for me. How can I thank you? First you found us a body—make that two bodies—then you found us a suspect."

"Not Jeri Tiker?"

"Yes," he said, as pleased as if he'd won the football pool.

I said, "But she didn't kill Augusta Willits."

"You're right about that," said Sanfuentes. "We figure that was Mr. Dobermann's work after all. He killed Augusta Willits to get that painting."

"So you admit Jeri Tiker didn't steal it?"

"Not from Augusta," said the cop. "Dobermann must have done that. When that guy's mind was set on getting something, there was no stopping him. He was probably taking the painting when Augusta found him in the office. So he panicked and put her out. Then he took the painting and stored it at the old Twin Palms."

"You have evidence of that?" I said.

"Not yet," said the cop. "But it all fits together. Miss Tiker apparently found out and went to the Twin Palms to get her painting back. There's no denying it was rightfully hers. It's just too bad she took matters into her own hands." The lieutenant shook his head sadly. "We'll have to prosecute."

"But anyone could have planted that painting in her studio."

Sanfuentes said, "We found mud on her sneakers, and we found footprints that match those sneakers outside the Twin Palms. And her bike tires are filled with the stuff. We know she was there this morning."

"When? Your evidence is all circumstantial, Lieutenant."

"But it sure points an accusing finger," he said.

"How did Jeri even know that Dobermann would be there?"

"She told us someone had called her to return the painting to her."

104

"Who?"

Sanfuentes shrugged. "She couldn't tell."

"So why do you assume it was Adolf?"

Sanfuentes shrugged again.

I said, "Besides, how could Jeri have carried the painting on her bike?"

"She's a very agile young woman," said the cop.

"Circumstantial," I said again. "Coincidental. You have no hard evidence." I sounded like a cop myself. "What about that cigarette in the mud?"

Sanfuentes shrugged. "Could've been anyone's."

"But a brand? It looked unsmoked."

"Good eyes," said the cop. "You're right. It wasn't smoked, but the tip was broken off, so we don't know what brand it was. We don't even know if it was filtered or not."

"But you can analyze the tobacco and the paper—"

"Hey, boy! You stop right there!" The cop's eyes glittered angrily. "I'm not about to spin the wheels at the lab up in Miami over a cigarette stub. If I thought it was important enough, maybe. But it was just a cigarette. You understand?"

"No," I said. "I don't."

"Then it's time you did," he said.

"What about the murder weapon?"

"What about it?"

"It was a T-shirt from the Countess Rulalenska's shop."

"That's right," said the cop. "And Miss Tiker had quite an ax to grind with the countess. She probably used the T-shirt to incriminate the other woman."

"Lieutenant, why is it that every time there's some evidence or a clue, you think it's the result of someone trying to incriminate someone else? Maybe it really was that first person after all. Maybe the countess did it."

"Nah," said Sanfuentes. "Why would she incriminate herself? No one's that stupid." He'd already resumed his cool, efficient manner after the brief outburst. "In the meantime," he said, "I'll say thanks just one more time for your help, and then you can go enjoy what's left of your vacation."

"That's it?" I said.

Sanfuentes nodded, then turned to go back to his office.

"Can I see her?" I said.

He faced me again, but with an impatient grimace.

"I don't know about that," he said uncertainly.

"I'm not going to help her break out. You can check me for files and explosives if you want."

Then he softened a bit. "Okay, the sergeant'll take you down. And Stan," he said, "let's keep things nice and even from now on, okay? I don't like headaches."

Sanfuentes returned to his office, and I'd gone from helper to headache in twenty-four hours.

The cell where they were holding Jeri Tiker looked almost comfortable. It was air-conditioned and brightly lit by a large area of glass bricks along the upper third of the outside wall. She, however, looked bleak and gray, with her head sullenly hanging down toward the floor. When I arrived she looked up briefly.

"These guys are complete jerks."

"They're doing a job," I said. It was a vain attempt to appease her and myself. "At least you've got some nice light in here."

"I'll remember that when I sublet it," she said. "But right now I need a lawyer, not a decorator. And I should be painting."

"I'll find you a lawyer," I said.

"Why bother?" she said glumly. "I can't afford it anyway."

"I can," I said.

She looked up from the floor.

"I'm rich," I said. "At least for a working-class slob."

"I can't pay you back."

"I'll take it in paintings."

That exchange seemed to restore some of the natural pink glow to Jeri's face, so I forged ahead and asked her to explain something that was bugging me.

"I saw the reddish mud on your bike tires, Jeri. You went to the Twin Palms this morning, didn't you?"

Jeri was mute.

I pressed her. "Sanfuentes told me you and Adolf had arranged to meet there, so there's no sense—"

"All right!" snapped Jeri. "I went there, yes. Dobermann told me he'd give me back my painting. At least I thought it was Dobermann."

"Was it a man?" I said.

Jeri replied, "I can never tell on the phone. I thought it was odd, him calling me. But I wanted that painting back, so I agreed to meet him. And when I got there, he was already dead."

"Yet in Camille's this morning you acted surprised."

"Yeah," said Jeri.

"Why didn't you tell me the truth?"

"Because I was afraid of this!" she said, indicating the jail cell. "Of being suspected and then arrested." She looked at me wanly. "And it happened anyway."

I said, "I'd better find you a lawyer."

"Do you think they might let me paint in here?" she said. "I've got nothing else to do." She described a small suitcase that contained paper, paint, brushes, and water dishes.

"I'll see if I can get the stuff for you, but I want a favor in return."

"What," she said.

"Don't lie to me anymore."

On the way out I asked Lieutenant Sanfuentes about letting Jeri paint in her cell. He grumbled briefly about releasing her art materials from everything he'd impounded, so I told him I'd bring in all new stuff. He finally agreed, probably figuring it would prevent another headache. Then I left the station and set out on my mission to find Jeri Tiker a good lawyer. But all I had to do was say it to myself a few times—lawyer, lawyer, lawyer—and the obvious answer came: Nancy L. Drew.

Okay, so maybe I had ulterior motives for engaging that particular Key West attorney, since she was also executing Peter Willits's estate. So what if she was a corporate lawyer, and the situation needed Perry Mason? Hadn't Cozy Dinette told me she was the best on the Keys? Why look any further?

I telephoned her office from a pay phone. Her secretary insisted that I'd have to consult Attorney Drew in person before she'd consider representing anyone. I tried to explain that the prospective client was already a client from a previous matter, but the secretary stood firm. It was a new case, and I would require an initial consultation. So with great difficulty I managed to get an appointment to speak with Attorney Nancy L. Drew, if I could be there in the next half hour. Then the secretary relaxed her severity for a moment and added, "There's no obligation, of course."

"Of course," I repeated. Then I trotted back to the Jared Bellamy House to get the Alfa, and drove out to Nancy L. Drew's office.

It was a modern single-level building overlooking a calm inlet called Garrison Bight on the north side of the island. A large sign erected in the parking lot out front proclaimed: LAW OFFICES OF NANCY L. DREW. Does any lawyer have a singular office?

I went in. Immediately the receptionist's guard went up, as though she wasn't prepared to deal with an actual client. It shouldn't have surprised me, since contemporary law is basically the production and controlled distribution of documents and other paper byproducts. And, save for the occasional courier bearing an urgent delivery, the lifeline of any law firm is really its fax machine. Human contact is not only unusual, it's undesirable.

I told the secretary who I was and that I had an appointment. She told me, yes, she knew, and that I should take a seat. I did, but I couldn't get comfortable. The room smelled musty. I'd heard that certain strains of bacteria thrived in poorly maintained air-conditioning systems, especially in the tropics. What rare tropical fungus was I inhaling with each breath? I had just about stopped inhaling altogether when the secretary finally led me into the great attorney's sanctum sanctorum.

Behind the massive desk in the domain of her chambers, Nancy L. Drew appeared to be in complete control, a massive woman seated in a massive chair. She had obviously consulted with makeup, color, and wardrobe specialists to whom she had paid exorbitant fees, which she then surely collected from her own clients. Apparently she had also consulted an expert in crystals, for on her desk sat a sphere of pure quartz atop a base of oiled rosewood. It was an unfortunate choice of desk accessory, for it made Nancy L. Drew look less like a successful attorney and more like a circus sideshow act—Madame Zara tells all.

"Mr. Kraychik," she said, looking up from her crystal ball.

"Thank you for seeing me on such short notice," I said.

"I'm always ready to help a woman in jeopardy," said the attorney.

"You mean Jeri Tiker," I said, just to keep things clear.

As I explained the situation to her, I realized how much I wanted to convince both the attorney and myself that Jeri was incapable of killing Adolf Dobermann. She couldn't be a killer, no matter how feisty her manners, or how provocative her art. It was impossible, I kept telling myself. Well, maybe improbable. Jeri was physically slight, but she was strong too, and agile, as Sanfuentes had noted. And Adolf Dobermann's body had been soft, and he'd seemed unsteady on his spindly legs. Jeri could have easily overpowered him. Hell, even I could have overpowered him. But I didn't have any motive. And Jeri may have. I kept all that from the lawyer though. All she heard was the good stuff about Jeri's art, and how unlikely it was that Jeri would have killed someone to recover her stolen painting.

I did ask Nancy Drew if there was a potential conflict of interest, since I knew she had a previous connection with Adolf Dobermann. The attorney said, "My affiliation with Adolf Dobermann was purely social. I would never do anything so irresponsible as knowingly represent a person whose case was in direct conflict with that of another client."

Sounded official enough.

Then Attorney Drew told me she would consider the case after she had consulted with Jeri Tiker personally, and to do that she required a retainer. I wrote the check quickly, nervously—god, all those zeroes! She raised one eyebrow, as if impressed with her ability to extort vast sums of money in the name of the law. I had a moment of doubt that her power might be illusory, that it might disperse like vapor when challenged by anything outside a law book, for I'd seen high-and-mighty lawyers brought down like Goliath by something as ordinary as rush-hour traffic.

As I held out the check to the great attorney, I said, "Why aren't you appealing the award to Augusta Willits?"

Nancy L. Drew's hand stopped just short of taking the check from my fingers. She set her eyes on mine, as the check hovered between us.

"Mr. Kraychik," she said, "your friend's dilemma has no connection whatsoever with the matter you've just mentioned."

"But you're the executrix of Peter Willits's estate, and Jeri is a legatee."

The legal terms caused Nancy L. Drew's lips to pucker up, as if preparing to kiss the sacred tomes that ruled the dispositions of estates and legacies and inheritances.

"That's another matter entirely," she said, taking the check, "and to discuss it with you would betray the confidentiality of other clients."

Blah-blah-blah was all I heard that time.

I said, "It doesn't make sense."

"You are not apprised of the circumstances."

"Apprise me then."

But Nancy L. Drew advised me that our time was up. She summoned her assistant to escort me from her office.

After the consultation, I drove back to the guest house to rest awhile before dinner. I wasn't sure how much I liked being wealthy. Word traveled quickly, and open palms appeared from all sides. I tried to focus myself on other things, like why I was in Key West. I was there to find myself. I was there to mourn Rafik. Who was Jeri Tiker that I should spend so much time and money helping her?

I got restless, so I called Nicole at Snips Salon. A talk with her, my adopted big sister, would help sort things out. But Nicole was out on an errand, probably buying a fifty-dollar lipstick for a special date that night.

I paced the room awhile, working up the courage to call Lieutenant Branco of the Boston police. Based on past times together, maybe he could advise me what path to follow at the moment. But after shakily dialing his number with cold sweaty fingers, I found Branco was out too. For him I didn't speculate on what errand, and I didn't leave a message.

I finally conjured up my dead lover Rafik. But all I could recall was a dreadful moment that had occurred partway through our brief life together. It was a guilt-laden flashback about the first fight, that inevitable moment many couples go through, the one that seems to conclude the initiation of the Great Love. As with

110

so many other couples, the fight resulted from the first infidelity, on my part no less. Looking back, that fight seemed to be the very moment that all the preceding courtship and passion had been leading up to. And once the fight had happened, would love continue? Or would it linger and stumble toward its inevitable death? I had told Rafik he could forgive me and forget my indiscretion, or else I could leave him. So he said he forgave me, and I stayed. But he never let me forget it.

So, my dear, dead lover, why am I in Key West?

But all he said was forget about it. Massage my back.

Nicole would have told me to forget about it too. Stop trying to save people. Let the police do their work.

And Lieutenant Branco would probably have told me to play my hunches to the end, until I got to the truth.

There was no question whose advice I'd follow, since it was exactly what I wanted to do anyway.

I looked at the clock. Six o'clock. It was time to shower again and head out to Ken Kimble's notorious pool party.

14

I decided to drive that evening. To avoid the tangle of tourists and traffic that crowded Duval Street, even off-season, I took Whitehead Street all the way across town to Ken Kimble's place, on the east end of the island. At one point along the way, I saw my anonymous admirer in the pink taxicab approaching from the opposite direction. But he passed me without pause or toot. Our mutually unrequited romance had already expired.

I found Ken's place easily. Like pretty maids all in a row, twelve snazzy new convertibles were parked neatly in the shade along the high wall surrounding his compound. All twelve ragtops were down. Any fabric boots had been fastidiously stretched and snapped into place. It was certainly a tidy group of guests in attendance that evening. I parked the Alfa at the end of the row, making an even baker's dozen. As I walked to the entrance, I realized the whole compound had the rare Key West feature of a ten-foot wall, all stone and mortar, surrounding its entire perimeter. Privacy was ensured.

I pressed the doorbell firmly. A few minutes later the heavy wooden door was pulled open by the host himself, Ken Kimble. He wore only a towel around his waist, and he was talking on his cellular telephone. I'd guessed right about him working out a lot. His chest and shoulders were well developed, the muscles dense and defined, yet oddly unsexy, as though they had been applied to him, rather than being part of an organic whole. Ken motioned me in, then quickly locked the massive wooden gate behind us.

He led me along a serpentine stone path that curved its way toward the big house. From behind I saw that Ken had managed to escape the accumulation of midriff flab common among middle-aged men. His broad torso tapered to a youthful waist and slim hips. I watched his firm butt moving under the towel. Again, it should have been sexy, but it wasn't. Maybe it was because the man himself was so removed from the moment. All that time he was murmuring monosyllables into the cellular phone.

The house itself was a grand old place, like something from the antebellum south. It was painted white, with black shutters. A broad columned portico ran along three sides of the building. As we ascended the front steps, Ken concluded his phone call. Then he turned all his attention onto me.

"I'm really glad you came," he said.

"I rarely miss a chance for something new."

"Good," said Ken. "Let's go through the house. Everyone is out back by the pool."

We passed quickly through the foyer, and I caught glimpses into the other rooms. One thing was clear. Ken Kimble really did collect art. Every wall in every room was covered with it, even works by art-world badboys like Mark Tansey and Jeff Koons and Bruce Nauman.

"I buy things before an artist is discovered," he boasted. "I like to think I help establish them."

If he had really bought all that art before the rest of the world had jumped on the wagon, then his ventures had already paid off handsomely.

I said, "Is that why you want some of Jeri Tiker's work?"

Kimble said, "When she simmers down, I'll approach her again."

"You may have to wait," I said. "She's in jail now."

The news seemed to startle him. "On what grounds?"

I hesitated before saying, "Murder."

"They think she killed Augusta Willits?"

"No," I said. "They think she killed Adolf Dobermann."

Ken Kimble's face went blank, as though he'd flipped a switch to halt any neurofacial activity that might betray his real reaction. Then he said, "That was the German fellow, right?"

"Right," I said.

Kimble ruminated awhile. Then he put down the cellular telephone and readjusted his towel, flaring it open long enough for me to get a good look at him. That's when I realized he had cultivated his body to serve merely as a magnificent proscenium for nature's generosity to him.

"No tan line," I said.

Ken smiled and covered himself with his towel. "Shall we join the party?" He led me further toward the back of the house. We arrived at a large open room with two mirrored walls and two others entirely of plate glass. The glass walls faced out onto the pool and the surrounding gardens.

He said, "You can leave your clothes in here."

But I hardly heard him. I was too astonished by what I saw outside.

It was like a photo shoot for *Intercontinental Male*, with fabulous young male bodies cavorting everywhere, except they were all naked. And not kind of naked. Really naked. There was a lot of laughing and fooling around too, everyone slick and wet. Some of the guys were half hard; some had happy, healthy prongs. Around the pool sat older men, lounging languidly with towels draped over their drooping flesh.

I said, "It's a saturnalia."

"Yes," said Ken proudly. "A movie that can't be made. I was lucky to find this place when I did. The masonry wall around the compound was built long before the new zoning laws, which make it illegal to build anything that high now. When I bought the place, I got it declared a landmark. Now the town can't force me to lower the wall to comply with the new restrictions."

"And without that wall you couldn't host gatherings like this," I said.

"Obviously," replied Ken.

He pointed to a stack of clean white towels, which seemed to be the limit of fashion for him and the older men around the pool. "You don't have to use one," he said suggestively. Then he gazed out over the poolside festivities and said dreamily, "They really are beautiful, aren't they?"

I said, "From that peek I got earlier, you can be proud of your body too."

Shameless hussy flatters hunky host.

Ken said, "A good body is a lifetime project. I work hard to create this." He ran his right hand over his left breast, grabbed the smooth firm flesh, then fingered small circles around the nipple. He faced me with a glowing smile.

I said, "How are your wife and kids?"

His mouth dropped open slightly, but he quickly retrieved the smile. "They're on holiday," he said lightly.

"So are you, from the looks of it."

Then Ken Kimble spoke to me seriously, as if from his heart.

"I used to enjoy provoking people," he said, "just the way you do. Then I learned to own and heal my truest self, and my life became much better. My wife and children accept the diversity of my personal needs."

Which probably wasn't too difficult from a posh flat in Kensington.

Ken went on. "Ever since I found the courage to admit my frailties, everything I touch comes alive with success."

"Maybe someday you can tell me how you manage that."

"That would be a pleasure," said Ken. He headed toward the door leading to the pool deck. "Take your time undressing," he said with an eager grin. "We'll watch from outside." Then he left me alone in the changing room.

The party frolic continued in and around the pool, with the laughs and squeals of pleasure and the big splashing jumps all muffled by the two walls of heavy plate glass. I looked beyond the pool full of slippery wet bodies and saw Ken talking on the phone again. I wondered if he ever participated. Or did he host the parties to entertain himself—live porn—to watch and to titillate while remaining oddly chaste on the phone?

I began removing my clothes and turned to face the two mirrored walls, which put my back to the audience outdoors. I happened to glance up into my own eyes in the mirrors, and I wondered, Is this me, about to strip and join an orgy in progress? And why not? Finally I was thin enough to show my body in public without shame. And I was single again and feeling very lonely. It would be a new experience. Finally I could let myself go in utter sexual abandon with no regard for the other person, except that he, or they, were there. At that hour of the day even the sun couldn't burn my sensitive skin. I had no excuse. My slacks and shirt were off. It was time for the briefs. I took a deep breath. You live only once, I told myself. Then as I pulled them down, I turned halfway around and looked outside again. Maybe it was the odd twisted angle of my head, or the delirium of being caught bare-assed "onstage," but all I saw out there was a bunch of rich older men fondling a bunch of young vibrant ones. I looked in the mirror again, into my own eyes, and I realized I just couldn't do it, just couldn't put myself out there, naked, with the rest of them. I pulled my clothes back on. And nobody seemed to notice.

With no reason to be on the outdoor deck, I wandered back into Ken's house. One of the display rooms for Ken's collection had an open space along one wall, as though a painting had been taken down, or else something was going up that hadn't arrived yet. There was a desk in there too, at a window that faced out onto dense shrubbery. No one could see me, so I went over to have a look at the desk, to see what kind of day-to-day business a big-time actor and art collector conducted in Key West. It turned out to be mostly junk mail. Even the wealthy weren't immune to the deluge of trash delivered daily to their doors.

Then I saw an envelope containing what looked like Polaroid photos. My fingers itched to have a peek at Ken Kimble's extra secret life, the one that even a poolside orgy didn't reveal. What a surprise to find that all the photos were various exposures—some dim, some overbright, some just right—of Jeri Tiker's painting, *Dinner of Uncertainty*, the very one I'd seen in the Crow's Nest office, and then at the police station. What was Ken Kimble doing with them?

"Looking for skeletons?" he said from the doorway.

"I think I found one. Where's the painting now, Ken?"

"You told me the police have it."

"I told you they had Jeri Tiker. How did you get it, Ken? Did you steal it from the Crow's Nest?"

He hesitated. "No, I didn't." He came into the room and took the photos from me. "But I did go to the Crow's Nest that morning. I wanted to reason with Augusta. I wanted her to stop her loathsome pursuit of Peter's estate."

"Loathsome? You had a personal interest, Ken. You were going to inherit half the Gulf Coast Theater with Edsel Shamb. That certainly gave you a good reason to kill Augusta."

He laughed nervously. "If I killed Augusta," he said, "it would hardly be for a piece of property."

"Then what would you kill her for? Hate? Love?"

Ken's nervous smile stopped, and his chisel-featured face relaxed, as though he was off camera and could be himself. "Your instincts are unsettling," he said. "I did hate her."

"And you loved her son."

"I loved him, yes," said Ken. It sounded like a confession.

I sensed he might talk to me on the subject of love. Most of my clients trusted me in that department too.

"Go on," I said.

"It wasn't the kind of love you mean."

"What kind is that?"

"There was no sex," said Ken. "I felt a familial, an eternal kind of love for Peter. It was pure and clean."

"Sounds lofty," I said. "Where did Augusta fit in?"

"She sensed Peter's desire."

"What about yours?"

"I told you, there was no sex. I didn't want to jeopardize my marriage, not then."

"So who decided to refrain from sex? You? Or Peter?"

Ken said, "Why is that so important?"

"Because sex changes everything, Ken—even friendships—no matter how moderne and sophisticated you try to be about it."

"Look," said Ken, "all I wanted to do that morning at the Crow's Nest was persuade Augusta to give up her contest against Peter's will. But I didn't kill her. Honest. She was already dead when I got there." His features were strained again, and his brow furrowed. "Can I trust you?" he said. "These things have been weighing so heavily on me. I must unburden myself. Do you understand?"

Ken was also rubbing himself against the edge of the desk, and the front of his towel was changing contour in a very obvious direction.

He said, "Is this a sub-rosa meeting of two adult men?"

"If that's what you want," I said agreeably.

The religious connotation he'd put on our discourse seemed to arouse him even more. Ken Kimble was certainly a case study for the psychosexual archives: He got hard telling the truth.

Ken said, "Augusta had hurt Peter so much when he was alive, threatened him with hellfire and all the other nonsense of her beliefs. And then she let him die that disgraceful, horrible, lonely death."

"Why didn't you do anything about it?"

"I tried! I tried to convince the doctor to put Peter on a morphine drip. We all did. But as next of kin Augusta held the power of attorney over Peter's death."

"Didn't he have a living will?"

Ken let out another nervous laugh. "Peter never believed he was going to die, poor soul. That's why he was so grandiose in his will. He never thought it would be executed. And there was no reasoning with him about it. So when the time came to decide how to treat his failing health, it was in his mother's hands. And Augusta quietly determined that her son had to pay for his sins, and so would everyone else he knew."

"The sins of the world visited upon her only begotten son."

Ken glared at me.

"Sorry," I said. "Who else was there at the end?"

"None of us were allowed to be with Peter when he died. But Cozy was at the hospital a lot, and so was—" Ken stopped himself, the same way Cozy had done on the outdoor deck at the Pier House earlier that day.

"Who?" I said. "Who was that other person?"

"I can't tell you," said Ken. "I gave my solemn oath to Peter on his deathbed."

"Was it a lover? A child?"

"Don't press me, please," said Ken. "The relief of telling you these few things is so great, I'm afraid I might slip and say more. And I swore to Peter I wouldn't tell—to my death!"

"Sounds like your connection with him was more than familial love." And the phrase "over my dead body" took on new meaning. "Let's go back to the painting then. How did you get it?"

"Someone gave it to me. Don't look at me that way. It's the truth. That's what you want, isn't it? The truth?"

"Yes," I said. "But who gave it to you?"

"I can't tell you."

"You mean you don't know? Or you won't tell?"

Ken looked at me desperately, but said nothing.

"Did it just magically fall into your hands?"

Still no answer.

"Okay, then how did the painting get from here back to Jeri Tiker's gallery?"

"I can't tell you that either," said Ken.

"Why not?"

"Because I don't know for sure."

"Any ideas?"

Ken shook his head remorsefully. "I'm sorry, but I can't say anything more without implicating someone else."

"Meanwhile an innocent person is in jail."

"I'm sorry," said Ken. "At least she's safe there."

His confession was apparently finished, for his towel had returned to a more regular contour.

Then Ken left me alone in that room. Apparently he felt I was

118

more trustworthy after he'd confided in me. That often happened at my other confessional too, the styling chair. The strange thing about Ken Kimble's story was, I almost believed it. And I hadn't laid a finger on his hair.

As I was leaving the compound to return to my car, one droopy old gent in a towel stopped me along the path and said, "Are you taking that nice pink body away from us? You're not shy, are you?"

"Yes," I lied. I even managed a demure blush, which only encouraged the man.

I looked back over the swimming pool and deck, and the lush gardens surrounding them too. Ken was on the phone again, and when he saw me leaving he made a frantic motion for me to stay. I gestured back, pointing to my wristwatch. I found my way out of the compound. The latch on the heavy outside gate closed itself securely behind me, and Ken Kimble's secret world was once again safe from intruders.

15

By the time I found a parking space and got inside the 707, I expected Cozy's show to be in full swing. But she was starting late. "As usual," whined the guy who was manning the PA system upstairs. So I killed some time at the 707's downstairs bar. It was a rough-and-tumble crowd, like members of a circus troupe rehearsing their acts behind the big top.

I ordered a Black Russian, and the barmaid raised her eyebrows. "Are you looking for some action?"

"I've seen enough tonight, doll."

"Seen or had?" she said. "You look beat."

I must have looked the way I felt. I took the drink and found an empty stool near the big open windows that faced Duval Street.

It was mid-evening, yet the tourists passed by steadily, seeing only what they wanted during their pleasant tropical vacation—the water, the fish, and the sun, all dancing to merry music in the dazzling light of Key West's center ring—while I had become entangled in the island's peculiar backstage life, all disjointed, dark, and contrapuntal.

Meanwhile, back inside the 707, a tall, energetic, and ruggedly handsome guy was making the rounds through the downstairs bar, greeting people like old friends. He had close-cropped hair, almost as short as mine, and a big cowboy-style mustache. He smiled like he was trying to sell his teeth, and he moved like he could easily sell his body. That's when I recognized him. It was Ross, the bartender from the Tulle Box. He approached me with a big grin on his face.

I said, "You sure look different without your cowboy duds, and with that new haircut."

Ross said, "Your fuzzcut inspired me."

"Is this how you spend your nights off?"

"I'm working, darlin'. Everyone needs a second job these days."

"Except maybe doctors and lawyers," I said.

Ross said, "That's when I started tending bar, when I was in medical school."

"You were in medical school?"

"Up in New York," said Ross. "But I got distracted and flunked out." He seemed completely at ease with the facts, or the fantasy, whichever it was. "Little by little I discovered tending bar was very satisfying work. I felt like I was helping people, really helping them. So I thought, why spend all that time and money learning how to patch people up when you can do just as much good for them behind a bar?"

Maybe he was telling the truth. After all, I'd done a similar thing, switching from psychology to hairdressing.

Ross continued. "And I always got offers to make some extra money, after the bars closed."

"Oh," I said, beginning to suspect the real nature of Ross's second job.

"Right," he said. "And now it's steady work for me."

"So you do sex for money?"

"Don't judge me too harsh, darlin'."

"I'm not judging," I said.

Ross's big brown puppy-dog eyes turned inviting. "Are you looking for company then?"

Our brief gavotte was interrupted by an announcement over the PA system, welcoming Cozy Dinette and the Family Style Meals to the 707.

"That's my cue," I said. "I came to hear Cozy sing."

"I'll catch you later, darlin'," said Ross.

I went upstairs for the show. But the only free seat up there was at the bar. And unfortunately it meant sitting next to that local charmer, the Countess Anastasia Rulalenska, who was there alone. I opted to stand.

Cozy began her first song, while I tried to avoid the countess. But it was hopeless, for the countess's turban that evening was a two-tone shocker—flamingo pink and key lime green—and its innate glow kept drawing my eyes that way. She waved her fingers discreetly to catch my attention. When I didn't respond, she resorted to getting one of the waitresses to summon me. Royalty was determined to have its way. I finally submitted and went to her. Without any greeting she barraged me with questions.

"Have you seen Kenneth? Is he downstairs? Did he leave any message? Did he forget this is a fund-raising event?"

I told her Ken would probably miss this party.

"How do you know?" she said.

"I just came from his place."

"Kenneth told me he was conducting business tonight."

I said, "Some people call it that."

The countess rummaged through her embroidered reticule and pulled out a cellular telephone. She unfolded it and punched in some numbers, then shrieked into it above Cozy Dinette's singing and the rest of the noisy club.

"Kenneth, where are you!" she demanded. "I am still waiting here . . . Yes, I know what you told me . . . I understand, but are you coming here? . . . Should I come there? . . . Oh . . . Oh! Why didn't you tell me that before? Bye-bye."

The countess snapped the little phone closed and tossed it into her bag. She said, "Kenneth is, er, occupied. Perhaps you will do me the kindness to accompany me outside and call me a taxi? A lady should not be alone in a public place."

I agreed and escorted her downstairs, if only to prove that social etiquette was known and occasionally even practiced by the feudal serfs. I phoned for a cab, and we waited for it outside the 707.

"You must have been disappointed," I said, "to lose your inheritance from Peter Willits."

"Young man, do not discuss those things with me."

"But you loved Peter. And when he died, he meant to leave you something. Except his mother took it from you."

"I am not alone," said the countess. "There were others. And I will find a way to get my air-conditioning."

I said, "Peter Willits left you more than air-conditioning. He left you Blue Water Tours, an extremely valuable source of income. In fact, your motive to eliminate Augusta Willits was probably the strongest of any of Peter's legatees."

"How dare you be so bold, when you are so ignorant?"

"Because I have nothing to lose, or to hide."

"Nor do I," said the countess.

"Didn't you try to reason with Augusta?" I said.

"Why should I do that?"

"Because Blue Water Tours was almost in your hands, and it was the most lucrative of any of Peter Willits's properties."

"Where do you hear such things?" said the countess.

The fact was, I hadn't. I was bluffing.

I said, "What about Adolf Dobermann?"

In response to that the countess grabbed at her throat, an ill-chosen gesture I thought, considering that Dobermann had been strangled with a T-shirt from her shop. I was about to pursue the delicate matter of said murder weapon and its apparent incrimination of Her Regal Fakeness, but that's precisely when the cab pulled up to the curb, and the countess scurried inside. She could move fast when she wanted to. From the open window she said to me, "It must require great effort from one with so little natural grace to be courteous."

"Takes one to know one," I replied.

The cab took off.

Meanwhile, from the 707's upstairs open-air club Cozy Dinette's voice crashed into the night air, twanging out the opening lyrics to her first number. I went back upstairs to hear her. Seconds later Ross was by my side.

"Did you hurt that fancy lady's feelings?"

"She hasn't got any," I said. "And she ain't no lady. But I am curious about all this new attention from you."

"It's not new, darlin'," said Ross. "I liked you the minute you walked into the Tulle Box the other day."

Up onstage Cozy was singing and waggling a warning finger toward the audience with the lyrics:

> "Don't let your eyes say yes
>   When your heart is telling you no."

I looked Ross straight in the eye. "How much?"

"For what, darlin'?"

"To spend some time with you."

"Spend time?" said Ross, all innocence and guile at once.

"Are you or are you not hustling tonight?"

"Well, sure, darlin', but—"

"Well, then, it's simple. I want to pay you for your time."

"Is that all you want?" said Ross.

I hesitated. "I don't know yet."

Ross grinned and said, "You're like a little lost lamb."

He was right. I had been feeling lonely and confused enough beforehand, but after the sights at Ken Kimble's pool party, my yearning for physical comfort had become an ache.

So Ross and I left the 707 together. On the way out I waved to Cozy Dinette, still onstage. She gave me a look of mock horror as she went on singing the blues. During the brief drive back to the guest house I argued with myself about why I was so ready to pay for sex. But then, why not? In my efforts to have a satisfactory sex life I'd tried everything from celibacy to self-abuse. I'd even tried love and marriage. The only thing I hadn't tried was a negotiated agreement with a paid professional. And here was Ross sitting in the roadster beside me—ready, willing, and with any luck, able—in his moonlighting persona of Mr. Love-for-Sale.

Up in my room I wanted to settle the financial side of our business right away, so once again I asked Ross how much.

He said, "What do you like to do?"

I groaned. "No gymnastics. Not tonight. Just pretend you like me."

Ross grinned and said, "But I *do* like you, darlin'."

"Good," I said. "You learn fast."

I placed four crisp fifty-dollar bills on the nightstand. I didn't want to appear cheap. And I did want him to spend the night.

"I hope that's enough," I said.

Ross glanced at the money, then looked back at me. In those lingering moments his brown eyes became warm and inviting. The guy was a real pro, quickly able to portray the kind of affection I needed.

That's also when I noticed he was aroused.

16

Somehow I attract the most unlikely people, sexually speaking. I'm no olympiad. I'm not even promiscuous. Sort of. But I do have some peculiar magnet for sexually gifted creatures. So it was with Ross. As the night progressed he did his job exceedingly well, so much so that we didn't really have sex, not if the act was limited to the fiery conjoining of loins, however protected by latex. I mean, we didn't do any of the poky things. Instead Ross did what I needed: I had asked him to like me, and he performed the task with conviction. I knew it was an act on both our parts, but it still felt pretty good. He left my room as the sun was coming up.

Shortly after that came a knock on my door followed by the abrupt intrusion of the houseboy carrying a big tray of food.

"Breakfast for two," he said.

"Kind of early," I said, "especially for something I didn't order."

"The owner thought you and your guest might . . ." He looked around the room, then listened toward the bathroom for giveaway sounds, then looked back at me, perplexed. "They said you had a guest."

"And they hoped you'd find us joined at the hip."

"Something like that."

"Sorry to disappoint you," I said.

The houseboy glanced toward the night table. Still lying there in the open were the four fifty-dollar bills I'd put out for Ross the night before.

"Looks like he forgot something," he said as he eyed the money hungrily.

"That's someone else's wages," I said, "but I'll take that breakfast." I gave him ten dollars for his trouble and sent him away. I drank the juice and started on the coffee. Though it was just after seven, I telephoned Nicole at home. She fumbled as she picked up the receiver.

"Too early," she growled.

"It's me," I said quickly. "Don't hang up."

I told her about finding Adolf's body the day before, and everything that had ensued from there.

Nicole said, "Darling, I love you, but it's a little early to appreciate your Nancy Drew exploits, so if you don't mind—"

"Nikki, wait'll you hear this . . ." And then I told her about the defense lawyer I'd hired for Jeri Tiker named Nancy L. Drew.

When I finished Nicole said, "It sounds like a three-ring circus down there."

"It's more like the sideshow, doll."

By that time Nicole realized I needed to talk, because instead of hanging up, she asked if I was having any fun.

I said, "Do you mean fun, or sex?"

"Well, well," said Nicole. "What's his name?"

"Ross."

"And what does he do?"

"He tends bar and he hustles."

"I see," she said. "Is he any good?"

"He makes a great martini."

"But does he make a living, Stanley? Or is he after your money?"

"He's after everyone's money, but he won't take mine."

"Aha," said Nicole. "And has this dalliance with a sex professional displaced your new lady friend?"

"Which lady friend?"

"Didn't you meet a woman you dared to compare to me?"

"Never, doll. You're incomparable."

"Thank you, Stanley. Just be careful you don't lead these new conquests on. Someone might fall in love with you."

"Nikki, one is a paid professional, and the other is a grown woman who accepts my sexuality."

"How naïve you are, Stanley. How old is she anyway?"

"Younger than you, but then, who isn't?"

"Pre or post?"

"No hot flashes yet."

"Then be careful, Stanley. She may want a child by you."

"Nikki, she's a cabaret singer."

"How's her skin?"

"Are you jealous?"

"Hardly. But really, Stanley, I am tempted to come down there and drag you home by the ears. Your blindness borders on self-destruction. First another woman, and now a hustler! What are you doing?"

She paused for a breath, and I said quietly, "You're screaming, doll."

"I am not screaming!" she screamed.

"It's okay, Nikki. I'm desperate, I'm lonely, and I'm miserable. But I'm okay. Honest."

"Now I wish you *had* taken the cat with you. You'd be forced to keep a glimmer of sanity just so you wouldn't neglect her."

"My little safety net," I said, and thought of Sugar Baby.

"And where is *my* little safety net, Stanley? If I don't hear your voice every twenty-four hours, I'm coming down there in person. Is that clear?"

"Yes, doll."

"Twenty-four hours," she said again. "I don't care what time it is. Just call and say 'alive' if that's all you have time for between your hustler and all the others."

"Cozy Dinette is not 'all the others.' "

Nicole roared, "Is that her name? Cozy Dinette?"

"She's an entertainer," I said.

"With a name like that? Oh, Stanley, it may already be too late to save you."

"Nikki, she's fun. You asked me if I was having fun."

"I did mean sex, darling. And I want you to call me. Agreed?"

"Yes."

"Solemn promise?"

"You've made your point."

"I doubt it," she said and then hung up.

Thus refreshed, I set out for another day of tropical fun and frolic, such as it was. My first errand was to tell Lieutenant Sanfuentes what I'd learned from Ken Kimble the previous night at his pool party: that he'd had *Dinner of Uncertainty* in his possession for a short time, and that it had been taken from his place, or so he claimed. But then I remembered my promise to Ken that our talk had been sub-rosa, and though I am a lapsed Roman Catholic, I couldn't violate that confidence. So, I told Sanfuentes about the painting, but without naming names, and I changed the rampant orgy to some anonymously hosted ordinary pool party. Well, the cop still didn't believe any of it. He said I was taking desperate measures, *lying* just to get my friend Jeri Tiker out of jail. He sat back in his chair, then rocked himself lightly, as if to comfort himself the way his mama once did. A few quiet minutes passed, and I sensed Sanfuentes wanted to tell me something. Finally he spoke.

"Just between you and me," he said, "strictly off the record, I don't have much of a case against Miss Tiker."

"Then why are you holding her?"

"It's my job to keep people safe."

"But Jeri hasn't hurt anyone."

"Are you dense?" Sanfuentes shook his head impatiently. "I'm trying to protect *her*."

"From whom?"

"That's what I don't know yet," said the cop. "See? Even I got questions with no answers, just like you. Difference is, it's my job. But you? You're supposed to be on vacation. So why don't you go now and have some fun, do some shopping, meet some new people."

"I've already done that."

"Yeah, so I heard," said the cop. "You had yourself a nice little time last night."

"I already told you, it was just a pool party."

"I meant the business in your room."

"How'd you know about that?" I said.

Sanfuentes said, "It's a small town."

I left the police station and walked to Fleming Street and passed by the Fleming Lemming, where I saw a line of gabby tourists extending out the open door. I peered beyond them and saw Joshua Aytem at the front desk inside. He was happily selling them little piles of things, all the while talking on the telephone. From what I could see of the goods, they were all Key West souvenirs—preselected, shrink-wrapped, and specially priced. No shopping necessary. No browsing. No thinking. Just a nice, safe little pile of Key West this, Key West that, and Key West et cetera.

When the garrulous mob finally disbanded, Joshua also hung up the phone. Had it been a prop merely to deflect the yacking tourists? He burbled enthusiastically to me, "That little army of shoppers just paid our rent for the next two months. I love tourists. I fly them in, I put them up, I sell them souvenirs, then I send them off on the conch trains and the glass-bottomed boats."

He flushed as he straightened out the pile of money he'd just taken in.

I asked him where Laura was. He told me she'd gone out on an errand. Then he said, "I hear you had a little adventure with some of our local culture last night. Or should I say local trade?"

"News travels fast," I said.

"Small town," said Joshua good-naturedly. "And you scored a small victory too."

"Victory?"

Joshua said, "Ross never sleeps with a john. He does his job, then leaves." Then he added with emphasis, "And he always takes his fee."

"You seem to know everything that transpired."

"Except the blow-by-blow," said Joshua, with his sexually hip inflection.

"Does everyone else on the island know too?"

"Just about," he said.

"How about answering a question for me then?"

"If I can," said Joshua.

"You said that all those items you just sold will pay two months' rent here, and I was wondering, who's your landlord?"

"Huh?" said Joshua. The sexually hip smirk was gone.

"Well, if Peter Willits used to own this place, and then Augusta got it, and then her church, does that mean your landlord is Augusta's church?"

Joshua replied flatly. "It hasn't come up yet."

"But it will. And then who will you make the check out to?"

"That's a good question," he said.

"Everyone knows who their landlord is, Joshua, if they have one."

The telephone rang and he picked it up. "Yeah? . . . What! . . . When? . . . Was anyone hurt? . . . Okay . . . Yeah . . . No."

Then he hung up the phone and said to me, "That was Laura. No wonder she's late. She was down by the marina when someone threw a firebomb onto one of the tour boats." Joshua sniggered. "I guess some unhappy tourist got seasick."

"Or maybe it was a sore loser," I said.

Joshua studied me warily, the way a loan officer at a bank might do. Then he said, "What are you driving at?"

"Wasn't the countess supposed to inherit Blue Water Tours from Peter Willits? Maybe she feels if she can't have it, no one can."

Joshua shrugged. "I'd better get down there and make sure Laura's okay. She sounded really shook up. You're going to have to find another place to park yourself."

"No problem," I said.

But before I was out the door Joshua asked me for five dollars. "Gas for the car," he said.

"Didn't you just rake in a pile of cash?"

"Oh, that's right," he said. "I forgot."

What else had he conveniently forgot?

I headed down Fleming Street toward Duval. A few minutes later I met Laura Hope riding her motor scooter toward me. She stopped, and I told her Joshua had just gone to the marina to make sure she was all right after the firebomb on the tour boat. She immediately called him on her cellular phone and told him she was on her way back to the Fleming Lemming, and that everything was okay.

Then I asked her the same question I had put to Joshua: Who was their landlord now that Peter Willits was dead?

She smiled brightly and said, "I assume we'll just pay the estate now."

"The estate of whom?" I said.

Her brow creased slightly. "Augusta Willits," she said.

"But she doesn't own the property anymore. Her church does."

"Then I guess we'll pay the church," said Laura. "Why does it matter?"

"Because all of Peter Willits's property belongs to somebody else now, and I wonder who it is."

Laura said, "Didn't you just say a church?"

"Doesn't it bother you to pay rent on property that was rightfully yours, and to a church no less?"

"What difference does it make?" she said. "A bank, a landlord, a church—someone always collects money for the roof over your head."

"Not if you own it outright," I said. "Or inherit it, as you were supposed to."

Her cheerfulness dispelled quickly. But who could blame her with me saying things like that? Then I asked her why Peter Willits had intended the property for her alone, and not jointly with Joshua.

"Where did you hear that?" she said.

"Small town," I said, using the same line people were throwing at me. "I wonder if there was anything more between you and Peter Willits than a love of books."

"Like what?"

"You tell me," I said.

Laura said, "Peter probably thought I wanted security and independence. Isn't that what you think too? That an intelligent woman like myself should leave Joshua, if only I had the means? And owning a business would give me that freedom. Maybe that's why Peter left the place to me alone. Well, just for your information, I don't want freedom. I love Joshua. Can you understand that? Can any gay man? Peter thought he knew better, and you probably do too. But I'd give that place to Josh in a minute and let him turn it into a garage if he wanted to. I've already given up everything important for him. Why stop now? Does that answer your question?"

"I was just curious," I said.

Laura revved the small engine on her motor scooter and zoomed away up Fleming Street, while I headed toward the marina to check out the earlier incendiary episode.

At the waterfront I found that my suspicions had proved right. A small crowd was gathered near one of the docks belonging to Blue Water Tours. Black smoke billowed from the open hatchways of one of the large tour boats. From within the throng of people shone a coral-colored silk turban, glowing brightly in the late morning sun. The Countess Rulalenska strained and stretched anxiously, trying to see above the people around her. I worked my way toward her, and when I was directly behind her, I spoke quietly into her ear.

"I hope their insurance didn't lapse."

She turned to me with a shocked look.

I said, "Who's running the company since you lost it?"

"Go away!" she muttered. Then she said to the man standing next to her, "Please, can you help me? This young man is harassing me."

But instead of helping her, the guy moved away, putting other people between him and the countess.

I said, "The word is out on you, Countess."

"How dare you accuse me? You have no proof."

"Your guilt is transparent."

Suddenly she shrieked, "Help! Police! Help!"

I quickly slithered away from her and out of the small crowd. That's when I came face-to-face with Ken Kimble.

"You left so quickly last night," he said. "I was hoping you'd stay longer. Had you made other plans?"

No doubt Ken had already heard the unexpurgated if fantastic account of my escapade with Ross the previous evening. And with everyone around me lying, I lied too, and told Ken I'd left his party because I thought I'd worn out my welcome.

"Wear out your welcome?" said Ken. "Never in my house." And he punctuated his remark with a flash of his expensive teeth.

"What brings you here?" I said, changing the conversational tack with the finesse of a lubberly seaman.

"Stassya called me," said Ken, "right after the fire broke out."

"Was she drawn by the crowd, or was she already here?"

Ken faltered. "What do you mean?"

I shrugged. "Odd coincidence."

"Is it?" said Ken.

"Blue Water Tours was supposed to be hers, wasn't it? From Peter's will? And now one of the boats is on fire. It's no wonder she's concerned."

"Yes," said Ken. "I'm sure that's why she's here."

"Do you know who's managing it now?"

"Who?" he said, as if I'd spoken in tongues.

I said, "Peter is dead. So who's running the company now?"

"I'm sure I don't know," said Ken.

"Somebody is," I said. "Somebody opens up, and sells tickets, and takes the boats out."

Ken said, "A corporation, no matter how small, is capable of operating whether its owner is dead or alive."

"Is that the same for the Gulf Coast Playhouse?"

"What are you getting at?" he said, finally and absolutely irritated with me.

"That property was supposed to be yours, I mean, along with Edsel Shamb."

Ken said quickly, "I don't have time for this nonsense. I must find Stassya." And off he went into the crowd to rescue the faux damsel in feigned distress.

I was heading away from the fire scene when I saw Lieutenant Sanfuentes conferring with someone from the fire department. I approached him, and Sanfuentes excused himself from the other guy and came toward me.

"You again?" he said. "Everywhere I look, it's you. I thought I heard a ruckus. Were you bothering someone in the crowd?"

"The lady in the silk turban," I said.

"The countess," said Sanfuentes with a wry smile.

"You might want to talk to her, Lieutenant."

"And why is that?" said the cop.

"Because she was supposed to inherit Blue Water Tours."

"So?"

"Well, she didn't. So maybe she's trying to put it out of business."

"Maybe it's just a coincidence," said the cop.

"And maybe it isn't," I said. "Just thought I'd mention it."

"Thanks," said Sanfuentes, "but I thought we agreed this morning I don't need your help anymore."

"I'm just talking, Lieutenant. Being friendly. We can talk about the weather if you want."

"Yeah, well, there'll be plenty of talk in that department soon. Weather bureau just announced a hurricane watch. You might want to get out of town while you can."

"I enjoy the forces of nature," I said.

"This isn't nature," said Sanfuentes. "This might be a disaster."

And then he turned and walked away from me.

17

Sanfuentes had instructed me to play the vacationer, and, evidence to the contrary, I can obey orders when expedient. It was noontime, already late for the first cocktail of any real holiday, so I set out to rehearse my former role as vacationing deadbeat in Key West. Despite the oppressive heat, I walked from the waterfront across town to the Tulle Box, protecting myself in the shady tree-lined arcades along Simonton Street. I hoped Ross might be tending bar that day, and he was. But when he saw me coming up the stairwell, he signaled me to go back down. A minute later he joined me and pulled me into a little alcove, out of sight and earshot of the hotel's lobby.

Ross leaned close and murmured, "Darlin', everyone's talking about us."

"I know," I said. "I don't understand the big deal."

"What's worse is they all know I didn't take your money."

It sounded like an accusation.

I said, "You forgot it—"

"I didn't forget!" he said, straining to control his whisper. "But did you have to tell everyone?"

"I didn't, Ross." I explained how the houseboy had seen the money on the nightstand where Ross had left it, and apparently he'd told everyone else at the guest house, and then the news hit the street, and the rest, well . . . ?

Ross apologized. "Sorry, darlin'. I thought you were bragging how you got me free. Folks hear that, they'll think I'm soft on you."

"You? Soft?" I said.

"You know what I mean, darlin'. But talk like that'll ruin my business."

"Then maybe we can stage a little transaction upstairs. I'll hand you some cash out in the open so anyone in the bar can see it. It'll be strictly business."

"That might work," said Ross. "And I'll give it back when we're alone, later."

"You don't have to, Ross. I believe in a day's pay for a day's work."

"Not between friends," said Ross.

"We're hardly friends," I said.

"You mean we're lovers?" he said eagerly.

I laughed before realizing the consequences.

His face drooped sadly. "I guess not," he said.

"Ross," I said, "we barely know each other. How can you throw out words like *friend* and *lover* when you're referring to us?"

He said, "Last night it felt like you really cared about me. Was that just an act?"

I said, "Wasn't it for you?"

Ross said flatly, "No."

"Oh," I said.

"What about you?" he said. "Were you acting?"

I didn't answer. I didn't know the answer. It hadn't felt like acting, but I'd thought it was. So, then, what was it?

Ross waited silently for me to solve a problem neither of us had anticipated.

I said, "How about for now we keep it business between us? I pay, we play."

"I don't want your money."

"What do you suggest then?"

Ross said, "Maybe we can keep it a secret when we get together."

"You mean, so people won't know there's no money between us?"

"Right," said Ross.

Now that was a change of pace, becoming clandestine lovers with a hustler to save *his* reputation.

I said, "We can try it, but all the walls in this town seem to have ears."

"Some of them have eyes too," said Ross.

"Then it's probably easier if we do it this way. We get together, I pay you, you flash the money around, and then you give it back later. Then we do it all again."

Ross said, "I love ya', darlin'." He gave me a big hug and a noisy kiss on the neck. "I'll go back upstairs and get settled. Then you come in and we'll do the skit with the money."

He went back up. I waited a few minutes, then made my entrance again. This time it was lights, camera, action!

"Hello, stranger!" said Ross.

"Hi, there," I said, and took a seat at the bar. "I think we have some unfinished business." I pulled out my wallet and removed the four fifties I'd earmarked for Ross's services the previous night. I said loudly, "You forgot to take something last night."

"Oh, yeah," said Ross matter-of-factly. "I must've had too much to drink."

I pressed the cash onto him, making sure the other patrons at the bar saw and heard. Ross took it and jammed it into his shirt pocket for all to see.

"Thanks for being so honest," he said.

"Sure," I said. "I might even call you again."

I almost believed our little scam myself.

"You want a drink?" he said.

I nodded. "Tini up with a twist, clean and double."

Ross set about preparing my drink. Then from the stairwell came the clatter of high heels running up the stairs, and finally the towering figure of Miss Cozy Dinette appeared at the top.

"Hey, Boston!" she yelled. "I saw you down at the marina. Quite a show, huh? Smoke and fire and everything else."

"What were you doing there?"

Cozy explained, "I got my hair done. Can't you tell?"

In truth, not a strand was different.

"Looks great," I said.

"Liar!" said Cozy, and she let out a laugh. Then she said to Ross, "I need to cool off, Rossina. I've been running around all morning. How about an apple spritzer, heavy on the lime."

"Which rum?" said Ross. "Light or dark?"

"None," said Cozy. "And no arguments."

Ross stalled, as though making a nonalcoholic drink for Cozy Dinette defied the laws of physics. Finally he jogged himself into action, and filled a giant tumbler with ice, poured in apple juice halfway up, then topped it off with seltzer. Four lime wedges finished the drink. Cozy grabbed hold of the tumbler and drank eagerly. "Really cuts the phlegm," she said. "Learned about it from a sky slut. It's the only thing that works in this heat."

While Ross tended to his other customers, I asked Cozy if she knew who was managing the Crow's Nest.

"Who?" said Cozy, as though the pronoun had no meaning.

"Yeah, who," I said, then explained that somebody was running the place since Augusta had been killed, and I wondered who it was. For that matter, who was managing any of the late Peter Willits's property?

Cozy said, "I wouldn't know."

"How about your property advisor? Would she know?"

"Maybe," said Cozy. "Boston, I wonder if you're having enough fun here. You're always worrying about things that don't concern you."

"What do you suggest I do?"

"That's easy," said Cozy. "Forget about the murders and stop chasing after Ross. They're both dead-end pursuits."

"I'm not chasing Ross."

"Is that so?" said Cozy. "Well, then don't encourage him."

"Why not?"

"You don't need him as a friend."

"I don't want him as a friend, Cozy. I want to keep him on the payroll."

"I think you should go see some strippers tonight."

I told her sure, I was willing to see more local culture. She told me where the best ones were. Then Cozy gulped down the rest of her spritzer and banged the tumbler on the bar. "See y'around, Boston." Then she left the bar.

Moments later Ross came over. He leaned close to me and murmured, "I got a little secret for you, darlin'. I know who's managing all that property Augusta stole from Peter's estate."

"You do?" I said.

"And it's not a person. It's a company."

"Have they got a name?"

"It's an odd one. Are you ready?"

I nodded eagerly.

Ross said, "It's called Mindful Lotus."

"How do you know this?"

"Darlin', I hear all kinds of things on this side of the bar. People think they're talking secrets, but everything comes over the bar loud and clear."

"Did you hear what I just said to Cozy about you and me?"

"Sure did, darlin'. But I know you didn't mean it."

Then Ross pulled away and spoke in a normal voice, for the benefit of the others in the Tulle Box. "So if you like strippers, you might do better with one of them." The remark lent more credibility to my persona of the lonely vacationer shopping for cash-and-carry sex.

On the walk back to the Jared Bellamy House, I stopped in at the police station to see Jeri Tiker. By that time Attorney Nancy L.

Drew should have met with her, and I was curious how that first session between client and advocate had turned out.

I found Jeri painting peacefully in her cell. She looked up. "It's actually good working here," she said. "There are no tourists to interrupt me."

"Then excuse this interruption," I said.

"I needed a break anyway," said Jeri.

I asked her if the lawyer had come by and how their meeting had progressed. Jeri told me Attorney Drew seemed more interested in finding out how much she knew about Adolf Dobermann's business dealings than with her whereabouts at the time of his murder.

I said, "Does she believe you're innocent? Does she want to represent you?"

"Yes to both questions," said Jeri.

"That's good."

"I'm not so sure. Look how she bungled Peter's will."

I assured her it would be all right. After all, Nancy Drew was supposed to be the best lawyer around. But really, what did I know? I left Jeri and headed back upstairs. The lieutenant wasn't in, so I used a public phone to call Nancy Drew's office. Even though I was paying the woman to represent Jeri, I still had to contend with her secretary, a dragon at the gate. I persisted, claiming that I had urgent matters to tell Attorney Drew in person, that I was old-fashioned when it came to the law, that I didn't trust the telephone and liked to confer face-to-face.

The secretary remarked, "A lot of good that'll do you."

But finally she yielded and gave me an appointment with the great lawyer, provided I could be at the office within fifteen minutes, no later. So it was rush, rush, rush, just like for the initial consultation. I ran back to the guest house, got the Alfa, and zoomed out to Roosevelt Boulevard.

I had raced all the way to Nancy L. Drew's office, but when I got there the secretary told me I'd have to wait. How long? As long as it took Attorney Drew to finish the matter at hand. I asked the secretary to announce me at least, but she snarled and said Attorney Drew was not to be disturbed.

"But I just called you," I said, "and you told me—"

"I know what I said! But the situation has changed and you've been pre-empted."

Big words from a small mouth.

She told me I'd be better off coming back some other time. I said I'd wait. She told me to suit myself. The airborne fungus, or whatever it was in that air conditioner, was stinging my nostrils again, so I told the secretary I'd wait outside.

She said quickly, "If you're going to wait, you ought to wait in here. I mean, it's so hot out there. And you don't want to miss Attorney Drew."

"I'm not going far."

The secretary remained uneasy. I sensed there might be something outside I wasn't supposed to see, which only drove me out the door faster. I wandered around to the back of the building, off the asphalt parking lot and onto a lush green lawn that faced out on the water. The perpetual rains had kept the green things healthy back there, despite the blazing sun. Also back there, parked close behind the building, right next to the rear emergency exit, was my old friend, the pink taxicab, idling quietly. I went toward it to peer inside the darkly tinted windows, but before I got close, it pulled slowly away from me and drove around the far side of the building. I followed it, and on the way passed the back windows to Attorney Drew's office.

The windows were all shielded by slatted blinds, which were shut tight. Nancy Drew was obviously engaged in a clandestine conference. I leaned close to the windows, hoping to hear or see something from within, but the glass was double-paned and perfectly soundproofed. What did come through loud and clear was the secretary's voice as she emerged from around the near side of the building.

"Attorney Drew can see you now," she said.

I wanted to linger out there and find out who was driving that taxi. But I realized the secretary's mission of the moment was to prevent exactly that from happening. So I went back with her through the front entrance of the building. The big glass-paneled door had just about latched itself behind us when I caught a glimpse of the pink taxi zooming out of the front parking lot.

In her office, Attorney Drew seemed slightly ruffled.

"Mr. Kraychik," she said too cordially, "Jeri Tiker's white knight. What brings you here today?"

"I wanted to discuss Jeri's case."

"I'm afraid that is now a matter of confidentiality between my client and myself."

"But I know something that might bear directly on it."

"Mr. Kraychik, I have found that when people offer information voluntarily, they usually have agendas."

"You mean motives?" I said.

"What do you want?" she said sharply.

"I want to help Jeri Tiker."

"Then I owe it to my client to hear you out for a few minutes."

"Especially since I'm the one paying for your services."

Nancy L. Drew smiled complacently and said, "That has never influenced me, Mr. Kraychik. But go on now, and quickly please."

I told her that I thought everything was interconnected: Augusta Willits's death, Jeri Tiker's stolen painting, Adolf Dobermann's death, and the subsequently recovered painting.

Nancy Drew said, "And just how do you connect the dots, Mr. Kraychik?"

"I can't. There's a missing link."

"And what do you think it is?"

"I think it's whoever is managing all of Peter Willits's property."

The lawyer said nothing.

"Do you know about a group called Mindful Lotus?" I said.

Nancy L. Drew smiled like a Buddha and said, "It sounds like one of those religious sects."

"I heard it's directly connected to the Willits estate."

The attorney replied, "Jeri Tiker's murder case bears no relation whatsoever to the Willits estates, and I strongly advise you to discontinue thinking along those lines."

"Who's managing all that property now?"

"That," said the attorney, "is entirely at the discretion of the owners."

"Exactly my point," I said. "Who are the owners?"

"Mr. Kraychik, I have nothing more to say on the matter."

"All right then," I said, "what about the pink taxicab that's been following me around the island for the past few days?"

Nancy Drew chortled. "A pink taxicab?"

"The one that was parked behind the building just now."

"Mr. Kraychik, do you realize how many pink taxicabs are on Key West?"

"But I recognized this one."

Her eyes narrowed like a predator registering its prey.

"Your blundering about like this may damage your friend's case."

"Why can't you tell me what it's all about? I'm paying you, after all."

"I don't care who's paying me," said Attorney Drew. "And I don't answer questions simply because people ask them. Now, if you'll excuse me, I'm not on vacation like you, and I have work to do."

"Then tell me what you're doing to prove Jeri's innocence."

"*That* is a very simple matter," said the attorney. "There will be no case against her. The only evidence is a painting of hers found in her own gallery, and some mud on her bicycle. Neither finding is even remotely incriminating. The charges will be dropped before an indictment is made. And now, my advice to you, Mr. Kraychik, is that you go and work on your tan. You look like you need it."

"I'm allergic to the sun."

Nancy Drew said, "Is that how you lost your hair?"

"No," I said. "I shaved my head. I'm in mourning. I came to Key West to find myself."

Nancy Drew said quietly, "Most people come here to lose themselves."

"How long before Jeri Tiker is released?"

The great attorney stood up, a dramatic gesture I suspected she reserved for her most intense moments of power. "The law works in its own time. Intrusions by outsiders often hinder that progress. So I urge you to get on with your vacation and leave the important matters to the professionals. Now if you don't mind . . ." She gestured toward the door.

I got up and went toward it. As I opened it to leave, Nancy Drew made her parting remark.

"And Mr. Kraychik," she said, "if you find yourself too restless, perhaps some companionship will help pass the time."

For that valuable advice I was paying Attorney Nancy L. Drew three hundred twenty-five dollars an hour, plus expenses. Ross's brand of no-frills service was a far better buy.

I drove the Alfa out to the vast public beach on the east side of town. I hoped the white sand and the blue water along the shore would help restore a sense of well-being after the legal consultation. I parked the car facing toward the water, then put on my straw hat and turned on the stereo. It was a tape of Smetana's "The Moldau," a piece Rafik had always dismissed as too sentimental. Now I could play it to my heart's content, and reconnect to my Czech forebears through the music they'd written. I kept it quiet though, so it wouldn't intrude on the gentle sounds of low tide on Key West. With the heat of the afternoon sun penetrating my light cotton shirt and warming the leather seat of the Alfa, and with the soothing music and the salty air, I was lulled into a pleasant dreamy state, and I lost track of time.

Sometime later I heard footsteps approaching on the gravel in the parking area. I opened my eyes lazily to see Edsel Shamb standing there. "This is the only natural beach on Key West."

I said, "Because Key West is a coral reef and not a land mass."

"Very good," he said.

"I've been reading my tourist guide."

I offered him a seat in the Alfa and he took it.

"Nice leather," he said.

"I didn't hear your car drive up," I said.

"I don't drive," he said. "I walk a lot. Isn't that what writers are supposed to do?"

"You'd know better than I would," I said.

"You'll forgive me," he said, "but I've got such good news I can't help telling everybody I meet. Can I tell you too? It's really wonderful. Hollywood just bought my pilot episode and they're contracting me for ten more. This deal puts me over the top financially. My life is secure forever."

"Sounds nice," I said. "Fame and fortune."

Edsel grinned. "Fame is hardly new," he said immodestly. "I've learned how to manage and enjoy that. But now I'll have the fortune too, and I intend to invest it wisely."

"Don't forget to spend some."

"Oh, don't worry," he said heartily, like one rich guy to another. "Well, enough about me. What have you been up to?"

"Nothing so glamorous as Hollywood," I said. Then I told him Sanfuentes had arrested Jeri Tiker, and that I'd hired Nancy Drew to represent her.

Edsel said, "I heard about the arrest. I think it was a big mistake. But you were wise to engage Nancy. She can certainly handle the case. Fact is, there isn't much of a case at all."

"Only murder."

"But there's no real evidence against Jeri Tiker, is there? It'll all blow over soon, and she'll be painting again."

"That's what Nancy Drew implied."

"There, see?" he said. "If she and I agree, it must be so."

"You're both usually socializing together too."

"Great minds in a small town must unite," said Edsel with a comfortable chuckle. "Just the way you and I are doing now."

Lucky me.

He gazed out over the calm water: Best-selling author appreciates nature.

I said, "Speaking of Nancy Drew, what is her connection to a company called Mindful Lotus?"

Edsel lowered his sunglasses and exposed his big eyes.

"You sound like prime-time television again, Stan."

"Naughty me," I said. "But what about Mindful Lotus?"

"Did Ross tell you this?"

I didn't answer. Why betray my sources when they were so adept at betraying each other?

Edsel went on. "If you spend any time with Ross, you'll hear a lot of interesting things that have little relation to the truth."

"How well do *you* know Ross?"

"Well enough," said Edsel. "And don't get on that track again. Men can be friends without sex, you know."

"So you and Ross are friends then?"

"You're twisting things."

"I'm trying to untwist them. All I asked was if you knew anything about Mindful Lotus."

"And the untwisted answer," he said, "is no."

"That was Nancy Drew's answer too."

"Great minds," said Edsel with another chuckle. "But don't forget, Nancy is part Teflon."

"Someone must know about Mindful Lotus."

"Perhaps they're not a local company. By the name, they sound foreign."

"Or trendy," I said.

Suddenly Edsel had to be on his way, and he moved to open the passenger door of the Alfa. I offered him a lift wherever he was going. He complained it was probably not on my way. I told him I had no plans.

"Besides," I said, "how big is Key West?"

Edsel then mimicked some generic character in a British TV sitcom. "Very well, sir," he said. "Take me posthaste to the Tulle Box, where I shall imbibe awhile."

On the way to the bar, I caught sight of the pink taxicab in my rearview mirror. I mentioned it, but Edsel dismissed my concern. "Those things are everywhere."

"But this one has dark windows, and for a while it followed me everywhere."

"Then what happened?"

"Now," I said, "now it just goes by."

"Maybe someone had a crush on you," he said.

"That's what Lieutenant Sanfuentes said."

"Did he?" said Edsel. "I would never have credited him with such imagination."

I said, "Straight people seem pretty tolerant here."

"Live and let live," he said, then added with a self-amused chuckle, "Fuck and let fuck." He took out a small black notebook and scribbled something down. "Lest I forget my own wittiness."

When I dropped him off, he invited me up to the bar for a cocktail, but I told him that I wanted to catch a short nap.

"Are you seeing Ross tonight?" he said suggestively.

"I have other plans."

"That's probably wise," he said, then closed the door and walked off.

18

I stopped in again at the police station to see Lieutenant Sanfuentes. He greeted me cordially and took me into his office.

"I'll assume this is a social call," he said, "because as far as I know,
we're not using your help anymore."

"I've been talking to people around town, and—"

"Uh-oh," interrupted Sanfuentes. "That'll send you in circles.
Everybody's got a *canción.*"

"A what?"

Sanfuentes smiled. "A *canción.* A song. Everybody wants to sing
for you."

"I haven't found that to be true, Lieutenant."

"Maybe you just don't like the tune."

"Have you got one too?"

"Sure," said Sanfuentes.

"Sing me some of it."

Sanfuentes smiled like he knew a secret. "Man," he said, "my
canción is a goddamned aria. You'd have to be some kind of head
doctor to listen to it."

"Try me," I said.

The cop became brusque. "What did you want to see me
about?"

I asked him if he'd figured out who set the fire down at the marina. He hadn't. I asked him if he'd spoken to the countess about
it. Again, he hadn't. I reminded him that she was supposed to inherit the tour company. He said he knew that. Then I asked him
if he knew who was managing Peter Willits's property. To that he
shrugged.

"Whoever owns it now."

"And who's that?" I said.

Sanfuentes didn't know.

"Lieutenant, I think Nancy Drew is involved with the disposition of Peter Willits's property."

"Of course she's involved," he said. "She's the lawyer for his estate."

"Right, and she wouldn't let all that property slip through her fingers without knowing the last detail of where every square foot of it went. She might even be managing it herself."

"And just how would she do that?" said Sanfuentes.

"Have you heard of a development company called Mindful Lotus?"

Sanfuentes made a crooked smile. "You know," he said, "if I was to pay attention to every real estate deal on this island, not only would I get no sleep, but a lot more serious problems would go unattended."

"Like murder, you mean?"

"Exactly," said Sanfuentes.

"But something isn't right, Lieutenant. I've asked everyone connected to Peter Willits's estate, and no one knows who's managing the property now. Somebody must be doing it, so why is it such a big secret?"

"Stan, I got enough on my hands trying to convict the guilty."

"How about acquitting the innocent?"

"That goes without saying," he said. "Why don't you go have some fun before that storm comes and spoils your vacation."

"Can I see Jeri Tiker?"

Sanfuentes grunted impatiently. "Go ahead," he said.

I went downstairs to Jeri's cell, where she was painting. She looked up and smiled at me. I wondered if maybe I should get myself jailed too. It certainly kept her in a good mood.

"I was just about to wrap things up," she said. "The light has changed anyway."

I glanced up toward the glass bricks high in the wall of her cell. The late afternoon sun had moved past, and along with it, the light.

"Are you comfortable here?" I said.

"They bring fresh water when I need it."

"They have to do that," I said.

Jeri smiled. "I meant for my paints and brushes. Lieutenant Sanfuentes even asked how much my paintings cost."

"I wouldn't have guessed him to be a connoisseur."

"He isn't," said Jeri. "And that's exactly the kind of person I paint for. I want people to enjoy my work, to invent stories about it, to become friends with it. I told the lieutenant if I ever got out of here I'd give him a painting, to thank him for being so nice."

"Nice? Jeri, he jailed you!"

Jeri said, "But I can tell his heart's not in it. He was doing his job, and there I was with a stolen painting in my studio. He had to arrest me."

I knew that wasn't true. Sanfuentes had already confided to me his real reason for keeping Jeri at the station: for her own protection. But I couldn't tell her that, so I remarked on the painting she was working on. Jeri's creation in the jailhouse studio depicted the flora and fauna around a lotus pond.

"Funny thing," I said. "I just heard about a development company called Mindful Lotus."

Jeri wasn't surprised by the coincidence. She said she often received psychic visions from the ether, which then appeared in her paintings. "Once," she said, "I painted a man falling through space in one of my works. Then a week later I learned one of my art school buddies had jumped off a building."

Her current opus, *The Pond*, was going to be a big work, and from what Jeri had just told me, perhaps also a psychically inspired version of the complex puzzle of the recent killings. Some of the aquatic animals showed a familiar look in their eyes, as though they were humans in disguise. One of them even looked remotely like me, and I said so to Jeri.

"Of course it looks like you," she said. "It is!"

"I'm a turtle?"

"No," said Jeri. "You have a hard protective shell around you right now. But that doesn't mean you're a turtle. My paintings show how I perceive things in the world. They're interpretations, not caricatures."

"What other breakthroughs in Key West personae did you make while painting today?" My voice was thick with sarcasm, for I was hurt by her portrayal of me as a lumbering turtle, especially since

I'd shed that extra weight recently. Jeri had even painted the turtle extra plump, like my former self. Did she perceive my true nature? Did she know that my slender, svelte figure was only temporary, and that I'd be round again all too soon? Oh, if only she had painted me as a menacing barracuda with deadly jaws, just for now, so there could be proof positive, some historical evidence that I had been fashionably gaunt and hard-edged for one brief moment.

Jeri said, "Joshua keeps appearing, but then he dissolves into something else."

"Maybe that's a reflection of your feelings for him."

"I don't think so," she said. "It doesn't matter how I feel about my subjects. The paintings don't have emotions."

"They don't?"

"How can they?" said Jeri. "It's just pigment on a surface. Where are the emotions hiding?"

I said, "The same place they do inside us."

Jeri looked at me uncertainly. "I don't think so," she said again.

"Maybe Joshua's elusive image means he's hiding something."

"Probably," she said. "Or else he's been near the police station today, or he's going to be, or he's been thinking about me. That happens when an image appears and vanishes—the person usually shows up in person. I mean, in the flesh."

I noticed in the painting a gecko devouring a palmetto bug twice as big as itself. "Who's that?" I said.

"The bug? Or the gecko?" said Jeri.

"Both."

Jeri said, "I don't really know. I can't tell until the eyes go in. That's when I know who the person is."

"No clue until then?"

Jeri shook her head no. Then she abruptly plunged all her brushes into a small bucket of water and swirled them violently. The water became murky, the color of dried blood.

"There!" she said. "Done for the day."

That's exactly when the guard appeared with a covered dinner tray for her. He left, and Jeri lifted the cover off the tray. Underneath was a succulent slab of grilled yellowtail, accompanied by risotto with pistachios, and baby asparagus nestled in a small boat of puff pastry with hollandaise sauce.

"Who on earth is cooking like that in jail?" I said.

Jeri replied, "I told you Lieutenant Sanfuentes was being nice to me. He orders my meals from outside."

"You've obviously made a hit," I said.

"No," said Jeri. "I think he knows he has no case on me, and he wants to make sure I don't sue him for false arrest."

Jeri Tiker was an astute young woman, which is probably why she was a fine artist too. Assured for the moment that she was in good hands, culinary and otherwise, I took my leave and went back upstairs. I was just leaving the station when I heard the voice of Joshua Aytem shouting from within, behind me, back inside the station.

"I didn't lay a finger on her!"

I followed the sound of his voice and found him being restrained just outside Lieutenant Sanfuentes's office. Joshua was facing my way, but he didn't notice me. He was too preoccupied by the powerful grip of two cops, one on either side of him. Lieutenant Sanfuentes was facing Joshua, with his back to me. He was questioning Joshua quietly. Joshua's replies, however, were anything but quiet.

"That's bullshit!" he said. "She's lying! Look at her and look at me! There's your evidence!"

I moved closer to the small gathering to hear better.

Lieutenant Sanfuentes said to Joshua, "Then why did your wife call us for help?"

"Because she's insane!" screamed Joshua. "Did you see a scratch on her? Huh? Tell me. Was there even a bump on the bitch? No! You have no grounds to hold me here."

He struggled against the two cops restraining him.

"I got grounds," said Sanfuentes. "You're drunk again. You stink of booze again. And I'm going to book and hold you till you're sober. Again!" Then he said to his men, "Take him downstairs."

That's when Joshua noticed me.

"Hey!" he yelled. "Come on, help me. You've got money. You

can pay my bail. I've got to get out of here. Laura can't run the business alone."

I went up to Joshua. Sanfuentes had been right. He reeked.

"I'm sorry, Joshua," I said. "I can't help you this time."

I could see pressure building up in the man. The two cops holding Joshua were hardly a match for his savage strength. Then he stopped his frantic writhing for a moment and tried to spit on me. He missed, and it only enraged him more.

Meanwhile Lieutenant Sanfuentes repeated the order to his men, but more forcefully. "Take him downstairs!"

The two cops did what they were told, while struggling to keep Joshua from breaking free of their grasp.

I said to Sanfuentes, "I didn't realize how strong he was."

Sanfuentes said, "Too bad that guy doesn't know a better way to let off steam. He's got a lot going for him, until he drinks too much."

"I hope you're not going to put him anywhere near Jeri Tiker."

Lieutenant Sanfuentes chuckled quietly. "We keep the boys and the girls separate here," he said. Then he added, "Although with those two it wouldn't matter much."

"What do you mean?" I said, for if he was disparaging Jeri, I was ready to defend her.

The cop said, "Haven't you heard anyone call their place the Flaming Lemming?"

"No," I said. "Is Joshua gay?"

"Not exactly," said Sanfuentes. "But that's another verse from my *canción*. Maybe someday I'll sing it for you."

He went into his office and closed the door.

I drove back to the guest house for a short nap before my big night out on the town, touring the strip bars. Before I got into bed I rummaged through the leather club bag that held my life's essentials. Somewhere in there was a blue chamois shirt, the final gift I never gave to Rafik. Since his death I had kept that shirt with me, like a souvenir of the Great Love that was destined for tragedy, a reminder that no matter what I had tried to do for love, it had never been quite enough. I held the shirt close to me, buried my face in it, tried to recall Rafik's distinctive scent. But all I smelled was pristine suede, for my man had never even seen the thing. Why hadn't

I known enough to bury that shirt with him, and instead keep some of his real clothing, the stuff that held his essence? But in the heat of my rage over his death I'd given it all away. I wanted no real reminder of him, nothing organic. Instead I'd kept that sterile new shirt.

Psychologists, do your thing.

19

After my nap I took a shower and put on khaki shorts and a short-sleeved cotton shirt, white with slate blue stripes. My vacation wardrobe was getting consistent exposure in Key West once the sun went down. At nine o'clock I walked to Duval Street and grabbed a late supper, then continued on to the bar called the Javelin. I didn't take the car because I anticipated a night of booze and debauchery. How else do you convince yourself that you're on vacation?

When I got to the Javelin, the place was already jammed with people. Through a series of sharp turns, the interior of the main bar was completely out of sight of any passersby on the street. Once inside I realized why. Up on the bar top was one of the Javelin's featured entertainers, just finishing up his "early" show. We got to watch his routine from below, like at an odd camera angle. He used the bar top like a runway, and moved along it with the slinky slow-motion grace of a giant serpent. He had already got down to basics, and was dancing in plain white crew socks and a white towel. As he gyrated and twisted he slid the towel around his body like a burlesque dancer with feathers, always concealing, never revealing the stark truth of sex. At one point, hovering above the rest of us watching from the floor, he cupped and supported his works in the open towel, and used the overhead lights to project a shadow of the stalwart rigging against the white terrycloth. Then he opened the towel flat and let go of it. Magically, it stuck to him, thanks to a large electric fan blowing like a wind machine from one end of the bar. The soft terry pressed against his loins, and showed the contours of his splendid muscles and a timberlike erection whose beauty Paul Bunyan would have revered.

The finale of the stripper's act was to secure the towel around his waist and then squat down on the bar to allow eager and willing customers to get to know him better in the privacy offered by the drape of the towel. All for a fee, of course. The most impressive patron was a tall stick of a man wearing an off-white, floor-length satin sheath with matching pumps, topped off with a platinum blonde headpiece fashioned into a cotton-candy beehive. He lingered quite a while in the netherworld of the stripper's towel. And when he'd finally partaken his money's worth and re-emerged to our side of life, not one single strand of that sky-high do was out of place. Now that's superhold hairspray. Cheers and applause followed.

I strolled to another part of the Javelin—a large outdoor area set under high tropical palms and open sky. It was dimly lit, almost romantic out there. I went to the bar and bought a bottle of mineral water. Refreshed by the fizzy fluid, I could focus better on the clientele in the outdoor lounge. They seemed oblivious to the entertainment within the other bar. In a faraway corner, where the darkness was densest and the palm fronds most concealing, I saw Joshua Aytem at a table with another person who was in shadow. Either Joshua had sobered up quickly, or else Lieutenant Sanfuentes had tired of his raging. But what was he doing in a male strip club? From all indications and protests, Joshua was straight. Perhaps a place like the Javelin offered a reprieve from all those heterosexual noises he made, even if they were true.

Joshua glanced my way. I waved, but he didn't respond. He turned back to his invisible companion. Moments later he left his table and came up to me.

"Did you enjoy the show?" he said cordially, as though nothing unpleasant had transpired at the police station earlier. Perhaps it was more of his selective forgetfulness.

"I prefer sex with a story," I said.

He grinned ghoulishly in the dim light. "I have a story that'll make a best-seller," he said.

I looked past Joshua's face and noticed his companion leaving their table. The form was unmistakable even under cover of darkness. It was Attorney Nancy L. Drew.

I said, "I'd rather hear the one about you and Nancy Drew."

Joshua looked back over his shoulder and saw the empty table. "Shit," he said.

"She's hard to miss."

Joshua said, "Can you keep a secret?"

"Depends."

Joshua then put on a little performance of his own, one that portrayed a married man caught in a compromising situation.

"Nancy and I have been seeing each other," he said. "Just socially. Nothing serious, y'know? We figured a place like this would be safe to meet. Not too many straights come in here."

"Straight people don't have a monopoly on gossip, Joshua."

Hell, the Telequeen Network was the prototype for the Internet.

Joshua pushed his act further. "What I mean is, if anyone saw Nancy and me in a place like this, they couldn't jump to the wrong conclusion."

"What conclusion is that?" I said.

"Isn't it obvious?" said Joshua.

"I'm wondering about a different conclusion," I said. "One that concerns a company called Mindful Lotus, which I think is connected to Nancy Drew. And from the looks of things here, so are you."

Joshua snarled. "It's none of your business."

"Why not, if you're conducting your business in public?"

"We have to do that."

"Why? To have plenty of witnesses around in case there's any gunfire?"

Just then I heard Cozy Dinette's voice call out behind me. "Hey, Boston!"

Joshua said to me, "Is that your date?"

"Cozy's my friend," I said.

"And Nancy Drew is mine," said Joshua with a cynical laugh. "Now we understand each other."

"The difference is," I said, "I don't care what people say about me."

"If they even notice," said Joshua.

Cozy came over and greeted us. "Funny seeing you in a place like this, Josh."

Joshua replied, "A good travel agent is familiar with all sides of local culture. I'd better go now. Laura's expecting me." Then he left us.

Cozy said, "That guy changes like the wind. One minute he's your bosom buddy, the next minute he'll sell you down the line."

I said, "Was he ever your bosom buddy?"

"Not exactly," said Cozy.

Then the bartender announced the next stripper that night, a guy named Pico Primavera. It sounded like a microwave entree. There was a wave of applause from the inner barroom. Then the music started. And who should leap up onto the bar in there but my personal hustler, Ross.

"Did they just call him Pico?" I said to Cozy.

"It's a stage name," she replied. "Come on, let's get closer. No need to keep it a mystery anymore."

"There's no mystery for me," I said.

We went inside. Onstage Ross was wearing blue jeans, white tennis shoes, and a snug white T-shirt. It was a classic costume of all-American masculinity, the kind of thing anyone would enjoy peeling piece by piece from a well-honed male body. Ross moved smoothly through his routine as he teased and taunted the audience, sliding up the T-shirt to show a nipple, tugging down the jeans to show some hair. Yet it was all done through an invisible wall he'd set up. He'd let you scrutinize his body, yearn for it, anticipate the next disclosure of flesh, all the while concealing the man who was making the body perform. It was only in that accidental glance, when our eyes connected for an instant, that I saw panic in Ross's eyes. The nature of his act changed abruptly. He stopped teasing the audience and just danced. Eventually they started making noises for him to take something off, and he responded by unbuttoning his jeans all the way, but his eyes looked at me in dire distress, as if to explain, "I can't help it. This is my job. It's what they want, so it's what I do." There was almost a sense that someone should interrupt his act and rescue him from ever having to take off his clothes for strangers again. Or maybe I was imagining it. I turned to Cozy and told her I wanted to go.

Cozy said, "Too much for you?"

"Let's just get out of here."

Cozy had her car that night, a gigantic white convertible, vintage 1959, back when tail fins bordered on hallucinogenic. In that magic open-air chariot we headed to our next stop, Pin-Ups. On the way I asked Cozy what she knew about Mindful Lotus.

She said, "Who told you about them?"

"More important is what you know."

"Boston," she said, "you're really getting involved in things you shouldn't be."

"That's everyone's stock answer, Cozy."

"Because it's true," she said.

"What's the big secret?"

"The big secret is," she said, but then stopped herself. "You know, Boston, I think you're swell, and I'll miss you when you're gone, so let's just enjoy our time together here, okay?"

"But you do know about Mindful Lotus, right?"

"I know a lot of things, Boston, and none of it's going to help you."

"How do you know that?"

"Trust me," said Cozy. "You've been in Key West now, what, a week?"

"Four days."

"There, you see? And I've lived here twenty years. So how could you possibly understand?"

"Understand what?" I said.

"That whatever you see and hear in Key West is only the tip of the iceberg."

Her metaphor didn't quite match the tropical climate, and I sensed Cozy wasn't going to tell me anything more about Mindful Lotus than she already hadn't. So we sailed onward to our next destination in the monstrous mass of gleaming sculpture that was her car. I turned and looked behind us, out over the trunk deck with its huge horizontal fins slicing through the night air, like gull wings spread to catch and hover in the tropical zephyrs. I almost expected the car to become airborne.

The feature at Pin-Ups that night was a show called "Big Bo Peep." The skit opened to the music of Bach's "Sheep May Safely Graze." A lone sheep wandered out onto the dance floor, played by a hairy muscular dancer cloaked in faux sheepskin and walking on all fours. He could barely conceal a big leather dildo strapped to one of his "hind" legs. Then Big Bo appeared, garbed in an absurdly oversized hoop skirt and bonnet. She hooked her shepherdess's staff onto one of the ceiling fixtures, and then swung herself like a big bell. With each passing arc she showed more and more of her firm pink bottom to all. The sheep noticed too, and bleated in happy distress. The music changed abruptly to an inane, throbbing track for heavy pelvic action. Big Bo released herself from the swing and did a quick change, doffing her hoop skirt and bonnet for roll-down chaps and aviator sunglasses—mirrored of course. "She" became "he" and proceeded to straddle the sheep playfully. More distressed bleating followed, until the sheep finally doffed its skin too, and became a masked leatherman in a half-harness, nipple clamps, and chains. "Animal" then overpowered "man," and despite the absence of raw sex onstage, the audience showered them with cheers and money.

I turned to Cozy, but during the show she'd vanished from my side. I quickly scanned the crowd and couldn't find her. So I went to the bar to get another drink and ask the bartender if he'd seen Cozy in the last few minutes. She was a Key West institution after all, so any bartender worth his or her salt would recognize her. But I was surprised to find Laura Hope sitting at the bar, talking to the bartender, so I snuck up behind her.

"Come here often?" I said.

Laura turned and, after an overfriendly greeting, told me she was looking for Joshua. "Have you seen him?"

"Not here," I said, selectively omitting the whole truth. "Why would he be in a place like this?"

Laura replied, "He said he was doing some research tonight."

"Are you doing research too?"

"No," Laura said quickly.

I studied her a moment, looking for the slightest sign that Joshua had beaten her, but Laura seemed absolutely fine.

I offered to buy her a drink, which she accepted. Then we moved away from the bar and I asked her if she'd enjoyed the show.

"That's not what I came here for," she said. She looked worried about something. I asked her about it, hoping the relative anonymity of a crowded bar would encourage her to talk. It did. "Whenever it gets to this point," she said, "I don't know what to do. See, I think Josh might be seeing someone else. He's dropped all kinds of hints. I think he actually wants me to find him cheating on me, so we can have a good fight and clear the air again."

"That's one way of maintaining a marriage."

"Whatever keeps him happy," she said almost blissfully.

I said, "What keeps *you* happy, Laura?"

"I've found all the happiness I need. I love what Josh awakened in me, and what he allows me to be."

Conjugally speaking, I sensed we might be approaching brackish waters, so I changed the subject and asked Laura what she thought of Jeri Tiker's arrest.

Without missing a beat she said, "I'm afraid I agree with the police. Jeri must have killed Adolf to get her painting back."

"Doesn't that seem out of character?"

Laura smiled. "You never know what's going on under a person's skin."

"Does that hold for you too?"

"Especially for me," she said, then threw her head back and laughed. Her neck and jawbone were very strong, and reminded me of that Australian singer, Dame Somebody.

"Do you like games?" I said.

"Depends," she said. "Are you flirting with me?"

"No," I said. "But let's pretend Jeri Tiker never made that painting. Okay? It's gone. It's off the earth. Now, who else might have killed Augusta and Adolf?"

"That's an interesting approach," said Laura. "And I suppose anyone on the island could have killed them. You, me, Joshua, anyone."

I said, "But what about some kind of motivation? Not just a random act of violence."

"Then I suppose I'd connect the killings to Peter's will."

"Augusta's son, you mean."

"Yes. And honestly, that was the first thing that came to mind when I first heard Augusta had been killed. But then I learned the painting had been stolen too, and I changed my mind."

"Go on," I said. "This is what I like."

"Mind games," she said wearily. "Josh prefers body games. So do I."

"Please go on, Laura. What did you think before you knew about the stolen painting?"

Laura replied, "Well, Augusta contested her son's will right after he died. I think it may have been the same day. That was a big to-do around here, the urgency of it all. She was his mother, for God's sake! He was barely dead, and there she was trying to grab his property back from everyone he'd left it to."

"Laura, do you know anything about a company called Mindful Lotus?"

She smiled broadly. "Where do you dig up these things? That's the silliest name I've ever heard."

"Nevertheless," I said, "do you know about it?"

"No," she said. "But if you want, I'll ask Josh."

"Do that," I said. "Maybe we'll both be surprised at what he tells you."

Laura gulped the rest of her drink quickly and said, "I think our little game is over now. I've got to get back home. Josh may have called there already."

"Call him from here," I said. "Don't you have your cellular phone with you?"

Laura looked at me blankly. "I lost it," she said. But she gripped her empty glass tightly, and I saw her knuckles whiten, even in that dark place. I also noticed again how strong her hands were, certainly strong enough to strangle a weak man like Adolf Dobermann. I looked back at her face. She was smiling contemptuously. Then she turned and walked off.

I made one more round of Pin-Ups hoping to find Cozy, but she was nowhere in there, so I left the place. I wasn't sure whether to be concerned that she'd vanished, or else annoyed that she'd deserted me. I decided to be cool.

Outside, Cozy's white convertible was still parked exactly where she'd left it, near the edge of the lot. I headed toward it, figuring I'd wait there for her to show up. As I was getting into the car, someone emerged from the dense greenery nearby. It was Ross.

He said, "I wish you hadn't seen me like that, darlin'."

"Like what?" I said.

"Onstage at the Javelin."

"You're a man of many talents."

"But that's not really me," he said. "I mean, it's just a little part of me up there."

I said, "Not so little."

"I mean a secret part," said Ross. "That's why I don't like friends to watch me strip. Onstage, I mean."

Cozy suddenly dashed out from Pin-Ups. "Boston!" she called out. "Where did you go?" Then she saw me standing with Ross. "How'd you get here, Rossina? I don't see that black stealth-hog of yours around anywhere."

"His what?" I said.

"My motorcycle," said Ross. "I took a cab," he said to Cozy with a big grin. "Imagine that?"

Cozy said to me, "I thought I lost you in there, Boston. I got worried."

"But you deserted *me.*"

"I'd never desert you!" she said. "I was going to give you a ride home."

"Well, we're fine now," I said. It had slipped out before I could edit it. Some part of me wanted to be *with* Ross. For however brief a moment in my life in Key West, Ross and I would be "we." I told Cozy I wanted to walk off some of the liquor I'd had. But she knew it was a lie, that I'd had hardly anything to drink.

She whimpered, "Okay." Then she got into her white starship and sailed off into the night.

I turned to Ross and said, "Did I do right? Do you want to come back with me?"

"What do you think, darlin'?"

"I think it's time for you to earn some extra money."

So we walked back along Elizabeth Street, saying hardly anything. Everything was quiet and wonderful, with just the sounds of our footsteps and the nocturnal creatures everywhere around us. About five minutes later I sensed a car approaching us from behind. It slowed down and followed us awhile. It was, of course, the fake pink taxicab.

"Damn," I said. "Who the hell is that?"

Ross turned around and looked too. Then he said, "Don't you know who that is? I thought you'd figured that out by now. That's Edsel."

"But he doesn't drive."

"Who says?"

"He says."

Ross smiled in the darkness. "Do you believe everything people tell you?"

"For starters."

Ross shook his head.

I said, "How do you know that's Edsel?"

"Because I used to drive him."

"You? All those times, that pink cab was you?"

"Mostly."

"Why didn't you ever stop for me?"

"I was on duty, darlin', working for him."

I said, "Like you're on duty now with me?"

"Not like that," said Ross.

"So if you're not driving Edsel anymore, who is?"

Ross shrugged.

Then the pink taxi zoomed past us and vanished into the darkness.

Up in my room at the Jared Bellamy House we slept like two young buddies sharing a sleeping bag at summer camp. It was all comfort and security—snuggling and caressing with tender little kisses. No tongues, no insertions, no throbbing anything. The consuming sex fires that Rafik had once ignited were still pretty much extinguished by his death.

20

Ross left at sunrise the next morning. An hour later I got up and showered and shaved. As I was leaving the guest house for breakfast, I heard a faint buzz among the staff about how much money Ross had got from me that time. Apparently he had flashed the bills before everyone's eyes on his way out, proving to them that our supposed love affair was over, and it was "cash only" between the Widow Kraychik and the town hustler. The staff never knew that Ross returned the money at our next meeting, our own little recycling program.

On my way to town I passed by the Fleming Lemming. That morning it was Joshua who sat outside, smoking and having a cup of coffee. Unlike Laura the previous day, he was not reading a book. I waved to him. He didn't wave back. Instead he muttered, "Thanks for telling my wife what was none of her business, or yours."

I asked him to explain.

He said, "How did Laura know I was out with Nancy Drew last night when I don't recall telling her myself? You're the only person who saw me at the Javelin."

"There were hundreds of people there," I said.

"Maybe next time you can keep your big mouth shut."

"Maybe next time you won't jump to conclusions."

I asked Joshua how he liked driving Edsel Shamb's personal pink taxicab.

"Where did you get that idea?" he said.

"I guessed it all by myself."

"Maybe you guessed wrong," said Joshua. "And what does it matter even if I am driving for him? Everyone's just trying to make a living down here. We're not all rich like you. Most of us need more than one job to get by, like your friend Ross."

"Is that what it is with you and Nancy Drew?" I said. "A job?"

Joshua narrowed his eyes. "Why don't you just forget you ever saw us?"

"That almost sounds like a threat."

"It's friendly advice," said Joshua.

I said, "But Nancy Drew doesn't seem like your type, I mean romantically."

"And what's my type?" he said.

"Someone meek and submissive, like Laura."

Joshua sniggered. "Shows what you know about people."

"So then, what is your job with Nancy Drew? Is it connected to the Peter Willits estate? I know she's directly involved with that."

"No kidding," said Joshua. "She's the executor."

"What about Mindful Lotus?"

Joshua bristled. "Will you forget about that!"

"Why?" I said. "Are you afraid I might discover the real connection between them and you? What is their business anyway? Property management? Or is it more specialized? How about stolen-property management? Is that what Mindful Lotus does?"

"It's property systems development," said Joshua. "It's a new concept in real estate, a stroke of genius, it's so simple. Mindful Lotus matches available property to the most appropriate buyer."

"Sounds like a big dating service."

Joshua said, "Someone like you would think like that."

"What do you get out of it, Joshua? A guaranteed cut of the tourist bookings on the properties? That would help your ailing finances at the Fleming Lemming."

Joshua flung his coffee toward me, but I moved quickly, and the stream of hot liquid just missed me. "People like you are a pain in the ass," he said.

"I try being friendly with you, but it doesn't work."

"Maybe you don't try hard enough." He got up and went inside.

I continued walking down Fleming Street toward Duval, and along the way I felt an odd sensation through the ground. At a regularly spaced interval—every few seconds—the island's coral foundation pulsed slightly with a thump, followed closely by the sound of metal colliding against metal far in the distance. *Thump . . . clank. Thump . . . clank.* As I followed the vibrations and the sounds to their source, the two sensations occurred more closely together. *Thump, clank. Thump, clank.* The epicenter of the activity turned out to be the parking lot behind the Gulf Coast Playhouse, down by the southwestern shore of the island.

There was a small crowd of people watching what was probably the only unbelievable sight in Key West. Sometime during the night a fleet of giant construction equipment had arrived, and that morning it was driving metal piles deep into the fragile reef. From what little I knew about marine ecology, that kind of mistreatment could destroy the reef, which is why such construction was absolutely prohibited on Key West. It would take a development company with cosmic clout to bypass the severe building restrictions that protected the reef. A development company would need unimpeachable power, a power of quasi-religious proportions, perhaps requiring even a lofty name, something like Mindful Lotus.

Close to the construction site was a stockpile of materials that looked like the prefabricated components of some kind of huge galvanized steel structure. From where the pilings were being driven, it looked as though it was to be erected in the parking lot between the Gulf Coast Playhouse and the shoreline. To my wild imagination, it almost looked like the makings of an airplane hangar. The Gulf Coast Playhouse was being transformed into something very different.

Ken Kimble and Edsel Shamb were among the crowd, both of them shaking their heads lamentably. I went and asked if they knew what was going on.

Edsel yelled above the noise, "Looks like someone got approval for a multi-story parking lot."

Ken added, "This will destroy the reef."

Meanwhile the machinery continued its relentless task, thumping and clanking its way through the delicately balanced ecology of a live coral reef.

"What about the playhouse?" I said.

"They haven't started work on that yet," said Edsel.

I asked the two men if they knew who'd hired the contractors. They were blank-faced, as though I'd asked if they wet their toothbrush before or after putting on the toothpaste.

I said, "*Someone* is paying them."

"You're right," said Edsel. "We should find out."

Ken said, "I'm going to Town Hall and get to the bottom of this . . . this disgrace!"

Ken turned and headed toward his car, a bright red Range Rover. It looked familiar, as if from some recent dream. By the shine of the paint, and the glint of the alloy wheels, and the dense spongy black of the safari-grade tires, the vehicle looked brand-new. Perhaps Madison Avenue had embedded an image of the thing in my subconscious as the perfect suburban transport for a queen, since a recent ad had called the car "Her Majesty's country carriage." But I'd seen it sometime recently, in real life.

Edsel said to me, "I'd better go with Ken. We're in this together."

"In what?" I said.

"Trying to save the playhouse, and the reef."

"You'd better hurry," I said.

He ran after Ken and got in the car with him, and they drove off to make a noise at Town Hall. They'd have to stamp their feet awfully loud to compete with the pile driver's villainous work.

I suspected Mindful Lotus was behind the work, so I decided to confront Nancy L. Drew about it. For that I needed my car, so I headed back to the Jared Bellamy House, picked up the Alfa and drove to the attorney's office.

Not surprisingly, the receptionist told me it would be impossible to see Nancy Drew without an appointment.

I said, "Why don't you tell the revered attorney that Stan Kraychik has been mucking around in a lotus pond, and he stumbled on a pile driver."

The receptionist looked at me dubiously, but made the call.

Nancy Drew agreed to see me.

"Well, well," she said as I entered her office. "It seems you've been putting your nose in places you shouldn't be."

"It's the only way to find the truffles," I said.

The culinary reference was wasted on her.

"Exactly how much do you know?" she said.

"I know there's a construction crew at the Gulf Coast Playhouse, which once belonged to Peter Willits. And I know that Mindful Lotus is a development company. So it doesn't take much to connect his estate to Mindful Lotus, which you told me had no connection whatsoever."

"And what do you expect from me?" she said, completely unimpressed with my perfect logic.

"Somewhere along the line in any business there's got to be an attorney. And in this case all roads lead to you."

Nancy Drew sank back comfortably in her big leather armchair. "An imagination like yours can be trouble."

"Because sometimes it hits on the truth."

Nancy Drew sneered.

I said, "Do you know who killed Augusta Willits?"

She shifted her body in the chair. "No," she said.

"What about Adolf Dobermann?"

She shook her head impatiently. "Mr. Kraychik, I'm a very busy person."

"I suspect Herr Dobermann was part of a business deal that went sour."

"Idle speculation."

"I saw you with him and Edsel Shamb twice. Don't tell me both times were just social occasions. Then I saw you with Joshua Aytem last night, and I know that Joshua is driving Edsel now. And Edsel leads me back to you, except now there's no more Adolf."

Nancy L. Drew leaned forward in her chair. She seemed to grow larger as she did, like those animals that swell up to ward off imminent threats. "You are wasting my time," she said. "If you don't leave here immediately, I'm going to call the police."

"Go right ahead. Ask for Lieutenant Sanfuentes."

She picked up the telephone and punched in a number. When the other side answered, Nancy L. Drew told them who she was and that she required urgent assistance at her office, that she was being harassed by a trespasser. Mind you, I was paying the woman. Then she looked me over and added that the trespasser was probably unarmed. She thanked the person, then hung up. It was all done with cool professional decorum.

I said, "If I didn't know better, I'd say you just called anyone but the police."

We watched each other silently while I listened for the wail of a police siren outside.

"I wonder," I said, "are you keeping secrets out of professional confidence, or are you afraid you might be next in line?"

"For what?"

"Two people have been killed."

"Why should anyone want to kill me?" said Nancy L. Drew.

"You tell me."

She looked at me warily, as though she was considering whether she could trust me. Perhaps all those years I'd spent at the styling chair had given me a trustworthy aura, a halo of light that encouraged people to let down their guard with me and tell the Real Dirt. Even lawyers.

"What are you afraid of?" I said.

"Nothing," she said quickly.

"That can be perilous," I said. "Is it Edsel? Ken? The countess?"

Nancy Drew said, "Look, I don't know where you came from, or why you're here. But I'm not telling you anything. Now please leave before they come. Please. For your own good."

There was an urgency in her voice that alerted me, as though she really was warning me for my own good.

"I'm not afraid of the police," I said.

"It's not the police you should be afraid of," she said.

I got up and went to the door. "Thanks for the tip," I said.

I got out of the building fast and headed for the Alfa. Just then a bright red Range Rover came tearing into the parking lot, all four new tires squealing. It jolted to a stop with no attempt to park properly. I braced myself to confront Ken Kimble, my would-be attacker in expensive sunglasses. He was ripping mad as he came toward me, but then he raced right by, barely acknowledging me. He obviously wasn't the person Nancy L. Drew had summoned to oust me. No, Ken Kimble looked as though he had other urgent business there. And he was very angry, so angry that he might tell me things he wasn't supposed to. Well, *quelle surprise* for Nancy L. Drew that instead of scampering off her property in fright, I would instead pursue Ken Kimble to soothe his savage breast.

"Hi," I said cordially, once I'd caught up with him.

"Yes, yes," he said as he tried to rush away from me.

I kept putting myself halfway in his path and gave him my earnest therapist's look, the one that never worked in the psych clinic but always worked at the styling chair.

"You seem upset, Ken."

"You have no idea," he said. "I've just come from Town Hall."

"What happened?"

"I have to see my lawyer," he said.

"Maybe if you talk to me you can dissipate some of your anger."

"I don't want to dissipate it!" he said.

"Anger isn't good," I said therapeutically. "It will only weaken your message." I struggled to control my gag reflex.

"Damn Ed!" said Ken. "Damn that coward! Do you know what he did?"

"Tell me, Ken."

"There we were, in Town Hall together, along with a noisy mob of irate residents, all of us trying to get to the bottom of the mutilation taking place at the Gulf Coast Playhouse. And finally, after trying to make sense to those damn bureaucrats, we got beyond the office that dispensed the building permits. Ed and I actually got behind closed doors and found out who's behind this whole thing."

"Mindful Lotus," I said.

That stopped his tirade. He pulled off his sunglasses. "Where did you hear about that?"

I shrugged. "You talk to enough people, you'll hear just about everything."

"Well, it's only a name," he said quickly, "though a badly chosen one, almost blasphemous, considering their wanton abuse of the reef. What's more important was to find out how they got permission to build, in spite of federal restrictions. And that's exactly when Ed bowed out. He told me—told *me!*—that we should surrender when facing a power greater than ourselves."

"Who is it?" I said.

"But I will not surrender. I will fight this to the death if I have to."

"Who is it?" I said again.

Ken looked at me. His eyes were murderous when he spoke.

"The judge," he said. "It was that same judge who decided for Augusta Willits when she contested her son Peter's will. It was the same judge who defeated Nancy Drew when she represented Peter's estate."

"And your interest in it," I added.

"Yes!" spat Ken. "It was the same judge who, as the executor of Augusta's estate, sold the Gulf Coast Playhouse to Mindful Lotus. It was the same judge who then allowed them the building permit that is now destroying the Gulf Coast Playhouse."

"Isn't there a conflict of interest in there somewhere?"

"Oh!" said Ken Kimble. "More than one, I assure you."

"Does this judge have a name?"

"What does that matter?" said Ken. "He's gone now, fled town weeks ago. Isn't that nice? A pious coward shits in your face and runs off with his share of the profits."

"But they'll find him."

"Who will?" spat Ken.

"The police, the FBI, the authorities."

Ken laughed. "How naïve!" he said. "Who knows better how to evade the strong arm of the law than a clever judge? No, my dear, foolish thing, that man is gone forever I'm afraid, and we are left with the detritus of his machinations."

I almost applauded, but Ken, bad actor that he was, couldn't leave the dramatic beat alone.

"And to think he was a deacon of a church!"

I reminded him that particular stamp of approval was pretty much defunct these days. Then I asked, "What can be done now?"

"That's exactly what I intend to confront Attorney Drew with."

I said, "She's not going to help you. She's involved with Mindful Lotus herself."

"What?"

"Nancy L. Drew is part of the corporation that now controls Peter Willits's estate."

"She can't be!" said Ken.

"Go ask her."

"But Nancy is on the board of the Key West Society for Historical Preservation. The Gulf Coast Playhouse is part of a heritage that must be preserved at all costs. If what you say is true, she has violated our trust. We may have to sue her, to have her debarred."

"To save the playhouse?"

"What else matters?" said Ken.

"What about your inheritance from Peter's estate?"

"My first concern is to save the theater and the reef."

"Good luck," I said.

And off he went to slay the dragon called Nancy L. Drew.

21

The implied threat from Nancy Drew's phone call never materialized. Perhaps it had been a bluff. Still, since I had the Alfa and it was lunchtime, I figured I'd eat somewhere out on that part of the island, just for a change from the relentless charm of Old Town.

I continued along Roosevelt Boulevard and soon faced a stretch of fast-food restaurants representing almost every chain known in America. Having spent the preceding days cloistered in the quaint corners of Key West, I'd neglected the other face of the island—the strip malls and, according to one superstore's logo, the largest supermarket in Florida if not the world. How had such incongruous structures been allowed on a finite place like Key West? Was it a metaphor for man's misuse of the earth? Or just further proof that the human species was genetically encoded for one-stop shopping in air-conditioned comfort?

I pulled into a burger emporium that advertised fresh salads and fish-thing sandwiches. Myself, I yearned for a decent burger, like from a dead cow. It was early afternoon, and except for a few tourists, the restaurant was deserted. It was exactly the kind of safe

haven an island resident might seek after a bitter fight with her husband, where she could lick her psychic wounds far from the ever-
watchful neighbors in Old Town. Which partly explained why I
saw Laura Hope sitting in a booth in a faraway corner of the dining area. She had turned herself away from the other tables, but I
still recognized her lustrous blonde hair.

The burgers in that place looked withered and pitiful, so I ordered a grilled chicken sandwich and an iced coffee, then took it
all with me as I headed toward Laura Hope's secluded booth.

"Mind if I join you?" I said.

She kept herself turned away from me and put a hand up to the
side of her face. "I'd rather you didn't," she mumbled.

I sat down across from her and spoke quietly. "You can talk to
me."

She shook her head without answering.

I said, "I won't tell anyone unless you want me to."

Laura shook her head again, but this time she also bit into the
tops of her fingers. Still, it wasn't enough to hold back the tears
that oozed from her eyes and streamed down her cheeks. She
spoke in a low quavering murmur.

"It almost doesn't matter," she said. Then she put her head
down on the table and sobbed quietly.

The few other people in the restaurant began paying attention
to us. I put my hand on one of Laura's. She had strong hands for
a woman, which I took as a sign of her internal strength, that she
would weather this crisis too, and survive. I cooed comforting lies,
things like, "It's going to be all right. Things will get better."

She lifted her head and said loudly, "I've done everything I can.
I've tried to do things right." Then she caught herself and lowered her voice. "You have no idea what I've done. I've sacrificed
things people could never imagine. But it always ends up with my
hurting him, then calling the police and telling them he hit me.
This time I'm afraid he may leave me for good."

"So you hit him?" I said, just to clarify the facts.

"Yes," she said. "It's always me who does it. But Josh deserves
it. I have the right to hurt him forever."

I thought of myself and my dead lover Rafik, and how we had
ritualized our sessions of bondage and battery. Joshua and Laura's

assaults may have seemed coarse, while Rafik's and mine had been ultra-refined. But didn't it all amount to the same thing? Lovers hurting each other to express God-knows-what.

Laura's sobs diminished. I moved my hand gingerly from her hand up to her hand up to her forearm, to give her one last reassuring squeeze. That's when I felt the odd sensation of . . . stubble! My fingers moved quickly over the skin to confirm the sensation. It was stubble all right. Laura Hope shaved her arms.

She looked up suddenly and pulled away from me.

"What are you doing?" she said.

Our eyes locked in a terrible challenge. I felt a slight ringing in my ears, and my heart was pounding.

Laura almost growled her next words. "Nobody knows," she said.

"Joshua?" I said.

"Of course he does!"

"Does anyone suspect?" I said.

"No," said Laura.

"Is it just . . ."—I faltered—"appearances?"

"No," said Laura.

"So . . ." I said with a cringe, "the knife?"

Laura explained the facts as though she was sharing a household hint for stain removal: She had had a sex change. "Four years ago," she said, "just before we came to Key West together. I used to be Lars. Now I'm Laura."

I had a rare moment of speechlessness.

Laura said, "Do I disgust you?"

"No," I said. "But I don't understand it."

"It's simple," she said. "Joshua couldn't face loving another man."

"But that's his problem. You didn't have to mutilate yourself—"

"It's not mutilation!" she said sharply. "I did it for love." Laura then looked at me desperately. "Haven't you ever loved someone?"

"I'm afraid so," I said.

"Then you should understand."

"I could never do what you did."

"There was no choice," said Laura. "It's what he wanted."

"Too bad you didn't meet someone willing to take you as you were."

"Yes, too bad," she said despondently. "And what a regal set I gave up too! The surgeon almost refused to operate. But love means sacrifice."

"And sacrifice means no payback," I said. "No guarantees, even if you had the surgery to secure Joshua's love."

"It should have worked," said Laura.

"But . . . ?"

"I'm not sure," she said. "Sometimes I want to cut Josh's things off, just to even the score. But then where would our sex life be?"

I certainly had no answer for that.

I said, "Your secret is safe with me."

"I doubt it," said Laura.

I said, "Sometimes a secret keeps people friends."

Laura gave a cynical little laugh. "Or makes them enemies."

Then she lit up a cigarette.

I said, "Did you ask Joshua about Mindful Lotus?"

She glanced warily around the restaurant then said, "No."

"I found out that Mindful Lotus owns all the property that was originally in Peter Willits's estate."

"Really?" said Laura. "Who told you that?"

"I don't recall," I said. "I talk to so many people."

"Yes," she said, "I know. But what you just said might explain the notice I received today. All future rent at the agency is payable to the ML Group. But who are they? How did they manage that?"

"I suspect they bought everything from Augusta's church."

"But she just died," said Laura.

"She didn't die, Laura. She was murdered."

"I know that!" she said. "But don't these things take time? How did all that property change hands so many times so quickly?"

I said, "I'll bet if the path to a big property prize can be cleared of all the legal underbrush, it would be a cinch to get whatever you want as soon as you want it. And the judge who cleared the path for Augusta's case was part of the plan. He was a deacon at her church too."

"And you say Joshua is involved in this?" said Laura.

"He was working for Adolf, wasn't he?"

"Yes."

"And now he's working for Edsel."

"According to you," she said.

"And Edsel and Adolf both worked with Nancy Drew. If Joshua's connected with them, he's connected to her."

Laura extinguished her cigarette. "I don't know what to believe anymore. All you do is create mistrust around you."

"I don't mean to, Laura. It's just facts." Facts? Why didn't I just admit it was mostly confabulation? "And honestly," I said, "your other secret is safe with me."

At that she sat up straight and said, "Would you please leave now? I have a lot to think about. God, I wish you'd never found me here. I wish you'd never come to Key West."

I said, "It's okay. We had our moment of intimacy, and now we'll be anonymous again."

"There's no way to undo any of this!" she said wildly.

I took my lunch back to the counter and had it wrapped to go. Maybe I'd feed the gulls later. The young woman eyed me suspiciously as she put it all in a bag. Then she told me to have a nice day. I felt as if I'd had a bad trick.

Outside I was just getting into the Alfa when a familiar white behemoth of a convertible pulled off Roosevelt Boulevard into the burger house's parking lot. It was Cozy Dinette.

"Boston!" she called. "What are you doing way out here? This is the wastelands."

"I like to see every corner of a town I'm visiting. What brings you here?"

She said, "I'm working up a new demo tape with my group at the radio station. But you don't want to be here, Boston. No one comes out here."

My pact with Laura Hope prevented me from telling Cozy Dinette how fertile the wastelands had actually been. I realized that Laura Hope might be watching us from inside the restaurant, so I asked Cozy if she wanted to go somewhere for a drink. Hell, it was almost cocktail time. It was always almost cocktail time in Key West.

"You buying?" she said.

"Sure," I said.

Cozy said, "Then let's go to Robby's Terrace."

"Isn't that the most expensive place in Key West?"

"That's why I asked who was buying," said Cozy.

"You lead the way," I said.

"That's what I like," said Cozy.

She got in her car, and I got in mine. As I was backing out of my parking space, I saw Edsel's pink taxi zoom by on Roosevelt Boulevard. Whoever was driving it that time tooted twice as he went past.

Robby's Terrace was a remodeled Victorian mansion on the east side of the island. In back was a luxurious stretch of private beach-front. The terrace for which the restaurant was named was a multi-tiered extension of the mansion's broad veranda, an outdoor dining area that cascaded all the way down the property to the beachfront. At that point, the bar, a large slatted deck area, crossed over the beach and into the water.

Cozy and I took a table near the edge of the deck. The tide was in, but the crystalline tropical waters around the deck were only a foot or so deep. I sat in the protective shade of an overhead umbrella, while Cozy gave her tan an afternoon feeding. We ordered cocktails and looked out across the water. The air was strangely still for the ocean, and Cozy remarked that a tropical storm might be brewing.

"You mean a hurricane?" I said, and explained that Lieutenant Sanfuentes had mentioned a hurricane watch the previous day.

Our waiter overheard me and corrected me when he came to take our drink order. "The watch might be stepped up to a warning tonight."

"Oh, great," said Cozy to me. "That's one Key West experience you don't need."

We ordered drinks. Then, recalling Cozy's obscure past with Edsel Shamb, I told her what he had told me about his recent TV contract, how thrilled he was about it.

Cozy said, "He thinks it's a guarantee of security."

"He did mention investing it wisely."

Cozy laughed. "I know Edsel, and that check will be spent before it's cleared."

The drinks arrived and Cozy took a big gulp of her Big Mama Mai Tai.

"Tell me about you and him," I said.

"It's an old story, Boston."

"Were you lovers?"

"It was a boo-boo," she said with obvious discomfort. Then she shrugged. "Live and let go."

"Is he really gay?"

Cozy said, "Straight as they come."

"Straight men occasionally cross over," I said.

Cozy said, "You're not one of those, are you—those gay men who think everyone else is hiding their gayness?"

"Funny," I said, "Edsel asked me the same thing. I don't think I am. But I still don't get the feeling he's a typical straight male."

"He's not pussy-crazed, if that's what you mean," said Cozy. "Ed is a writer. He doesn't have to prove he's a man. His characters do it for him."

"Who does it for you, Cozy?"

She almost guffawed. "Boston, I got a whole string of men, but they're all past tense. Why do you think I sing the blues? I'm the one who chases down those troubled, brooding, lost and lonely young men. And then I try to patch them up with big mama's love. And then they get better—finally!—and that's when they discover why they were so lost and lonely in the first place. They wanted da-da. I've got a goddamned magnet for closet cases. Sometimes I think I ought to hang out a shingle and make some real money as the great gay emancipator."

"And Edsel doesn't fall into that group?"

"No!" snapped Cozy. "I told you it was a mistake. Haven't you ever made a mistake?"

"Plenty."

"That's all it was," she said with finality.

She lowered her sunglasses and looked at me like a cornered animal preparing to strike. She said, "I'm not sure I like you right now."

"You're seeing the unlikable me."

"Maybe you should let it go, Boston. The rest of you is so nice."

"I've learned it's better to walk the bitch occasionally, even if she does bite."

"Remind me to stay clear," said Cozy. Then she aimed her gaze beyond my head and remarked, "Now here comes a couple for the books." As I made a motion to turn she said, "Don't look yet."

"Why not?" I said. "You think people don't know the back of my head?" I turned to see Ken Kimble and the Countess Rulalenska waiting for the hostess to seat them.

Cozy said, "This is my cue to leave. I don't care to share the air with her."

"The countess? You're going to leave me here alone just because she arrived?"

"It's less risky than staying around and killing her," said Cozy. As she got up to go she said, "Do you have any message for Ross? I'm heading over to the Tulle Box, and he'll probably be there now."

"Tell him I have a new dance step for him."

Cozy strutted off the deck. When she passed the hostess's desk, she turned back to me and blew air kisses. "Love you, Boston!" With that gesture I felt I had finally arrived in Key West society, for I had received the same air kisses as Camille.

A few moments later, as Ken and the countess were led past my table, her regal highness spoke in a voice loud enough for me to hear. "Such a vulgar display!"

Ken replied, "They're harmless, Stassya."

As they passed, Ken nodded almost imperceptibly, as if doing more might encourage me to join them. Hell, I know when I'm not wanted. So I waited until they were seated at their table for two, then I went over.

"Do you mind if I join you?" I said.

"Oh!" exclaimed the countess, as though I had asked to sniff her shoes. "But there is no room here, and we are staying for dinner."

"I'm sorry I can't dine with you," I said, "but I'd like to buy you both a drink."

The countess became flustered, while Ken said, "By all means, pull up a chair and sit down. We should be buying you a drink, since you're the guest in our town."

I chirped gaily, "Then let's all buy each other a drink."

The countess squirmed in her chair. "Is there time?"

"Of course," said Ken.

"What are you celebrating?" I said.

"Eh?" said the countess.

"Isn't Robby's Terrace the kind of place people come to celebrate?"

"Some do," said Ken. "For us it's just a good place to eat."

I said, "I thought maybe you'd had some success with Attorney Drew this afternoon. Did you manage to get a stop-work order on that equipment that was wrecking the reef this morning?"

Ken's face got a sudden queasy look on it. The countess flashed her eyes angrily at him, and then at me.

"No?" I said. "Well, did you at least demand that she appeal that bogus decision for Augusta Willits, so that the Gulf Coast Playhouse can go to its rightful owners, you and Edsel?"

Ken said, "I don't think it's wise to talk about these things in public."

I asked the countess, "Was there much damage to that tour boat? If the appeal goes through and you get the company back, you might have to fix it yourself."

The countess turned to Ken with a desperate look. "Please, Kenneth," she said, "you must send him away. I cannot tolerate his presence."

Ken said to me, "This is very upsetting. Would you mind leaving us now?"

Instead I asked the countess what she knew about Mindful Lotus. She didn't answer. Big surprise. Then I asked her if she'd known Adolf Dobermann before he came to Key West.

She said, "Where do you hear such things?"

"In my imagination," I said.

She bolstered herself up proudly in her chair and spoke as though making a pronouncement to the huddled masses. "I will not discuss these matters with a commoner. Kenneth, do something!"

Ken said to me, "If you won't leave, then I'm afraid we'll have to excuse ourselves. Stassya and I wanted a nice quiet evening, just the two of us."

"Maybe you should have stayed home."

"I expected more of you," he said. "I hoped you'd understand. Now I'm asking you please not to bother us anymore."

"Okay, you win," I said. "But before I go, would you mind telling me one thing?"

"If it gets you away from here any sooner."

"Are you really trying to save the Gulf Coast Playhouse? Or is that just an act, a bad act, to conceal a project to convert it to something else?"

I glanced toward the countess and saw her warn him with her eyes. Danger, danger! A commoner is asking too many questions.

Ken said to me, "I want to save the playhouse. Period."

"Then why all this secrecy about it?" I said.

The countess interrupted, "Please, Kenneth. We must go inside. I feel a chill."

Sure, doll. A chill at ninety-two degrees Fahrenheit.

Ken said, "There's nothing secret about anything I do."

"Enough!" said the countess. She rose from her seat and looked me square in the face. "We will not acknowledge you in the future."

Then she put out her arm for Ken to take, and the two of them went inside, leaving me to wonder how she had acquired her regal pretensions, and why she had any hold over Ken Kimble.

I paid the waiter for the cocktails Cozy and I had ordered. Back in the car the cold leftover sandwich on the floor had little appeal, so I went in search of more modest viands for myself.

22

One way of careening from the sublime to the ridiculous in Key West is to go from Robby's Terrace to the Paradise Deli on the other end of the island (or vice versa, depending on what food means to you). Robby's Terrace might challenge your culinary wits and your credit card, but the Paradise Deli could really work your alimentary canal.

I pulled the Alfa into the deli's small parking lot, alongside the only other car there, a misty champagne-colored Japanese touring sedan, like something an attorney might drive. It was six P.M., and I got to the door just as the owner was locking up. I pleaded with her that I just wanted something to go. In truth, I wasn't even hungry, but I knew I'd have to eat something sooner or later. The owner yielded to my pleas on the condition that I order a cold sandwich only.

Inside, a television was blaring the six o'clock news: The two recent murders had been solved already. But I knew it was media pablum to assuage the fears of Key West citizenry. By the time the real tourist season arrived, the killings would be just another bit of island folklore. Was I the only person who wouldn't believe the culprit was a transplanted painter from Wisconsin with no motive?

I ordered my sandwich and looked around the joint. In a secluded corner of the deli, back where one of the workers had already begun washing the floor, a lone table was still inhabited by two people. The lingerers were Nancy L. Drew and Edsel Shamb, together again. I aimed myself toward their table, stepping over the wet floor on the way. The floorwasher grumbled and swore at me. I apologized, but I sounded glib, like some callous twit who chirps, "Sorry," after spilling India ink on your white linen slacks.

Nancy L. Drew was about to launch heartily into the second half of an enormous grinder, while Mr. Shamb fussed daintily with a small Greek salad. Nancy stopped mid-bite when she saw me approaching. Perhaps she was shy to eat in front of me, a relative stranger. Or maybe she didn't care to disclose one of her obvious secrets, the fact that she consumed piles of food.

I greeted them brightly. "How are the Hollywood writer and Key West's most powerful attorney?"

Edsel smiled and replied that life was beautiful.

Nancy Drew held her sandwich to her mouth—caught in a freeze-frame—while she scrutinized me.

I said, "I'm not interrupting anything important, am I? Are you two chewing as friends? Or is this a power snack?"

Nancy L. Drew put her sandwich down.

I said to her, "What's new with Mindful Lotus?"

A mask appeared on her face, the one that made her an attorney and not a human being, and thus she remained mute.

I went on. "Did you and Ken Kimble work out that problem with the Gulf Coast Playhouse? He said there might be a conflict of interest with you because of that judge."

Nancy L. Drew replied coldly, "This is harassment."

But Edsel asked her, "When did you see Ken?"

Nancy didn't answer him, so I did.

"Earlier today," I said.

"How do you know about it?" he said to me.

"I was there."

Nancy L. Drew said brusquely, "This discussion is completely inappropriate."

"Not really," I said. "A conflict of interest for a big lawyer in a small town is pretty much everybody's business."

Edsel said to her, "You didn't tell me you talked to Ken."

Nancy Drew advised him to shut up.

"Okay," I said. "Let's forget Mindful Lotus for now. Let's talk about people—who's alive and who's dead, who's winning and who lost."

Nancy asked Edsel to call the police. He told her to calm down.

I said, "Someone killed Augusta Willits, and someone killed Adolf Dobermann, and all of us know it wasn't Jeri Tiker."

"Why not?" said Edsel.

"No real evidence," I said. "And no motive either. Besides, she's an artist."

"So?" he said. "Artists are passionate people, capable of thoughts and deeds unknown to ordinary folk."

"So are writers," I said. "Maybe you did it."

Nancy Drew interrupted. "Don't talk to him, Ed. I'll get a restraining order on him first thing tomorrow."

But instead of agreeing with her, Edsel said, "Loosen up, Nancy. Let's have a little fun with him."

He must have been bored.

"This poor young man is confused. Perhaps we can set him straight once and for all." He sniggered and added, "I don't mean sexually, of course. But let's say, just for the sake of a little party game, that I did it. Okay? I killed Augusta Willits. So, Mr. Sherlock Holmes from Boston, what is my motive?"

180

"Yours is connected to the Gulf Coast Playhouse."

"Is that the best you can do?"

"That's what my instinct tells me."

"Instinct leaves so much room for error."

"Actually none," I said, "if you listen honestly."

Nancy L. Drew added, "Everything is instinctive. You just have to make choices."

Her observation sent me into momentary mental orbit.

Edsel said, "All right, Stan, I'll level with you. Here's my real motive, and this is the truth. Yes, I was supposed to inherit one half of the Gulf Coast Playhouse from Peter Willits. But Peter's mother contested the will. So I killed her to make sure I got the playhouse. But it didn't work. End of story."

"All of this is moot!" said Nancy Drew. "You did not kill Augusta Willits to get the playhouse because it was already part of her estate."

"And why didn't *you* appeal that award?" I said.

"In a case like that," said Nancy L. Drew, "the judge's decision is final."

"Sounds like a TV game show," I said.

Edsel laughed and said to me, "Well, if you want to continue *your* game, you'll have to include Ken Kimble among your suspects too."

"I do," I said, "along with everyone else who was supposed to inherit property from Peter Willits."

"Jeri Tiker is on that list," said Edsel.

"But she's not connected to Mindful Lotus," I said, "while the rest of you are, however indirectly."

He said, "Laura Hope isn't."

"No," I said. "She isn't. At least not yet."

"Neither is the countess."

I said, "I'm not so sure."

Then Nancy Drew fairly shouted, "This is *really* inappropriate!"

The owner of the Paradise Deli called out that my sandwich was ready. I nodded and waved. Then I turned back to Edsel and Nancy. She had picked up her sandwich again, but he seemed eager to continue our game.

He grinned broadly and said, "Okay, Stan, here's the other half of my confession. Ken is my partner in crime, theatrically speaking. We're a team, like the Lunts, or May and Nichols, Comden and Green, Cronin and Tandy. We're part of that great tradition."

"They were all performers," I said.

"We are too," said Edsel. "Ken and I both have purely selfish motives to preserve the playhouse. I've always wanted to write for the stage, and Ken has always wanted to establish himself as I believe he puts it 'a credible and legitimate theatrical force.' And what easier way to build a reputation than in one's own theater? That's our personal motive for wanting to save the playhouse, beyond its historical and cultural value. And Nancy represents us in our efforts to regain what is rightfully ours. So there you have it." He popped a big black olive into his mouth and chewed. "Now," he said, "what do you propose for our next round?"

"I'm curious about your other partner, Adolf Dobermann."

Nancy L. Drew continued chewing mutely on her sandwich.

I said, "The two of you and Adolf were always meeting together in public, and now it's just the two of you. So I have to wonder, what did Herr Dobermann do to get himself eliminated from this snug little scenario you've created with Mindful Lotus?"

The buzzword "scenario" caught Nancy Drew's attention.

"Enough!" she said. "Any further discussion of this matter in my presence is unethical."

"What's unethical," I said, "is your representing both Mindful Lotus and Peter Willits's estate."

Edsel added, "Don't forget Jeri Tiker."

Nancy L. Drew glared at him.

"Hey!" yelled the owner of the deli. "You want this sandwich or not? We're closed now."

Edsel said to me, "Too bad, Stan. I guess you'll have to leave. We must do this again sometime."

"What about you two?" I said.

"Nancy and I have arranged to stay here after closing."

Nancy L. Drew said, "For some privacy."

I sensed I wouldn't squeeze much more from those two, so I took my sandwich and a beer and headed for the door. As I left the place I turned back to Edsel and said, "How do you like Joshua's driving?"

182

"Huh?" he replied.

"Isn't he driving you now, in that pink car?"

"You've been hallucinating," said Edsel.

"I could swear that's what I heard."

"And you believed it?"

"Why not?" I said.

He replied, "Do you see a pink car anywhere outside?"

"Maybe Joshua dropped you off, and he's waiting for you to phone him to pick you up. You all have cellular phones, and—"

His laugh stopped me. "You have an explanation for everything, don't you?"

"I try."

I sensed that he thought he'd dismissed me with that laugh, but on Nancy Drew's face I saw a worried look.

I left them to continue their secret deliberations, and drove myself out to a deserted area near the electric power plant. I wanted to watch the sun go down, but far from the madding crowd that gathered every night to witness the event behind Old Mallory Square.

I parked the Alfa and climbed along some rocks that formed a jetty out onto the water. Alone with my sandwich and beer, I sat and watched the sun descend slowly into the Gulf of Mexico, its shape refracting and distorting like a cosmic egg yolk as it sank into the water. I thought of my dead lover, and how seldom we'd shared the typical romantic moments, things like watching the sun go down, or the moon come up, or the clouds or the stars. Our time with each other had been spent mostly in sex, and the intervening moments spent with the physical and emotional preparation for the next randy session. There had been almost no quiet growth together, the stuff that lifelong marriages were made of. I'd expected it was going to happen later, as if by magic, when we grew old together and discovered that we really did love each other, beyond the obvious response of our organs. But we never got the chance to find out. All I had was the remembrance of delirious orgasms past. That and four and a half million dollars.

The sun finally submersed into the glassy water. I finished half my sandwich, threw the rest along the rocks for the gulls to enjoy, then headed back to my car. As I was walking along the narrow road to get there, I heard another car approaching. It tooted its horn friendly like, as if to alert me of its arrival.

I turned to see the pink taxicab approaching me. I waved at it, to signal Joshua to stop. But instead of slowing down, the taxicab revved its engine to a roar, then engaged its tires with a terrific squeal and came charging at me.

I froze in its path like a startled animal. Instinct wasn't kicking in the way it was supposed to. Come on, legs. He is going to hit you. Save me! But nothing happened until the image of Sugar Baby flashed before me, pining for me in Rehobeth, New Jersey. And then with one vigorous catlike spring, I leaped from the road into the dense foliage along the side.

The cab sped by.

I caught my breath. I was saved for the moment. But the cab screeched to a halt and went into reverse. Then, back-up lights ablaze, it careened toward me again. But I had the advantage, for the back windshield was opaque like the side windows, and Joshua could barely see through it. He'd have to rely on the outside rearview mirrors. As long as I kept myself out of their range, I was somewhat safe. Still in reverse, the cab swerved erratically out of control trying to locate me in the dimness.

I sought shelter by dashing back to the shoreline and scrambling along the rocks in the opposite direction. I headed toward the waterfront, which would be safer and more populated. Behind me though, through the still night air, I heard the thud and crunch and groan of metal against metal. Joshua was destroying the Alfa, which I had left parked along the side of the road, alone and vulnerable.

I found a pay phone and called Lieutenant Sanfuentes at the police station. I'd neglected to memorize his private beeper number, so I had to go through the ordinary channels. But the lieutenant had gone home. The nerve, keeping regular hours! I left a message for him to call me at the guest house. Then I headed back there myself, looking behind myself all the way.

Up in my room I phoned Nicole in Boston, but her answering service told me she was unavailable. I turned on the television set, but nothing appealed to me. I finally gave up and showered and cleaned my teeth and tried to settle down with Edsel Shamb's book, but even that couldn't put me to sleep.

The phone rang about an hour later. It was Lieutenant Sanfuentes. I told him what had happened and where. He said he'd send a crew out and have a look. I also mentioned what had transpired shortly before, in the deli with Edsel and Nancy L. Drew.

Sanfuentes said, "You think the two events are connected?"

"Why not?" I said. "Everyone's got portable phones. It would be easy for Edsel or Nancy to alert Joshua that I'd left the deli with a sandwich and beer."

I could almost see him shrug.

"I don't know, Stan. Sounds to me more like maybe you found a way to get Joshua really mad at you." His voice had that insinuating curlicue in it.

"Like what?" I said.

"Haven't you been talking to his wife?"

"Is that a crime?"

"Depends," said the cop.

"Will you arrest Joshua?" I said.

"We'll find him first and talk to him. Then we'll see."

"But he tried to kill me," I said.

"You already told me that," said Sanfuentes.

"What if he decides to come here and get me?"

Sanfuentes said, "Then I'd suggest you stay alert. Don't go out, though. I'll call you as soon as my men have anything."

"Thanks," I said. But I wasn't exactly relieved.

As it turned out, Lieutenant Sanfuentes didn't call back that night. Nor did I go out. So it was back to the good ol' days, just me alone. I didn't even have my cat there to purr contentedly in my lap while I tatted shade-pulls for the local churchwomen's auxiliary. Some vacation.

23

Next morning I called Lieutenant Sanfuentes's private number and waited for his call back, but it never happened. With the Alfa wrecked, I needed an alternate set of wheels fast. So after a flimsy continental breakfast in my room, I arranged to borrow a bicycle from the guest house.

As one of the houseboys adjusted the bike seat to accommodate my long legs, he advised me to return soon because the hurricane alert was being stepped up to a warning. I thanked him for the advice, and told him I was from New England and had seen hurricanes before. He smiled and said, "Not like these."

I peddled out to the same remote place where I'd left the Alfa the night before. The car was gone, probably towed away by the police. The only clues were the streaks of tire rubber and the scatterings of shattered glass and plastic on the road. As a car, the Alfa had meant nothing. It was just another hunk of metal with carefully timed explosions going on under the hood. But it did have sentimental value, for it had been a gift from a fine old friend. And it had made my tyro brand of sleuthing a lot easier, even glamorous. Unless I rented a car immediately, I was going to be a two-wheeled detective.

Then a surge of anger welled up. How dare Joshua destroy my car, a gift from a friend no less? Heedless of any further danger, I peddled back to the Fleming Lemming to confront him directly. On the way there I turned down an overgrown stretch of road that looked to be a shortcut. A huddle of squad cars was up ahead, flashers blinking nervously in the early morning light. Off the side of the road was the pink cab. The front and sides were dented and scraped with black paint where it had rammed into the Alfa.

Lieutenant Sanfuentes saw me and motioned me over to him.

"What a coincidence," he said. "I was just about to send for you."

"I was looking for you too, Lieutenant. I wondered what happened to my car."

"There's nothing to tell you that can't wait."

"You found it then?

"Last night," said Sanfuentes. "It's totaled."

"I guessed as much. Oh, well, it needed gas anyway."

"Is that a joke?"

"Humor helps me cope, Lieutenant."

"Well," said Sanfuentes, "someone didn't show too much humor there." He pointed toward the pink cab. "Found it this morning."

"Trouble?"

"Have a look," he said, and led the way.

Inside the cab, splayed across the front seat, was the body of Joshua Aytem. One side of his head had been blown open by a massive gunshot wound. The gun was still in his hand, an apparent suicide.

"What a mess," I said.

"Just like your car," said Sanfuentes. "Totaled."

"Why would he do that?" I said.

"Maybe he didn't," said the cop. "You know, most times people shoot themselves, the gun flies out of their hand. But look how neat this one is, sitting right there in his palm."

"You think someone killed Joshua?"

"It's a very real possibility," said Sanfuentes. "Didn't you tell me he wrecked your car last night?"

"Yes."

"So maybe you decided to get even for that."

"Lieutenant, I wouldn't kill someone over a car."

"What would it take?" said Sanfuentes.

I didn't answer his question.

"I'll tell you how it looks to me," said Sanfuentes. "You come down here from that big city up north, and you got your fancy little car with you. And you did something that got Joshua pissed off, and then he did something that got you pissed off, and you didn't know what to do next. So maybe you came here to settle the score, and things got a little out of hand."

"I called you last night, didn't I? Would a guilty person call in the police?"

"Depends," said the cop.

"And where did I get the gun?" I said.

"Easy enough in this town," said Sanfuentes. "So maybe you got a gun and arranged a meeting with Joshua, and, well, you might be the kind of guy whose blood boils over pretty fast."

"It takes one to know one, Lieutenant."

"Watch it!" he said. "We didn't have trouble like this before you came on the reef."

"Don't blame me if your town is an epicenter of crime."

"Okay, okay," said the cop. "All I'm saying is, I never had headaches like the ones I'm getting since I met you."

"Why don't you check the registration on that gun before you start accusing me."

"Easy!" said Sanfuentes. "I'm not accusing you. I'm just thinking out loud. Don't you do that sometimes?"

"Who found the body?" I said.

"We got a call this morning. And yes, we traced it. Came from a phone booth."

"Man or woman?" I said.

"Hard to tell," said the cop.

"Any name?"

"What do you think?" said Sanfuentes.

"I think the killer would be pretty stupid to do that. Have you notified Laura Hope yet?"

"The wife?" said Sanfuentes, with a wayward little gleam in his eye. "We're looking for her now." Then he told one of his crew to take impressions of the bike tracks by the side of the road.

"Bike?" I said. "Or motor scooter?"

"Can't tell yet," said Sanfuentes. "Might even be a motorcycle."

"Or a velocipede," I said, trying to deflect his suspicion from Ross.

"A what?"

"A circus bike," I said to Sanfuentes. "At least you can't blame Jeri Tiker for this one."

"I guess not," said Sanfuentes.

"And you already know she didn't take the painting either."

Sanfuentes grunted much the same way Branco did in Boston. I wondered if all the rookies in the police academy learned how to make that distinctive, noncommittal, manly grunt. Then Sanfuentes reminded me not to leave town without telling him.

I said, "Isn't it time you let Jeri go?"

He said quietly, "You know why I'm keeping her."

"What if we have to evacuate for the hurricane?"

"There ain't no hurricane," said the cop. "It's all a ploy to distract the natives. See, they get restless off season, and they need a little excitement, so the weather bureau tells them to run out and buy cases of Sterno and batteries."

I looked at him incredulously. "You're kidding, right?"

He said flatly, "Humor helps *me* cope too."

"What about my car?"

"It's on Stock Island," he said. "Trust me, Stan. It's not worth fixing."

"I just want to see it."

"I'll take you there later," he said.

I got back on my bike and rode into town. On the way I met Ross coming the other way on a big black motorcycle. (Rafik's had been red, which proved I wasn't repeating a behavior pattern. Right?) I told Ross what had happened to Joshua, and how he'd come after me the night before and tried to run me down in the pink cab.

"I was pretty shook up," I said. "I was kind of hoping you might come by last night. I could've used the company."

"Sorry," said Ross. "I was, uh, busy."

"It's all right. You have to take work when you get it."

"There's some things I can't tell you, darlin'."

"It's okay, Ross. There's no strings between us."

"No," he said. "No strings. But you ought to rent yourself a car, in case we have to evacuate."

"Can't we get out on your motorcycle?"

"Not in a hurricane," said Ross.

Just then a red Range Rover passed us.

"I've seen that thing before," I said.

Ross said it was Ken Kimble's new car, just a few days old.

I told him I knew that, because I'd seen him get into it at the

Gulf Coast Playhouse. But I'd also seen it sometime before that, and I couldn't recall when. Again I recalled the notion of "Her Majesty's country carriage." Then also came an association to Key West's local majesty, the Countess Rulalenska.

Ross's voice broke into my mental meanderings. "You want to get together tonight?"

"Sure," I said easily.

Ross grinned, then revved the motorcycle's engine and rode off.

I apologized to my dead lover, explained to him that it was only a visceral response I had for Ross, a loneliness that was easily solved by physical companionship. I was convinced that my heart, or what was left of it, was still my own.

I turned up Whitehead Street, to pay a call on the Countess Rulalenska and probe the subconscious link I'd made between her and Ken Kimble's car. But her shop was locked up. Yet through the thin walls of the converted cottage I heard sounds within—her heavy footsteps, and cabinet doors being opened and slammed shut. I knocked heavily on the door of the shop. The countess opened it, and couldn't conceal her surprise and displeasure at seeing me.

"I was expecting someone else," she said in her high regal tone.

"Sorry to disappoint you," I said.

"I am not disappointed," she replied. "I am annoyed. Now, please, I must prepare for the storm. You should leave town yourself." Then she added ominously, "While you are still able."

"How are you planning to get off the island?" I said.

"Kenneth will drive us."

"Where is he now?" I said.

"He has matters to attend to," she replied.

"Joshua Aytem is dead," I said.

The countess sniffed coldly and said, "Really? What has that to do with me?"

"He used to work for your friend Adolf Dobermann."

"Adolf Dobermann was not my friend," she said. "And Joshua was a very, er, colorful character. But I had no business with him. Now, please, will you leave?"

Just then a wild gust of wind tore a huge palm branch from a nearby tree and crashed it against the roof of the porch outside.

The countess cried out in alarm. Then, as the wind just as quickly receded, she regained her composure.

"Are you leaving?" she said again, but this time she almost sounded afraid I *might* leave her alone.

"Not yet," I replied.

"Very well," she said. "I must pack my valuables." She went back into the shop, and I followed her.

Her valuables consisted of all the original artwork that she transferred electronically to some of the expensive T-shirts she sold. That art was irreplaceable, especially at the paltry sum for which it had been obtained. The countess rolled each one up separately and inserted it into a cardboard tube, then inserted that tube into a second waterproof plastic tube.

I said, "Did you ever see that missing painting, the one called *Dinner of Uncertainty?*"

"Why do you ask me that?" she said.

"I know that you and Ken Kimble are close friends, and he collects art. I also know he had the painting for a while."

"Who told you?" she said.

"I saw Polaroid snapshots at his place. So, I wondered if you ever saw the painting when he had it."

"Where is he?" she said impatiently, looking toward the door.

"Why don't you call him?" I said.

"He is not at home," she said quickly.

"But you all have cellular phones," I countered.

"The storm has interrupted our service."

"Countess," I said, "did Ken take that painting from the Crow's Nest?"

"Of course not!" she said. "He is innocent."

"Do you know who did? Was it Adolf Dobermann?"

"Adolf," she muttered resentfully. "Where is the great Adolf Dobermann now? He thought he was so clever. Hah!"

"Clever? How?"

"He was a braggadocio," she said. "He was always trying to put himself above me, because I am a true aristocrat, and he was just a commoner with money. He told me how he would outsmart his partners. He was going to buy all of Peter's property from Augusta for himself."

"For Mindful Lotus, you mean?"

"For himself!" she insisted. "I know nothing of any lotus thing. Why do you always say that?"

"So, did Adolf kill Augusta?" I said.

"I am sure of only one thing," she said. "I have no blood on my hands."

"There wasn't blood on Augusta Willits or Adolph Dobermann, though he was strangled with one of your T-shirts."

The countess arched one eyebrow. "That was a clever ruse to incriminate me."

"Why?" I said. "Who?"

"Someone who was envious of me."

As if on cue, there was an ominous knock on the door. Then the door was unlocked from the outside and flung open, all done quickly in a single three-part gesture: knock, unlock, open.

"He's dead!" cried Ken Kimble before he realized the countess was not alone. He looked at me and muttered, "What are you doing here?"

The countess explained how she had mistakenly opened the door earlier, thinking I was Ken.

"Stassya, I told you I'd let myself in," he said shortly.

"You did, Kenneth, but I am so worried that I forgot. Don't be angry, please. We have much to do before the storm."

"Yes," he said. Then he turned to me. "Unless you want to help me board up the place, you're only in the way here."

I agreed to help, and he quickly explained what had to be done, which was basically to batten down the shutters from inside the cottage, then to install fiberglass panels across the large glass picture window at the front of the store. So into temporary enforced labor I went, bartering drudgery for clues.

Ken and I went outside to install the fiberglass panels along the front of the store. My task was to balance a large panel upright while Ken fastened it to the porch floor. I saw his red Range Rover parked out front, and finally the repressed memory was freed, and I remembered where I'd seen the car before. It was no wonder I'd forgotten the moment, for I'd just witnessed the second corpse in two days. I murmured quietly to Ken to keep the countess from hearing us.

"I saw your new car at Jeri Tiker's gallery the day Adolf Dobermann was killed."

Ken looked up at me from where he was kneeling on the porch floor. He squinted his eyes.

I said, "Why did you lie to me, Ken? You're the one who returned *Dinner of Uncertainty* to Jeri's gallery."

"I was never there that morning," said Ken.

"But there's no mistaking your car. You may think because it's new, people wouldn't recognize it. But you made the mistake of buying a very distinctive car."

"I told you, I wasn't at the gallery that morning."

"Then maybe someone else borrowed your car, and returned the painting for you. Are you protecting a guilty person?"

"Who's guilty?" he said aloud.

From inside the shop the countess called out, "Kenneth? Did you say something?"

Ken called back, "These damn panels are the devil to latch, Stassya!"

I said quietly, "What's happening at the Gulf Coast Playhouse?"

"I was able to get a temporary stop-work order."

"Who issued it?"

Ken glared. "Nancy Drew."

"What did that take? Blackmail? Or bribery?"

"I think you may have misunderstood her," said Ken. "She was very agreeable to the idea of halting construction."

"That's not what you said the other day outside her office."

"My reaction then was based on the misinformation you gave me."

I said, "What about your friend Edsel?"

"What about him?" said Ken irritably.

"Are you sure he really wants to preserve the Gulf Coast Playhouse?"

"Of course he does! Ed loves the theater."

"He also loves Hollywood. Maybe he has other plans he hasn't told you about."

Ken said, "Ed and I are professional friends. I'd know if he was lying to me."

"Did he know about Adolf's plan to buy all the property directly from Augusta?"

"What are you talking about?" said Ken.

I nodded toward the interior of the shop. "Your friend Stassya just told me about it. Sounds like Adolf had a neat little plan to cross his partners."

He said, "Stassya told you that?"

I nodded again.

Ken said, "Tell me exactly what she said."

I did—the whole story—then added, "I assumed you knew everything too."

"Well, I didn't," he said, now angry. "Why would she tell you, of all people, and not me?"

"Beats me," I said. "I wonder if she told Edsel too."

"I'll find out," said Ken.

"Sounds like your friends are keeping things from you."

"Shut up!" said Ken.

Where had all his blissful self-realization gone?

I said, "Now will you tell me what you were doing at Jeri Tiker's gallery the day Adolf was killed? As I recall now, the car was dripping water slightly, as though it had just been washed."

"Enough!" said Ken, as if a stinging insect was bothering him. The last of the panels was secured and he stood up. He said, "You seem to thrive on mistrust. I can see you enjoy the idea that Ed would betray me, that he'd use anything I've told him against me."

"It's not unknown, even among friends."

"You're wrong there," said Ken. "Unlike you, I trust my friends unconditionally."

"That's too bad," I said.

We went back into the shop, where the countess was still struggling to fasten the same shutter she'd been at when we left her to go outside. Ken went over and latched it with a simple, strong gesture.

"Thank you, Kenneth" she said. "It takes a man to do things right."

But I saw a troubled look on Ken Kimble's face. He didn't seem to be on home ground at the moment. Perhaps my cynicism had sparked new doubt in his relationship to his friend Edsel Shamb, and to his confidant, the Countess Rulalenska. For her part, the countess seemed oblivious to any uneasiness from Ken.

But when I finally left them alone in the shop, I heard their anxious voices through the thin walls.

"He saw my car, Stassya."

"Who will be next, Kenneth?"

Then their voices became low and undistinguishable.

I got on my bike and continued riding up Whitehead Street. On the way I tried to make sense of what I'd just got from the countess and Ken: Adolf Dobermann had planned to buy all of Peter Willits's property directly from Augusta. And that could only happen if she won her contest of Peter's will. And she had, but it was after her death, so everything went to the church, and Adolph was left high and dry. Then why had he been in those meetings with Edsel Shamb and Nancy Drew if he was an independent agent? Maybe he was a double agent?

The other odd thing was, no one seemed to be grieving over Joshua Aytem. So I decided to express my condolences to his recent widow.

24

I headed northward to the Fleming Lemming. I hoped the police had notified Laura by that time, so I wouldn't be bearing the message of her husband's cold-blooded murder. I was getting a little hungry too, peddling around in the gusty wind. So on the way I stopped at a natural foods market on the waterfront to pick up some snacks to share with Laura, widow to widow.

In the market I ran into Cozy Dinette. When she saw me, she was surprised, and even a little nervous.

"Boston," she said, "I'm buying throat lozenges. This is the only place that sells the ones I like." She held up the tin, and I recognized the imported brand used by many opera singers.

"You don't have to explain," I said.

"No," she replied, "I don't, do I? What are you doing?"

I told her I was going to see Laura Hope, to comfort her after what had happened to Joshua.

"What happened?" said Cozy.

"Someone snuffed him."

"No!"

"True crime," I said. "Honest."

"Joshua?"

I explained how he had wrecked my car the previous night, then he was found dead that morning. "It looked like suicide," I told her. "But I don't know how anyone has the courage to put a gun in his mouth and actually pull the trigger."

"Boston," said Cozy, "getting up in the morning is what takes courage. Shooting yourself in the mouth is just plain stupid. So who found him?"

"The cops."

"That's a relief. Did they question you?"

"Oh, yes," I said. "Sanfuentes was even making noises that I had a good motive to kill Joshua, but I don't think he meant it."

"That's way off base," she said. "Sometimes I think the lieutenant has his head up his—"

"Cozy!"

"Well, what do you want me to say? He's a cop."

"I kinda like cops."

"Boston, that just proves what a sick little puppy you are."

But I was willing to bet that Miss Cozy Dinette would change her tune if she met Lieutenant Vito Branco of the Boston police.

"Anyway," I said, "I'm taking some food to the Fleming Lemming so Laura and I can sit and commiserate like two young widows."

"If I know you," said Cozy, "you have other motives."

"Kind of," I said.

"If you want to get on Laura's good side," said Cozy, "take her lobster salad. It's her favorite."

I grunted like a cop. "Expensive taste."

Cozy winked to emphasize her feminine wiliness. "Which is exactly why Joshua never let her have it."

"Laura won't have to worry about that anymore."

Cozy said, "I wonder if she'll be able to manage on her own. She doesn't seem capable of taking care of herself."

I said, "If my instincts about Laura are right, she'll recover from Joshua's death real fast."

"Ooh, you're hard, Boston. Cold and hard."

"Am I?"

Cozy made excuses about being late for rehearsal again, and left the market in a hurry. I ordered a lobster salad for Laura Hope. For myself I got a large, peach-studded frozen yogurt, half of which I devoured on the way to the cash register, the other half on the way to my borrowed bicycle.

When I got to the Fleming Lemming, it was locked up. I knocked, and the blinds separated slightly. Between the slats Laura Hope's face appeared looking flat and gray. She'd obviously heard the news about her husband. I waved, and she opened the door a crack.

"I come bearing gifts," I said, holding up the bag with the lobster salad inside.

"I want nothing."

"Not even lobster salad?" I said.

She yielded. "Maybe I ought to eat something," she said. "Why are you doing this? We're not exactly friends."

"Partly to apologize for upsetting you the other day, and partly because you could probably use some company right now. I recently lost someone I loved too."

"Apology accepted," she said gruffly, and took the bag. Inside the office, she opened the container eagerly, then sniffed at the salad as if to make sure it was safe to eat. "How did you know?" she said. "I was dreaming of lobster for lunch."

"Sometimes I'm psychic," I said.

Laura poked out a piece of claw meat and popped it into her mouth. She closed her eyes while she chewed it. Only after she swallowed the morsel did she open them again. She looked surprised to see me still standing in front of her.

"Did you want something else?" she said. "Or are you content to watch me eat?"

"That's not one of my peculiarities," I said. "But I would like to ask you some questions."

"Ah," said Laura. "So this is more than an apology."

"Yes," I said.

She put the salad down and resumed the work she'd been doing when I arrived—packing and protecting her precious signed first editions. She slid each one first into a sealable plastic bag, then placed it into a large plastic crate with a waterproof lid.

I watched her a few moments, then said nonchalantly, "Did you know that Joshua was coming after me last night?"

"Was he?" said Laura.

"First he tried to run me down with that pink car. When he failed at that, he wrecked my Alfa."

Laura said, "Did you come here to comfort me? Or to accuse my dead husband falsely, when he's not even alive to defend himself?"

"Laura, he was involved with Edsel Shamb and Nancy Drew and Adolf Dobermann. Two of the four people are dead."

"Do you think I don't know that?" she said. Then she went back to the salad and picked through it until she found a big chunk of tail meat. She put it in her mouth and chewed until her eyes began to glaze over again.

I pressed forward. "Aren't you bothered by his death?"

Laura snapped her eyes open. Then with an odd smile she said, "It's a tragedy, isn't it?"

"What if it wasn't suicide? You could be in danger yourself."

Her eyes gleamed at the discovery of another hunk of tail meat. "I'm not afraid," she said. "Not like you, who thrives on high drama."

I said, "What did Joshua know that got him killed?"

Laura shook her head slowly. "You know," she said, "I forgot to ask him." Into her mouth went the lobster flesh. "And now it's too late." She chewed deliberately, swallowed, then said, "I'm sorry, but I don't know anything about his business with those people. And this salad is excellent—I really appreciate it—but talking to you is just too much for my nerves right now." She pushed the salad away, as if she couldn't eat another bite.

I said, "The police found bike tracks near the place where Joshua was killed."

"Really?" said Laura.

"Don't you drive a motor scooter?"

"Along with a few thousand other people on Key West."

"But you're the dead man's wife."

Laura said, "You ask too many questions, and you jump to wrong conclusions. And besides, every time I talk to you something bad happens."

"Like what?"

"Like what!" she said. "Joshua's dead! That's what."

"You can't blame me for that."

"Why not? You got him very upset. Maybe the two of you arranged to meet last night, and things got out of hand."

"That's what the police think too."

"So what *were* you doing out there by the power plant?" Then she added sarcastically, "Feeding the gulls?"

"That's exactly what I was doing," I said. "That and thinking about my dead lover."

"You're pathetic," said Laura, as she pulled the salad back toward her and popped another chunk of lobster into her mouth.

I asked her, "Aren't you afraid that whoever killed Joshua will hurt you now?"

"It was suicide," she said as she jabbed the fork into the salad, and once more shoved the container away from herself.

"What if it wasn't?"

Laura said, "Aren't *you* afraid? Perhaps you and I should be afraid together. Or maybe of each other." Then Laura smiled blissfully. The lobster salad must have activated her endorphins. Either that or she was on heavy-duty tranquilizers to cope with her husband's murder. She spoke dreamily. "All I know is, Joshua's dead. Now if only you'd leave town, things might really get better again."

Reduced to playing the role of chief obstacle to true world peace and inner healing, I left the Fleming Lemming and headed to the police station to see Jeri Tiker. I knew she would have stopped painting, because the sky had turned an awful brownish shade of blue, like a bad bruise. It was the first sign that foul weather might actually lie ahead.

As I peddled to the police station I saw Cozy Dinette's big white convertible pulling out from the back lot where the cruisers were parked. She went the other way and didn't see me.

Inside the station Lieutenant Sanfuentes told me he had called Lieutenant Branco again. "I wanted to check up on you one more time—just to make sure."

"Sure of what?"

"That I can still trust you."

"What's the verdict this time?" I said.

"You're still clean."

"That's good."

"Yeah," said Sanfuentes. "But if you ever thought about getting serious about this business, you better get used to people checking up on you. And get ready to come out looking bad a lot too, 'cause when you're really cooking on a case, you smell kinda bad just before you crack it."

I sniffed at the underarms of my shirt. "I must be close, then," I said. But I knew the olfactory spasms were more likely due to all the pedaling around I'd done on the bike that day. I wasn't any closer to a solution than when I'd found Augusta Willits with that alarm clock jammed down her throat five days ago.

I told Sanfuentes everything I'd seen and heard since our grisly rendezvous that morning over Joshua's body. Then I told him I saw Cozy Dinette pulling out of the station's back lot on my way to the station.

"Was she in here?" I said.

One of the cop's eyes twitched nervously, only once.

"Not that I know of," he said. "Maybe she was turning around."

I said, "Like this is the only driveway on Simonton Street."

"Look," said Sanfuentes, "Miss Dinette's situation is, er, kind of delicate, as regards us, I mean—the police."

"Why's that?" I said.

"She smokes too much."

"Lots of people smoke," I said.

"Yeah, and lots of people buy cigarettes too."

"Oh," I said. "You mean she *smokes.*"

Sanfuentes looked at me. "Isn't that what I said?"

"So? Is that such a big deal, I mean here?"

He said, "It's a big deal when you hold clearance sales on your overstock. Miss Dinette runs a regular cottage industry."

"But you look the other way?"

Sanfuentes nodded. "Sometimes that's the best solution. Don't make a big deal over it, okay?"

"Sure," I said.

"What's important between you and me right now," said the cop, "is I want to get this guy before we have another body on our hands."

"Do you want my help again?"

"Did I say otherwise?"

"You officially stopped me the other day."

The cop set his jaw firmly. "Did I? I don't recall that."

"When are you going to let Jeri Tiker go?"

"How many times have I told you why I'm keeping Ms. Tiker here? Your memory's getting a little dull, Stan. So I'm also going to remind you not to go yapping about any of this, okay? I don't want people to start thinking I'm some kind of patron of the arts, y'know?"

"Certainly not."

"I'm a cop."

"Does Jeri know why you're keeping her here?"

"I think she understands whose side I'm on without me saying so many words."

"You can trust me, Lieutenant. Jeri Tiker is still your prime suspect in the death of Adolf Dobermann."

"Now you're talking straight," said Sanfuentes.

Which was a genetic impossibility.

I noticed Jeri's painting propped up on the floor behind the lieutenant's desk, and I asked him if I could take it down to her cell for a bit.

"You got an idea?" he said.

"Something might be hiding in that painting that we can't see."

Sanfuentes chuckled cynically. "You mean like a microdot with secret information hidden somewhere?"

"I mean the painting itself. Maybe there's a message on that canvas that meant so much to Adolf Dobermann that he had to steal it from the Crow's Nest. He even killed Augusta Willits to do it."

"Sounds farfetched to me," said the cop. "I think that painting is a painting. That's all."

"Jeri may know something more. There's nothing to lose, Lieutenant."

"I guess there's no problem," said the cop.

I took the framed canvas downstairs to Jeri's cell. She was just putting her paints away when I arrived.

"Oh, good!" she said enthusiastically. "A visitor from the real world. The sky just turned brown and I can't paint anymore."

I said I'd figured as much, then told her about the impending hurricane. Jeri hadn't heard a word about it. I guess Lieutenant Sanfuentes really didn't believe in false alarms. Jeri noticed *Dinner of Uncertainty* in my arms.

"What are you doing with that?" she said.

"I thought we'd have a little art appreciation class."

I set up the painting on her easel.

Jeri looked distressed. "If I had known all the trouble that painting was going to cause, I would never have done it."

"Don't say that," I said. "You can't be a real artist and worry about people's reactions to your work."

"Real-shmeal," she said. "How would Norman Rockwell have felt if one of his magazine covers drove someone to murder?"

"Do you think he was a real artist?"

"What do I know?" said Jeri. "Once I'm out of here I'm going radically commercial."

"Fine, fine," I said. "But for now let's focus on the work at hand. Why has this painting caused such a stir? It seems innocent enough. It's colorful, and the characters and the situation are provocative. But why did Adolph steal it?"

Jeri said, "I don't know. It's not even my best painting. I don't understand why anyone would want it badly enough to kill for it. Maybe because of who's in it."

"Who?" I said.

"This is a real event that I painted."

"It is?" I said.

"Is that important?"

"Jeri, it could hold the key to everything that's happened in the last five days."

"A painting?"

"When did you paint it?"

"I finished it about a month ago, but the actual event took place long before that."

"And Adolf Dobermann wanted to buy it right after you finished it?"

"No," said Jeri. "No one knew I'd painted it, just like all the stuff I do. But Adolf saw it hanging in the Crow's Nest, and that's when he got all fired up over it."

"Yet you didn't sell it to him."

Jeri said, "For fifty dollars?"

"Cheap bastard."

"I know," said Jeri. "But if this painting incriminated him, wouldn't he have bought it no matter what price I told him?"

"I suppose you're right," I said. In my hurry to find a clue, I'd missed that myself. Maybe Sanfuentes was right. Maybe it was only a painting. Still, I asked Jeri to tell me who was in it.

"There's Ken Kimble," she said, and she pointed to a dark-haired young man with a milky complexion in the foreground.

"Very flattering," I said.

"Not really," said Jeri. "Look beyond the youth."

I did. Then I gasped. The face, though superficially attractive, had the mesmerizing stare of a bloodthirsty predator.

"Wow," I said. "Who else is in there?"

Jeri replied, "Everyone who was there at the restaurant that night."

She pointed to each character on the canvas as she named their real-life counterparts. And as usual in her paintings, no one resembled who they really were. Edsel Shamb was portrayed as a swarthy Middle Easterner with short gray hair and a shifty eye that confronted the observer directly.

Joshua Aytem was an expressionless chocolate-colored giant at the bull's-eye center of the portrait, while Laura Hope was a very tan blond man at his side. Apparently Jeri knew the truth about Lars becoming Laura, even if no one had told her the facts.

At another table in the background she'd painted the Countess Rulalenska, also chocolate-colored and of indeterminate sex. Alongside her was Cozy Dinette, whose image resembled a very masculine cross-dresser. Cozy would not have approved.

"Who's this in the foreground?" I said, "with the face turned away."

"I don't know," said Jeri. She sounded a little defensive. "Whoever it is was facing away from me that night."

"Maybe it's you."

"I wasn't at the table," she said.

"What about the body? Was it big? Or slender?"

Jeri said, "I don't remember."

"Was it Adolf?"

"He didn't arrive in town until after Peter died."

"How about Nancy Drew?"

Jeri said, "I don't recall her being there."

"She'd have good reason, being Peter's attorney."

"Maybe," said Jeri, "but I don't think so." She was sounding a bit irritated.

"What about Ross?"

"Your hustler?" said Jeri. "Peter would never be seen in public with someone like him."

"Well, is it a man or a woman at least?"

Jeri shrugged. "That never matters in my paintings."

"What about in your mind?"

"It doesn't matter there either."

There was one more character on the canvas, a waiter, standing and dominating the entire picture as he took everyone's order. I asked Jeri to identify him.

"That's Peter Willits," she said.

"But he was already dead."

"No he wasn't," said Jeri. "I told you, I did the painting a month ago, but the actual event happened when he was still alive."

"But why did you make him subservient?"

"He's not subservient!" said Jeri. "Look where he is. He's so big he doesn't even fit on the canvas!"

"But he's waiting on them."

"No," said Jeri. "They're waiting on him. They're waiting for him to die. He invited them all out to dinner that night to discuss his estate."

"Just like that? Come to dinner, I'm doing my will?"

Jeri nodded. "Peter knew he was going to die, and he was a very picky person. He wanted everything in perfect order after his death."

"Morbidly compulsive."

"Practical," countered Jeri. "He wanted things to go smoothly."

"For all the good it did," I said. "He forgot to invite dear Mummy Augusta to dinner."

Jeri said, "I think that was intentional."

"And look how it all turned out."

Jeri said, "That's why the title works—*Dinner of Uncertainty*. No one at that table knew what was going to happen, even though it was all being planned out to the letter."

I said, "How did you know all this, I mean about the dinner? Did they pose for you?"

"I was sitting nearby."

"But you weren't at the table?"

"I already told you, no."

"Jeri," I said, "if Peter arranged that dinner for all the people he was naming in his will, why didn't he include you? You told me he was leaving you the Echo Me Gallery."

Jeri looked down. Then she said quietly, "I lied. He did invite me, but he didn't want any of them to know. See, he wanted me to paint them all. He wanted to commemorate the event of making his will."

"So he commissioned *Dinner of Uncertainty?*"

"Yes."

"And they never guessed what was happening?"

Jeri laughed. "They knew I was sketching them, and they loved the attention. I think most people are vain. But no one knew that Peter wanted me there."

So the question remained, Why did someone want that painting so badly?

"By the way," I said, "why does everyone have only three fingers?"

"Where?" said Jeri.

"Look," I said and pointed.

Jeri squinted. "Laura Hope has four."

Perhaps that was Jeri's unconscious compensation for Laura's loss of another more critical appendage.

I said, "But no one else does."

Jeri shrugged again. "I never noticed it until now."

"It's not a criticism," I said.

"I don't care if it is," she replied.

I thanked her for her help, then took the painting back upstairs to Lieutenant Sanfuentes's office. He'd already gone home for the day, since it was early evening. The hour reminded me that I'd showered only once that day, so I peddled back to the Jared Bellamy House thinking about Jeri Tiker's painting, but could make no sense of anything I'd learned about it from her explication. Was it, after all, only a feast of neuro-optical stimulation?

25

The staff at the Jared Bellamy House were trying hard to suppress their panic about the impending hurricane. They insisted there was absolutely nothing to worry about, just another bad storm, happened all the time. But it all sounded forced, like a bad rendition of strength under pressure. At any moment I expected some anxious anonymous queen to elicit a Fay Wray scream from the front desk.

Up in my room I made a phone call. It was six o'clock, and I knew Nicole would still be at Snips Salon. When she came on the phone, she scolded me.

"Why haven't you called sooner?"

"I've been busy, doll."

"Too busy for your real friends? I've been worried sick."

"I can't keep track of time down here," I said. "It either drags, or else it slips away too fast."

"It's time to come home, Stanley. We've been watching the weather reports here. That storm looks dangerous."

"It may be too late, Nikki. There's talk of an evacuation, and I don't have a car anymore."

"What happened to yours?"

I explained the Alfa's tragic fate.

"Then fly back," she said.

"No seats," I said.

"Rent a car."

"Too late, doll."

It was all lies. I probably could have left the island if I really wanted to. But some part of me wanted to experience a natural disaster firsthand. I'd seen murder and I'd lost love, so what new thrill was left for me except a record-breaking hurricane? (Bungee-jumping was out—acrophobia.)

"What about the trains?" said Nicole.

"I'd still have to get to Miami."

"So you're stranded there."

"Kind of," I said.

"Just what you wanted, probably."

"Kind of," I said again.

Nicole heaved a sigh over the phone. "Stanley, I think we're due for a long talk when you get home."

"Nikki, I'm still planning to work part-time at the shop."

"That's fine, Stanley, but lately the only feeling I have with you is worry, and I'm exhausted. You've said there's nothing worth living for, and that morbid state of mind is creating a big problem."

"For whom, Nikki? You? Or me?"

"Both of us."

"I'm coming out of it," I said.

"Your behavior shows otherwise. Now, if you're going to insist on pursuing this dangerous kind of life you seem to crave, I'm going to insist that you get special training in self-protection. You have no idea what you're doing."

"Gosh, doll. Thanks for pointing that out."

"I'm not going to sit by quietly while you continue to endanger yourself. I won't tolerate it."

"Are you breaking up with me?"

"I'm serious, Stanley. Don't get smart!"

"You're *too* serious, Nikki. What is there for me to lose?"

"Your life!"

"Big deal," I said flatly.

"Then what about me?" she said. "Don't you care how I feel?"

"You'll recover."

"Damn you, Stanley. Then what about the cat? If something happens to you, who will feed her?"

"You will."

"Really?" she said. "You know how I feel about domestic animals."

"But you like Sugar Baby."

"Only if you're alive," said Nicole. "Otherwise, she's just another cat."

"Do I sense an ultimatum, doll?"

"Yes," she said. "I've talked to Vito, and he agrees with me. When you return to Boston, you are going to learn self-defense. You probably should learn to use a gun too."

"Perry Mason never had a gun."

"Perry Mason never existed."

"Nikki, I don't need a gun."

"It's time to grow up, Stanley."

"Since when is wielding a gun a sign of maturity?"

We'd reached another impasse of absurdity. Eager to get off the phone, I lied again and told Nicole that I had an appointment that night. Once again she didn't believe me. I promised to call her with daily updates, especially if the storm did arrive.

She said with a resigned laugh, "If it turns out as bad as they predict, the phones will probably be out."

I apologized for upsetting her. She said it didn't matter, that I always did whatever I wanted to anyway. Then I said good-bye, and Nicole, as usual, hung up. Through all our years together I always wondered if our bickering was a peculiar strength or a subtle threat to our friendship.

I showered and set out for some supper. I decided to walk to La Diosa del Mar, and have dinner in the downstairs dining room. The air had cooled already, and was blowing in strong gusts. As I approached Duval Street I saw that it had been made one-way, going eastward, and with all parking prohibited. Heavy traffic was at a standstill. I crossed between the three lanes of crawling cars and continued down to Whitehead Street. Likewise, Whitehead had been made one-way traveling eastward, and it, too, was clogged with traffic. People were obviously getting off the island and driving up the Keys before the storm arrived. I wondered where they were going. To Miami? Would it be any less dangerous there? Or would they all have to travel further north? Or further inland? Why not just stick around like me and hang on to a tree? Or did they know something I didn't? Like the fact that trees got uprooted and blown away in a tropical hurricane? I imagined myself straddling the trunk of a palm tree, whirling high in the vortex of the storm, soaring over the causeways clogged with cars trying to escape the Keys. I'd wave and yell, Hello down there! Fine weather for ducks, eh?

I needed food, and fast.

The dining room at La Diosa del Mar was lively and packed with people, all the fools like me who intended to stay on the island and ride out the storm. I heard Cozy Dinette singing upstairs in the Tulle Box cabaret. Her song was "Stormy Weather." I'd go upstairs later and see her. Maybe Ross was working too, and I'd confirm our night together.

There were no tables free in the dining room so I nestled onto a vacant stool at the very end of the shorter arm of the L-shaped bar. The barmaid set a napkin in front of me almost before my fanny was on the stool.

She barked above the noise in the bar. "Everything's half-price tonight. We're celebrating the hurricane."

Frivolity thrived as doomsday approached.

I ordered Napoleon cognac, a double, and asked for a menu.

She said, "The filet is excellent. Just arrived in town. It's a beautiful piece of meat. Probably the last chance you'll have if we get that storm."

How could I refuse? I ordered it rare. Then I put a fifty-dollar bill on the counter to let her know I appreciated her attention.

The cognac arrived in a snifter the size of a fishbowl. Not too obvious. I lifted it to my face. The barmaid had warmed the snifter to help vaporize the cognac more easily. She was a pro. One deep breath and I was floating again.

The barmaid took the money off the bar and said, "I'll keep this on account for you."

I asked her if Ross was working upstairs at the Tulle Box that night. She gave me a big smile and said he was working his "other job" at the Javelin.

I scanned the room for a familiar face, but none shone from the crowd. Then in a dim corner opposite me I saw the powerful mass of Attorney Nancy L. Drew sitting alone in a booth. From my vantage point I realized for the first time that Nancy L. Drew, despite her power-laden girth, was relatively slender on top. Had she been the missing person in Jeri Tiker's painting? A half-empty pint of beer sat before her, but no food. She kept looking toward the doorway, like a sad little girl waiting for someone special to arrive. I imagined how she'd fought her way through law school, then continued the battle to carve her particular niche in Key West. And there she was, sitting alone in a dark noisy bar with a glass of beer her only willing companion, at least for the moment. Poor Nancy L. Drew.

Meanwhile, upstairs, Cozy Dinette had made a smooth segue into "Raindrops Keep Falling on My Head." Apparently the set was a medley of precipitation-inspired numbers.

Then, as if waking me from a dream, the barmaid placed a heavy platter in front of me. I could feel the heat from the plate rise up. The filet looked wonderful. I sliced off an edge of beef and put it in my mouth. It quickly disintegrated into a warm, bloody, peppery mass. For the moment, my theory that humans are not natural carnivores expired. I was in the equivalent of cat bliss. I almost started purring.

Then I saw someone join Nancy L. Drew at her dark booth. It was Laura Hope. She looked around nervously, as though she was afraid to be recognized by anybody. Laura was, after all, supposed to be in mourning for her husband, found earlier that very day. From what I could see, Nancy did most of the talking, while Laura did or said almost nothing, so I assumed it was Nancy who wanted something from the other woman. But no sooner had I surmised that than the tables turned, so to speak, and Laura was leaning forward and verbally challenging Nancy L. Drew—quite a feat when facing off an attorney. Nancy did little but sit stoically and take occasional gulps of beer.

What could the two women possibly want from each other? Perhaps Nancy wanted to know more about Laura's involvement with Joshua's business deals, just as she had about Jeri Tiker's connection to Adolf Dobermann. For her part, perhaps Laura wanted to know more about Nancy's personal involvement with Joshua. Perhaps Nancy was proposing that Laura become her associate, much the way Joshua had seemed to be Edsel's. Perhaps . . . what? What was wrong with me? I was doing it again. I was using intuition, and carelessly too. I was imagining ridiculous things that could have been easily settled with a few hard facts. But what else could I do? I hadn't yet learned how to transmogrify myself into a fly on the wall.

The barmaid appeared and put two more plates in front of me, one heaped with slender steamed asparagus, the other with long crunchy french fries. I nibbled at a spear, then ate two hot fries. Now I had a balanced meal. When I glanced back toward the booth where Nancy Drew and Laura Hope were sitting, I saw that in the intervening moments they'd got up and were on their way out the door. What kind of PI was I going to make, so distracted by the arrival of food that I'd missed their exit? I faced a horrible decision. Should I leap up and follow them? Or should I finish the excellent meal in front of me? What was I made of? What would Perry Mason have done? Come to think of it, he never ate, except at the very end of a case, after good triumphed over evil. Back on earth, what would Lieutenant Branco have done? He would have forsaken the steak and followed the two women.

But I wasn't Perry Mason, and I certainly wasn't Lieutenant Branco. I slapped the filet between two hunks of bread, threw in a handful of asparagus spears, and wrapped it all in a napkin. Perhaps it would become a trendy new fast-food item, *filet mignon à porter*. I slid off the stool and headed toward the door, but then went back to my place and jammed three long hot fries into my mouth for good luck. The barmaid told me I'd forgotten my change. I told her it was hers. Upstairs, Cozy Dinette had just launched into "Pennies from Heaven."

Alas, those valuable seconds I'd wasted making a decision and wrapping up my food had given Nancy Drew and Laura Hope time to get away. But now? The car traffic was still heavy on Duval Street. And they couldn't have disappeared on foot so quickly. Then I heard the buzz of a small motor scooter from a nearby alley. The tiny engine strained to accelerate under the combined weight of Laura Hope and Attorney Drew behind her. Still, within moments they vanished up a side street.

After my dramatic exit from La Diosa del Mar I was too embarrassed to go back inside, so I continued on foot toward the waterfront, sandwich in hand. Already I regretted leaving the fries behind so impulsively. The wind had picked up and was blowing more steadily, making the temperature the most comfortable it had been since my arrival. Maybe the occasional hurricane was Mother Nature's way of cooling things down in the tropics.

I came to the Gulf Coast Playhouse. As Ken Kimble had told me, construction had halted, thanks to Nancy Drew's stop-work order. With any luck damage to the reef had been minimal. The playhouse loomed in the darkness before me. All was quiet except for the welcome wind—welcome to me, that is.

Then I heard voices resonating against the brick walls of the old theater. Two men were arguing, and I recognized their voices.

"Damn you, Ed! All along I thought you were with me."

"I am, Ken. I always have been. It's going to turn out all right."

"How can it ever be all right?"

"Ken, I told you, it's not the way it looks."

"Tell me, then. Tell me what it really is."

The two men continued talking, but too quietly for me to hear them. I moved cautiously toward the place where their voices came from. As I neared them, I made out bits of their continuing argument.

". . . to get control back in our hands."

"What good will that be . . ."

". . . the playhouse will always be preserved."

"History? History!"

". . . performances too. Film and television . . ."

"That's enough, Ed! You've betrayed me."

"I've betrayed no one, Ken. You're clinging to the past."

"We'll see who's clinging to what."

Then from around the corner came Key West's own movie star manqué, Ken Kimble. He moved toward me, stopped short when he saw me, then muttered softly, "Get out of here. Now! This is none of your business, nobody's business. Do you understand?"

The other voice called out from behind the playhouse. "Who's there, Ken?"

"No one," he said.

But then Edsel Shamb appeared from around the building, his gray ponytail silhouetted in the dim light. He recognized me and said, "How do you always show up where you don't belong?"

I answered, "A cop I know in Boston says—"

"Exactly how much did you hear?" interrupted Edsel.

"Enough to know you guys are having a serious disagreement."

"He's harmless," said Ken.

I sensed Edsel studying me in the darkness.

"Maybe you're right," he said to Ken. "What can he do about little misunderstanding between us?"

I said, "It sounded a lot more serious than that."

Ken said to me, "Why can't you just shut up, for your own sake?"

"It's a character flaw."

Edsel snorted and said, "If this was a script, I'd send you to rewrite."

"But it's not," I replied. "And I'm right here, in your face."

Ken said, "Let's go, Ed. Leave him alone. He's harmless, I tell you. Come on."

Then he took the other man's arm and led him away.

It was odd, how one minute they'd been arguing violently, and the next thing they were placating each other over me, the harmless if annoying faggot. Sometimes it was the hardest role I ever played.

The two men continued on toward the waterfront, while I turned back and headed east toward the Javelin, to reunite with my holiday hustler.

As I strolled into the place, Ross had just finished his spot in the night's lineup. He was stepping down off the bar with his clothes slung over one arm, and he grinned broadly when he saw me.

I asked him, "Hard day at the office?"

"I'll show you hard, darlin'," he said. "Do you have the car?"

"What car?" I said.

"I told you to rent us a car."

"You did?"

"How could you forget?" said Ross. "I finished early tonight so we could get a head start."

"Hardly matters now," I said. "The traffic is jammed all the way up Duval and Whitehead Streets."

Ross shook his head woefully. "I can't believe you forgot to get a car, darlin'." He quickly scanned the Javelin's bar. "I might be able to get us one." He nodded in the direction of an elderly gent. The old man responded with a ravenous leer of desire when h caught Ross's eye. For me he showed only contempt.

"One of your johns?" I said.

"He collects cars," said Ross. "That's all that counts now. I'll see if he has one with a full tank."

"What'll you have to do for it?"

"Do you care?" said Ross.

"Theoretically," I said, "yes."

"Good," said Ross. "All I have to do to get a car out of that guy is make him a promise."

"One you'll keep?"

"Are you telling me my business?" His eyes flared angrily. "You set up the rules up, darlin', remember? No strings, you said."

I plucked at his G-string. "Except this one."

Ross said, "I'll take it off right here if you want me to."

"I'll do it myself later."

"Is that a promise?" His eyes were eager.

"Yeah," I said. "That's a promise."

That was me portraying a tough guy, which was sometimes an easier role to parody than the annoying harmless faggot one I always got stuck with. Ross went and spoke to the old gent. Then he came back, and for the moment we forgot about the car and the promises.

Back at the Jared Bellamy House, the night took on a disquieting feeling of finality, as before a significant event. First came a big confession from Ross, as if he wanted me to know the utter truth about himself before we drowned in each other's arms in a raging typhoon. His secret was very simple. For many years Ross had conducted a discreet business arrangement with none other than the late Peter Willits. It was supposedly the best-kept secret on the island. Still, I should have guessed it. For his discretion regarding the arrangement, Ross was to inherit the old Twin Palms guest house, the same place where Adolf Dobermann had been killed.

"Why are you telling me?" I said.

"Because I might not get another chance like this, darlin'."

"You didn't have anything to do with Adolf's death, did you? I mean, just to get the place back for yourself."

"How could you say a thing like that, darlin'?"

But he never answered me.

For the rest of the night Ross and I played doctor—one the physician, the other the shrink, then vice versa—as we explored each other's bodies and psyches in my luxurious chamber at the Jared Bellamy House. However playful we were though, I knew our connection had breached the boundaries of biology and economics, and that I had surrendered my heart that night.

26

I woke to the sound of heavy rain buffeting the windows of my room. It was seven-thirty, and the morning sun had left our galaxy for good. My legs sought Sugar Baby under the blankets, where she always cowered during a storm. Then I remembered she wasn't with me. Alas, neither was Ross, my pal *de nuit*. With all the rain and wind outside, where could he have gone? What had drawn him from the secure warmth of my bed to the harsh elements outdoors? What urgent mission beckoned him? An assignation? Mine was not to ask. People in Ross's line of work, like taxi drivers, were busiest during bad weather.

He'd left a note on the nightstand: *See you later.*

Verbose he was not. Then I finally remembered: He was going to wrangle a car from one of his johns. But so early?

I called for room service, but was told that the house staff had been reduced to a skeleton crew, due to the storm. I'd have to fend for myself regarding food. I showered and dressed. Downstairs, the desk clerk advised me to catch the last evacuation bus out of town, which was scheduled to leave at noon. I thanked him for telling me, but I had no intention of leaving the island that way, on a cattle car.

I donned a plastic poncho compliments of the house, and took one of their bikes to Camille's. But the cafe was closed, boarded up in fact. The few other people who were out walking in the storm were wearing sunglasses, despite a sky dark with rain. I ended up at Fausto's Market, where I bought some fruit and crackers and yogurt, which is about all that was left on the shelves by that time. The bottled water was completely sold out. I had a vague feeling of panic about that until I realized all I'd have to do, if necessary, was stand out in the storm with my mouth open. I'd only have to watch for windborne geckos and palmetto bugs.

I was munching my makeshift breakfast under the portico outside the market when I saw Laura Hope on her way in. She was almost completely concealed by her poncho.

I said, "Nice weather for ducks."

Her reply was an irritated smirk.

I said, "How's your friend Nancy Drew?"

"We're not friends!" she snapped.

"You're friendly enough to give her a ride on your motor scooter last night."

"You're mistaken," said Laura.

I told her what I'd seen the previous night at La Diosa del Mar: that she'd met Attorney Drew, they had talked briefly, then left the place together.

"So what?" said Laura.

"What was the meeting about?"

"Mind your own business!" she said. "You ought to leave this place, now, for your own good, before it's too late."

"Everyone's telling me that."

"You have no idea what these hurricanes are like," she said. "If you stay, anything could happen to you."

She headed into the market as if to escape from me, then changed her mind and came back out. She scurried around the building to the side parking lot. Moments later a big imported sedan, champagne-colored, appeared and maneuvered gracefully onto Fleming Street, then turned onto Simonton Street and headed west toward the marina. I got on my bike and tried to follow the car, but they had the advantage of internal combustion over my Slavic metabolism, and they got away.

I rode past the marina anyway, which is where they seemed to be headed. But the office for Blue Water Tours was dark and locked up tight, which wasn't surprising. Who'd go out on a boat in that weather?

Then I biked past the Gulf Coast Playhouse. All was deserted there too. The heavy construction equipment stood dormant in the gray wetness, and the temperamental outbursts and blustery indignations of Edsel Shamb and Ken Kimble had left no echoes.

Peddling my way in the wind and rain, I once again thanked my Czech forebears for the genetic hand they'd dealt me regarding legs. Despite the harsh weather that morning in Key West, I found myself enjoying my waterlogged excursion.

I made a brief stop at the police station. My soggy appearance must have belied my enjoyment of the elements, because Lieutenant Sanfuentes exclaimed, "What the hell happened to you?"

"I'm surrendering to a power greater than myself."

Sanfuentes shook his head. "You're gonna be surrendering to pneumonia if you don't watch out."

"How can you get pneumonia in Key West?"

"Because your body loses heat no matter how warm you think it is, and once your temperature drops, the bacteria find a welcome home. That's how." He punctuated his explanation with a sharp nod of his head.

"Thanks for the medical lecture," I said. Then I asked him if I could visit Jeri Tiker.

"Sure," he said. "She's got company right now, but I'm sure they'll let you know if you're interrupting anything."

"Who is it?" I said.

Sanfuentes replied, "Who else would come out in this weather? Her attorney."

I took the stairway down, stepping extra quietly, hoping to conceal myself in the stairwell and overhear Nancy L. Drew's conversation with Jeri Tiker. It worked, however briefly.

Nancy Drew said to Jeri, "Is that your final decision then?"

"Yes," said Jeri.

"I have to tell you," said the attorney, "how disappointed I am at your response to my effort to help you."

"It's not that I don't appreciate it," said Jeri.

"Who can blame you?" said the lawyer. "You certainly are comfortable here."

Then Nancy Drew called the guard to let her out of Jeri's cell. That's when I emerged breezily from the stairwell, as if just arriving.

Nancy Drew said to me, "Are you still in town? And out in this weather?"

"Just like you," I said.

She pulled on her raincoat. "Nature doesn't control my life."

That's when I noticed an odd discrepancy in the attorney's ensemble, for despite the British raincoat that protected her trademark billowing silk, and the Italian leather bag, and the nylons, and the color-coordinated manicure, Attorney Nancy L. Drew had shod her feet that morning with deck shoes, as though she was about to participate in the annual yacht club regatta.

I said, "Where did you take Laura Hope this morning?"

"To the market," she said. "Isn't that where you saw us?"

"Where did you go after that? I tried to follow you, but I lost you."

Nancy Drew gave me a blank stare. "Of course you did."

The guard came and unlocked the cell door and let Attorney Drew out. She went to the elevator and entered. When the door slid closed, I said to Jeri Tiker, "What was that all about?"

"She wanted to pay my bail and get me out of here."

"Why didn't you go?" I said.

"First off," said Jeri, "I'm comfortable here. I know that sounds strange, but all I have to do is eat and sleep and paint, which is my idea of heaven."

"And why else?" I said, although I had my own suspicion of the second reason.

Jeri confirmed it by saying, "Don't you think it's strange that my attorney waited until now, in the middle of a hurricane, to get me out of here?"

"I do," I said. "I wonder what she had in mind."

Jeri said, "All I know is I'm warm and I'm safe, so I'll stay. In fact, the lieutenant told me he has to camp out at the station too, until the storm passes, because there'll be all kinds of emergency calls. And he said with me painting down here, it wouldn't be so lonely for him."

"Aw," I said. "Isn't that nice?"

"I think so," said Jeri.

"What, you like him now?"

"Once you get below the surface, he's really a nice guy. Aren't you cold in those wet clothes?"

"No," I said. "And it's warm outside, really."

"You can still lose a lot of body heat."

"That's what the lieutenant said."

"You'd better go change," said Jeri.

"Maybe you're right," I said. "I'll see you after the climax."

"The climax of what?"

"The hurricane."

On the way out of the police station, Lieutenant Sanfuentes intercepted me and told me I shouldn't be outside anymore, that the storm would only worsen.

"Are you ordering me indoors?" I said.

"I know better than to order you anywhere," he said. "I just thought I'd advise you, because from what I see, you don't know what you're doing. You're soaked through, yet you're riding a bike and paying social calls in the middle of a hurricane. You ought to go home, Stan. Get in a hot tub, then get in bed with a good book."

"Sounds great," I said. Except all I had to read was Edsel Shamb, and matching wits and muscles with a raging hurricane was preferable to that.

Once again I set out into the storm, but in the brief time I'd been inside the police station, the wind had picked up drastically, so much so that staying vertical on the bike was impossible. I dismounted and walked it along the sidewalk.

The traffic was moving slowly but more steadily. Then a titanic white convertible pulled up to the curb beside me. The passenger's window lowered itself electrically. From inside the car I heard Cozy Dinette yell, "Boston!"

I straddled my bike and went to the open window. Like other folks who were out, Cozy had her sunglasses on, despite the obvious unnecessity for them.

She said, "Are you crazy riding around in this rain?"

"I kind of like it," I said. "Man against the elements."

"Why haven't you left the island yet?"

"Look who's talking," I said.

"Yeah, but I am crazy. And I live here. Besides, I've got to keep the troops entertained when the lights go out."

"How are you going to do that?"

"What, you think I can't sing without a microphone?" She brayed one of her noisy laughs to prove her vocal strength. "What are you doing now?"

"Quack, quack," I replied.

"Forget it," she said. "Get in."

"Where are we going?" I said.

"Just get in!" screeched Cozy. "Drinks are three-for-one at the Tulle Box."

"What about the bike?"

"Throw it in the trunk," she said. "It's open."

I did as she told me, but then the trunk lid wouldn't close. I went around to her window and told her it was going to fill up with water.

"Do you have eyes?" said Cozy. "Will you just get in the damn car!" I did, and as we pulled back into traffic she explained, "There's plenty of holes in the bottom of that trunk to let the water drain out. This is a great car for kidnapping people if you want to keep them alive."

And off we went, crawling along through the wind and rain, for a hurricane happy hour at the Tulle Box.

Cozy pulled her car into an empty space in front of La Diosa del Mar, with the Tulle Box upstairs. Traffic had pretty much thinned out at that end of town. Gusts of wind buffeted the car, making it sway and bounce on its springs. Rain pelted heavily against the windshield.

"Here you go," said Cozy. She left the motor running.

"Aren't you coming in?"

She hesitated then said, "I've got one small thing to take care of. I'll be back in a bit."

I got out and closed the door, but before I could get the bike out of the trunk, Cozy drove off in the heavy rain. I called after her, but instead of slowing down, she accelerated, taking full advantage of the open street ahead of her.

Inside the hotel lobby the fireplace was going. The desk clerk looked bored, probably because all the guests had fled the island, at least those with any sense. The fire beckoned to me, and I realized I was feeling a slight chill from my wet clothes. I went and stood in front of it to warm myself. The scene was pretty ridiculous, a blazing fire in Key West.

I heard the sounds of hurricane merriment echoing down the staircase from the Tulle Box. After five minutes, Cozy still hadn't shown up, so I went up to celebrate hurricane happy hour on my own.

I hoped to see Ross tending bar, but it was the other guy, the lesser god. Seated around the bar was a group of hurricane drinkers, among them Edsel Shamb, Ken Kimble, and the Countess Rulalenska all in a row. Edsel motioned me to sit near them at the bar. The countess and Ken greeted me coolly. Edsel was more cordial.

"What's keeping you here?" he said. "I was sure you'd be off the island by now. It's not love, is it?"

"Is that what's keeping you here?" I said.

At that moment the bartender placed a frosty martini in front of me. "First one's on the house," he said. "After that they're two for one."

Honestly I would have preferred a cup of herbal tea to ward off the chill I was feeling, but I never refuse a free drink, especially a martini. I thanked him, then took a big gulp. I turned back to Edsel to continue our *joustus interruptus*, but was thwarted by the countess, who was suddenly standing up and fastening the buttons of her raincoat. She pleaded with Ken Kimble to leave immediately. Ken explained to Ed that he and the countess really did have to leave the island right away. It was almost too late, and they had been delayed far too long. The roads might even be closed. Ed apologized as though he had been the cause of their delay. Yet something had obviously been important enough that they all meet for a drink before the other two evacuated the island. Then finally the countess and Ken Kimble left the bar and went downstairs.

Edsel turned to me and said, "Now where were we?"

"You and Ken have certainly kissed and made up after your fight the other night outside the playhouse."

"Oh," he said with a dismissive wave of his hand, "we always bicker. That's the strength of our friendship. It's the proof of honesty and trust for another person when you can speak your mind without holding back."

Perhaps he was telling the truth. After all, Nicole and I had exactly that kind of friendship.

He added, "You saw Ken just now. Did he look like someone who was angry with me?"

"No, but why did he delay his departure? Was it just to bid adieu to you? That sounds like love to me."

Edsel grumbled, "It was strictly business."

"Between friends?"

"Sure," he said. "Don't you engage in commerce with your friend Ross?"

"Cute," I said, catching his double entendre.

Meanwhile from across the bar a man called out to me, "Is Ross with you?" It was the older gent Ross had pointed out at the Javelin the previous night, the one with extra cars in his garage. He went on, "That young brute is going to lose a lot of clients if he can't keep his appointments better."

I asked the man to explain, and he said that Ross had arranged a meeting that morning, but had never showed up.

"He's usually very professional," said the man.

"I know," I replied.

Edsel interjected, "Domestic problems?"

"Not at all," I replied curtly.

But I knew something was amiss, so I left the bar and went downstairs to use the public phone, in relative privacy. I called Lieutenant Sanfuentes and reported Ross as missing.

"Missing how?" said Sanfuentes.

"I don't know where he is." I explained the situation with the older john upstairs in the bar, how Ross hadn't shown up for his appointment.

Sanfuentes listened patiently, then asked, "Has your, er, friend ever missed an appointment with you?"

"What are you getting at?"

"Just answer me," said the cop. "Has he ever not shown up when he said he would?"

"Well, yes."

"So this is not unusual behavior," said the cop. "Right?"

"Yes, but—"

"We can't consider a person missing just because he misses an appointment in one of the worst hurricanes in history."

"But, Lieutenant—"

"Stan, you want my advice? Forget about it. You're taking the attentions of a known male prostitute too seriously. You know what I'm saying here?"

"I disagree."

"That's your right," said the cop. "But I got more urgent matters on my mind, so we'll have to talk about this later."

Then he hung up on me.

I went back upstairs, where Edsel offered me a ride back to my guest house.

I said, "I thought you didn't drive."

"I don't," he said. "While you were downstairs the bartender called a cab. When it comes, you're welcome to ride with me."

"But I'm staying on the other side of town."

He said, "You're on my way. I'm heading over to the Pier House."

"The Pier House? Near the marina?"

"Yes," he said. "I've got some business there."

"Now?"

"Sure," he said. "You can't let a little rain rule your life."

Nancy L. Drew had expressed a similar notion at the police station earlier. Perhaps it was the standard island trope reserved for stormy weather.

Edsel reminded the bartender to put everything on his tab. He was oddly magnanimous that day. Maybe the presence of natural destructive elements had put him in a good mood. The cab that came for us was one of those big pink ones.

"Just like yours," I said.

He replied, "Mine will be a stretch version."

Once inside the cab I noticed that he was wearing deck shoes too. I asked him about it, and he said, "They're not just for boats, you know. Excellent traction." Then he advised me to get into some dry clothes. "It would be a shame," he said, "if you caught your death of cold."

"I'm hoping for a more dramatic end," I said.

"Maybe I'll write one for you," he said with a self-amused chuckle.

The cab pulled up to the Jared Bellamy House. By that time the evacuation traffic had almost disappeared. I suppose it had to stop sometime.

"Here you are," said Edsel. "Time for your bath." Then he looked out the cab window at the place. "It looks closed up."

"Never," I said.

I thanked him for the lift, then got out. The cab took off quickly, as if I'd launched it on a rampage, with its tires spinning and skidding on the watery road.

The only trouble was, the Jared Bellamy House really was locked up. The owners had evacuated. Now what? Here I'd been peddling around the island in some furious race against time, and for what? To be locked out of my guest house? I mean, what was I doing? Where was I going and *what* did I have to go on at the moment? There was the local hustler who didn't keep his appointments, the local singer who seemed to appear everywhere I was at any given moment, the piles of local property snatched from their rightful beneficiaries, a corporate lawyer with a custom-made wardrobe, but wearing deck shoes, a commercial hack on the precipice of Hollywood notice, also wearing deck shoes, the tor-rential rains—the water, the boat shoes, boats, a lawyer, quack-quack, Blue Water Tours. It was a desperate hunch, but what other kind of hunch was there for someone like me?

I found a pay phone and called Lieutenant Sanfuentes again, but another cop told me he was out of the station, on a "real" emer-gency. I left a message for him. "Urgent," I said, and told him I was going to the waterfront, that I suspected Ross's body was somewhere down there.

The sergeant replied that Lieutenant Sanfuentes had other pri-orities.

I told him I'd already heard that litany. "Just tell Sanfuentes where I'm going," I said, as if omitting his rank sounded tougher. "By the time you guys believe me, half the island will be massa-cred." Then I hung up.

Meanwhile the hurricane had grown fierce. The wind battered me with rain that felt like needles—no, *nails*—driven through my clothing. I was caught in a travesty of martyrdom as I stumbled my way on foot toward the waterfront.

27

The wind and rain were gusting violently, pushing me around, knocking me off balance. Only fools like me and maybe an overzealous meteorologist would be out in a raging hurricane.

The waterfront was deserted. Every craft was secured to its mooring, for whatever good it did. The smaller boats bounced around in the choppy water like toys in a bathtub, while the larger ones tugged their lines tautly enough to strum a tune on. A sign over the entrance to the longest pier read: BLUE WATER TOURS. At the far end was moored the largest of the tour boats. Another sign hung further down the pier It was heavy metal yet was being blown about like paper. It advertised a wondrous glass-bottomed vessel. In balmier weather I imagined hoards of vacationing Midwesterners, free at last from their landlocked status, cooing delightedly at the aquatic circus within the coral reef and the tropical waters.

But that dark and stormy afternoon, all the drama was above the water. The big glass-bottomed boat rocked and lurched precariously in the huge swells, its bow occasionally rising up out of the water at thirty degrees. My sensitive tummy reeled at the sight.

Then, at one particularly bad swell, through the howling wind and great crashes of water, I heard someone scream briefly, as though startled by the suddenness of a world turning topsy-turvy, or unexpectedly violent. It was a powerful throaty scream, strong enough to travel through the storm, even through the steel hull of the tour vessel. Someone was on that boat.

I made my way along the wharf, which swayed and twisted with every rise and fall of water, like an aquatic roller coaster. I stopped to gather my wits and my courage, and my balance too. What if I fell in, me who can't swim? I tried hanging on to the cord railing, but it was too slick with rain, and it moved contrary to the wharf, making me more unstable. So I let it go and stumbled toward the tour boat unassisted. It was a runway walk that would have tested the most champion drag queen, in flats, without a cocktail.

With the boat and the wharf heaving and lurching against each other, I caught only brief glimpses inside the main cabin. But I did see lights further down the boat's hull, so I moved closer toward those windows. There was a sturdy piling at that point too, so I had something relatively solid to hold on to. Still, with the endless counterpoint of yawing and pitching between the tour boat and the wharf, I saw only fragments of the drama within the boat's main cabin.

Nancy Drew and Edsel Shamb were inside. Both of them gripped a brass railing that surrounded the large glass viewing window mounted horizontally in the boat's hull. But they weren't admiring the watery world beneath the boat. They were facing their victim. They had bound Ross, my holiday hustler, down on top of the glass. He'd been stripped naked and secured to the viewing window with nylon mooring rope. It would have been a pretty sight looking up into the boat's hull from underwater, and seeing Ross's meaty backside pressed against the heavy plate glass. But topside, Ross's nakedness made no sense until I realized his two captors were torturing him. They had put some kind of small dark things all over his body, but with the motion of the boat and the wharf, I caught only glimpses. It was like watching forbidden vignettes through a peephole, Pasolini-like, where your imagination filled the unseen frames with horrors or, depending on your particular perversion, delights more extreme than any portrayed on the film. Except it wasn't a film, and Ross's torturers weren't acting. He must have realized that too, for in those fleeting moments when I saw his face, he seemed almost to be taunting them, smiling defiantly, as if he was in full control of the situation. Such bravado! Or was there a hint of pleasure too? Perhaps he realized his chances of surviving the episode were nil, for what did the other two care about one more killing? Yet even in his last moments of excruciating, delectable pain, Ross was trying to enjoy himself, a professional to the end.

How can you not love a guy like that?

There wasn't time to run and call for help. I had to get on that boat and save him. But the boat and the wharf were pitching wildly in opposite directions. One went up while the other went down. One tilted to the right, the other to the left. I hung on to the piling until I could determine the period of sway between the two water-borne objects. And the next time around, when the boat and the wharf were moving most closely in unison, I made my daring leap from land to sea. I sprang myself upward and forward—thank you, legs—and landed splat onto the deck of the boat with a heavy wet thud. I prayed that Edsel and Nancy hadn't heard me from down below.

There was no time to lose. I scrambled as quietly as I could along the heaving wet deck toward the hatch that led down into the main cabin. I slunk down the metal stairway, keeping in the darkness, dripping wet, hanging on to the railing for balance, while I listened to Nancy L. Drew and her cohort.

"That ought to keep him still," said Nancy.

"Did you have to hit him there?" said Edsel.

"Did you have to scream?" replied Nancy. "Someone might have heard you."

"Who's going to hear us out here? I thought the plan was to get him to talk, not beat him unconscious."

"Someone had to do something," said Nancy. "He wasn't co-operating, and you were just standing there ogling him. I still don't know why you wanted to strip him."

"I told you, it's research," said Edsel.

Attorney Nancy L. Drew snorted and said, "Let's just hope the hairdresser knows less than he pretends to."

I crept down another step and peeked into the cabin. In the center was the viewing glass. On top of the glass lay Ross's bound body, trussed up like a succulent holiday roast on a huge banquet table. His tan, taut skin was splattered with an amber viscous fluid, like motor oil. Were they about to set him on fire?

Edsel said, "How much longer do we wait for this mysterious person?"

"As long as it takes her to get here!" said the attorney.

"Why won't you tell me who she is? There are only so many women—"

"Because, Ed, you're not a partner. Until that Hollywood check clears, you don't own any shares. Technically you have no right to be here now, except I needed someone to help me kidnap this traitor."

"I gave you a goddamn cashier's check, Nancy. I have a right to know."

"You have no rights."

"*You* had no right to stop the work on the Gulf Coast Playhouse. The money I gave you more than covered that. And you promised once you were paid—"

"Giving the go-ahead on that part of the plan was premature," said the lawyer. "A mistake. I had to stop it."

"You'd better not cross me, Nancy."

To that, Attorney Nancy L. Drew laughed.

Meanwhile, from the stairway, I heard someone else boarding the boat. Was it friend or foe? Cop or mere mortal? Enemy or deus ex machina? It was none of the above.

"Boston!" yelled Cozy Dinette into the stairwell. "What are you doing here?"

I tried to shush her, but it was too late. Nancy Drew and Edsel Shamb were already hauling me out from the stairwell into the main cabin. Cozy followed us in there. Before anyone spoke, she saw Ross on the viewing table and exclaimed, "Rossina! Why are you here? Is this a gig or a gag?"

But Ross didn't answer.

"Her?" said Edsel, glancing between Nancy Drew and Cozy Dinette. "We've been waiting here for Cozy?"

Nancy Drew didn't answer him. Something had caught her off guard, and I couldn't tell if was my arrival or Cozy's.

Cozy said, "Why is Ross here, and tied up like that?"

Nancy Drew explained. "I had doubts about his allegiance, and I worried that he'd gone over to the other side. I had to find out. But I didn't anticipate his potent allure, enough to bring the tail-wagging little Bostonian around to rescue him."

"*Woof,*" I went.

"Rescue him?" said Cozy. "What for? What are you doing here? It looks like some kind of pagan ritual."

"That was my idea," said Edsel. "Research for my next book."

I said, "Still plagued with doubts about your masculinity?"

"Shut up!" said Nancy Drew. "Let's get down to business."

"What is the business?" I said.

Cozy said, "Nancy told me she found a way for me to get the Crow's Nest back."

"Don't hold your breath," I said.

Edsel said to Nancy, "If Cozy's in, I'm out."

"That's fine with me," said Nancy Drew. "Mindful Lotus never needed you anyway, you or anybody else." She sneered at the little group gathered around Ross's body on the viewing glass. "Look at the lot of you," she said. "I don't know how I ever expected things to go smoothly with a cast like this. We've got a hairdresser and a male whore. Then there's you, Cozy—a third-rate cabaret flop."

"Hey, what are you picking on me for?" said Cozy. "I just came here to get my property back."

"One stinking piece of Key West property," said Nancy Drew. "The Crow's Nest. And then you, Ed. I thought you might be smart, but all you are is a sniveling ineffectual little . . . writer!"

"Look who's talking," retorted Edsel. "You've done nothing but push papers around."

"Papers!" spat Nancy Drew. "You call them papers? Without those *documents*, you'll own nothing."

The big boat tilted upward in Nancy Drew's direction.

"You can't take all the credit," said Edsel.

"Of course I can," said Nancy Drew.

The boat lurched again, and Edsel shifted on his feet to keep his balance. Something crunched under his deck shoes. He cringed. Nancy Drew smiled.

"You're grasping, Ed. That's good. You realize you've lost to me."

"Never," he said.

"You're a loser," said Nancy Drew. "Everything you do is a failure. Even your idea for torturing Ross didn't work. Look at him. Covered with honey. Honey! And where are the instruments of torture? Palmetto bugs! Gone! Run away. And Ross *enjoyed* it, you fool! I'm the one who had to show him we were serious. I'm the one who hit him where he felt it. Not you, not Edsel the Loser." She cackled maniacally and chanted, "Edsel the Loser, Edsel the Loser."

Verily, verily, Attorney Nancy L. Drew was an abomination to her namesake.

Edsel defended himself with his last piece of armament. "I've got a best-seller out there. You can't top that."

"So what?" said Nancy Drew with a taunting laugh. "You still can't write."

"You're jealous," said Edsel, his authorial pride clearly wounded. "You're nobody."

"On the contrary," said his opponent. "I am Nancy Drew."

"Is that a gun?" said Cozy.

"I have empowered myself," said Nancy Drew.

Sure enough, Nancy Drew had a gun on us.

Edsel shook his head and muttered, "Ever since she read that damn book about women and wolves—"

Then, as if to challenge the attorney's declaration of complete and confident selfhood, the boat lurched up violently and knocked Nancy Drew off balance. She grappled desperately onto the rail, slipped again, and then her gun went off, followed instantly by another gunshot, and somehow Nancy Drew went down to the floor. Ross stirred slightly on the viewing window. Edsel's mouth and eyes were hanging open. Meanwhile, Cozy Dinette held a smoking gun in her hand.

"You've got one too!" I said.

"Of course I do, Boston. Haven't you figured out anything yet?"

Edsel stammered, "Wh-why did you d-do it?"

"She was going to kill you, Ed." Cozy looked at the weapon in her hand. "Jeez, my aim sure is off today. I only meant to graze her."

I saw that Edsel Shamb had peed his pants.

"Cozy?" I said anxiously. "Are you the killer?"

"Boston! What is your problem?"

Edsel began rambling to himself. "You killed Nancy," he said. "You killed her. Okay, so I didn't trust her, or any of that business with Mindful Lotus. She and Adolf made decisions without me. I knew that. I knew they were going to sell Peter's property to a European consortium, and I'd be left out in the cold. I was screwed. But I wouldn't have killed her. Why did you kill her?"

"How did they get the property?" I said.

"What?" he said.

"The property," I said. "How did Nancy and Adolf get it?"

"They paid off some judge to award it all to Augusta Willits. Then when she died, the property would go to the church, and from there to Mindful Lotus."

"But that could take years," I said.

He said, "They knew Augusta was terminally ill. The doctors gave her six months."

"Except Augusta conveniently got herself killed," I said, then turned to Cozy. "Thanks to you."

"Boston!" said Cozy. "Stop saying things like that. You don't understand. And don't look at me that way."

"How should I look at you, Cozy, with that gun in your hand and Nancy Drew dead on the floor?"

Then, through the wind and rain and choppy water, we heard heavy clomping on the deck overhead. The cloven-hooved tread was unmistakable.

"The countess," I said.

Cozy said, "It's about time you woke up."

The countess clomped her way down the metal stairs. She entered the cabin wearing a phosphorescent blue turban and wielding a gun. She held on to the hatchway as she gazed at Ross lying naked on the viewing glass.

"So many times," she said, "so many times I warned Peter about him. He was only good for trouble." She surveyed the cabin. "Where is the attorney?"

Edsel said, "Cozy shot her," and pointed to where Nancy L. Drew was lying on the cabin floor.

The countess said to Cozy, "Now I see I cannot trust you." She aimed her gun at Cozy.

Cozy was looking at the gun in her own hand, the one she'd just fired at Nancy Drew, as if she'd forgot how to use it.

Then the countess shot her, just like that. And Cozy went down. That's when I almost peed my pants.

Edsel said shakily, "You can't just kill us all."

"Why not?" said the countess. "I shall go to Australia, while my tour boats here will make me rich."

"You can't do anything without Nancy Drew's signature," said Edsel. "And now she's dead."

The big boat lurched up suddenly, and the countess let out a scream as she grabbed for the brass railing. She held it to regain her balance, but I noticed in the dim light that her skin had taken on a green pallor.

"What am I to do?" she said. "Is this the final solution, then, with nothing settled for me? The attorney promised me I would have my property. Who would think an accident would make so much trouble?" The countess shook her head dismally.

"What accident?" I said.

She explained, "I went to see Peter's mother that morning, trying to make sense to that stubborn woman."

232

"Augusta Willits?" I said.

The countess nodded. "But she would not listen. And she talked and talked about selfish foreigners who would not leave her son alone. Can you imagine? I have royal blood, yet she dared to call me a foreigner. Augusta would not keep quiet that morning, she went on and on, and she drove me insane. Insane, I tell you. I had to stop her from saying anything more. I was desperate. And so I picked up the only thing I could find in that office."

"The small clock," I said.

"Yes," she said. "I do not know what made me do it. I have never done such a thing before. I am certain that I was completely insane at that time. How else can anyone explain what I did?"

"You killed her."

"I did not intend to hurt her, only to stop her mouth. But I had pushed the small clock too far back and then held it there too long, and it stopped her breathing. Then everything was quiet. I had a feeling of great relief. And even to this very moment, with us all standing here, I believe the world is a better place without that woman."

Edsel said, "I never suspected you."

"That was my protection," she said. "No one would think I would kill anyone. I am too refined."

I said, "There are some who might disagree."

She glared at me. "Say whatever you want, foolish commoner. After today I will never have to hear your voice again." Then she continued her story. "I would have escaped if someone did not see me leaving the Crow's Nest after the accident."

"Adolf Dobermann," I said.

"Yes," said the countess.

"Did he see you do it?"

"No," she said. "But after he thought about it, he guessed that I was guilty. And he did not hesitate to blackmail me. He even dared to stoop so low as to extort merchandise from my shop."

The cad!

"How did you kill him?" I said.

"I knew Adolf would be interested to buy the Twin Palms, so I told him that Peter had entrusted a special paper to me—a codicil I believe you call it—which gave to me the right to sell the property."

Edsel looked hopeful. "There was a codicil?"

The boat lurched and the countess slumped a little lower. She also got a little greener.

"She's lying," I muttered.

"Do not use that word," said the countess. "It was the only way to settle the injustices brought onto me by Herr Dobermann. I told him a story, and he was so greedy he believed me. Then I waited for him at the Twin Palms. That man was soft, so weak, he was almost sickly."

"His wallet certainly wasn't," said Edsel.

"I deserved to take that from him," said the countess. "He had stolen so much from me."

I asked, "Did you trick Jeri Tiker into going to the Twin Palms to get her painting back?"

The countess shrugged. "Someone had to look guilty."

"And you took the painting back to her gallery."

"Yes," said the countess.

"And you used Ken's red Range Rover to do it all."

The countess replied woozily. "I told him I had to take Herr Dobermann's large shipment of merchandise to the post office, and he believed me, poor thing. Before I returned the car, I took it to be washed because of the mud. And Kenneth never imagined that I could do such things."

Talk about denial.

"What fools men are!" said the countess. She was limp and quite green by that time, and was grappling desperately onto the brass railing around the viewing glass. "Fools!" she said again, aiming the epithet at Edsel. "From the beginning Adolf was deceiving you and the lawyer. He stupidly boasted to me that he would acquire all of Peter's property directly from Augusta, but unfortunately the accident made that impossible. Still, Adolf had another plan, one more joke to play, his best one he said. You know that overseas company you were all planning to sell the property to?"

Edsel uttered the words like a holy chant: Das Neue Kapitalist Holidayische Resorten-Grabben Gesellschaft GmBh.

"Yes," said the countess. "That one. It belonged to Adolf." She laughed a cruel disarming laugh. "Americans will never understand the dark side of business."

It didn't sound so devilishly clever to me, buying the same property twice.

But despite the countess's fabulous peroration, she had one glaring performance flaw: She was utterly seasick. And during the woozy silence that followed her last words, I saw my chance to get away. I had to save myself, for without me alive who was going to save Ross?

I turned and tore up the metal stairway.

Behind me the countess shouted to Edsel, "After him!"

Up on deck it was like the raging storm in *Moby Dick*, all wind and rain and tidal waves. Well, maybe not tidal waves.

Edsel was soon up the stairs after me, and he somehow had got hold of a gun—Nancy Drew's or Cozy's, I guess—because he came out of the hatchway firing wildly.

I scrambled about for shelter on the listing deck. He fired again. I made a dash for cover behind a huge metal vent pipe, but the boat tilted up suddenly in front of me, knocking me off balance and off my feet. I grabbed onto the decking to keep myself from sliding off into the water. Edsel fired again, and that time he connected with my thigh. It hit like a knife on the end of a baseball bat. So much for the strongest part of my body. Was Fate trying to break my spirit? But it was no time to get picky about gunshot wounds. Better one to the densest, fleshiest part of me than a direct hit to the heart or brain.

Then I made a quick, perhaps stupid decision. Out there on the pitching deck, warm blood flowing into my cold wet pants, I decided to play dead while watching my pursuer through squinted eyes. It was risky, because Edsel might come and shoot me in the head, just to make sure. But with all the motion of the boat, he'd have to come close to do it, and with that advantage, I had a slim chance of survival. If he came within range of my legs, I'd kick him down with the good one—maybe—and get that gun away from him. I heard him stagger toward me as the boat heaved and lurched in the water. I half expected the coup de grâce to my head, but instead I heard the countess clomping unsteadily up the metal stairs leading onto the deck. Then she appeared in the hatchway.

"What happened?" she asked, holding tight to the stair rail.

Edsel stammered. "I . . . I . . . shot him. I think I killed him. I can't believe I killed someone. This is awful."

The countess yelled back, "Are you sure he is dead?"

"I . . . I think so," replied Edsel. "My God! What have I done?"

"Get a hold of yourself," said the countess. "You must shoot him again, in the head, just to make sure."

"No!" he said. "No, I can't. I don't want any more blood on my hands."

"Blood?" squawked the countess. "You worry about blood? What about all the minds you kill with your writing?"

While they argued over the delicate matter of my demise, I slithered ever so cautiously across the pitching deck, using the giant swells to help me slip little by little away from them.

"Since you're so smart," said Edsel, "you kill him."

"I cannot," she said. "There is too much motion, and I cannot stand by myself. Don't be so weak. Just shoot him!"

"No," Edsel replied. "I've done enough."

"Very well," said the countess. "Help me off the boat, then, and I will shoot him from the dock. He knows too much. He must be eliminated."

"And then what?" said Edsel. "Will you kill me too?"

"Why should I?"

"I know as much as he does."

Too bad you don't know when to shut up, Edsel.

Then the boat lurched up again, high, forty-five degrees, maybe more. My grip was tentative, and I felt my body slipping on the deck. I grabbed cautiously with my good leg, trying not to bring attention to myself. But I couldn't stop my body once it began moving, and finally I slid off the deck like an omelette from a frypan.

"Look, look!" cried the countess. "He got away!"

The water was warm, but it was deep and deadly turbulent. The salt stung my wound. I stifled a cry, for that would only provoke the countess or Edsel to shoot me in the water. I grappled onto the hull of the boat, searching for any patch of friction to keep my head above the water.

"You must shoot him!" cried the countess. "Quickly! Go! I cannot. You must do it now!"

"No," said Edsel. "You do it."

"*Akh!*" she said. "Weak, foolish men!" And despite the wind and the rain and the pounding waters, I actually heard the countess clomping up the last few stairs and coming out onto the deck. She yelled at Edsel. "Since you force me to shoot him, I must now apologize to you."

"No!" cried Edsel. "Not me! Don't! I don't want to kill again. *Please!*" he wailed. "Don't make me shoot! *Don't!*"

I heard the volley from up on deck, then silence. The rain and wind continued. Not even murderous humanity could change its course. I waited for whoever had survived the onslaught to lean out over the deck and finish me off too. But it never happened. Instead the boat lurched up again, higher than it had so far. It almost looked like the huge slick hull was going to tip and capsize onto me. Just as I felt myself being pushed under, I sensed two bodies plummet past me into the water.

The boat righted itself, and I saw the two of them, Edsel and the countess, floating a little distance away from me, bobbing almost calmly in the raging water. They stayed like that a few moments, then sank slowly. The countess made a particularly lovely picture, with her phosphorescent blue turban slowly unwinding as she sank into the turbulent depths.

That crisis past, I realized I could work my way around the tour boat's hull, to the wharf, where I could embrace one of the sturdy pilings rather than struggle to stay afloat with a tenuous hold on the boat's slippery hull. By the time I slid my way around the boat, the Coast Guard and the cops arrived. They cleared the cabin of bodies at the same time they rescued me, sloshing around in the dark heaving water. I told them that the countess and Edsel had slid off the deck into the water.

They laid me on a gurney next to Ross's, just as they wheeled Attorney Nancy L. Drew's body away. I guess the world just wasn't big enough for two Nancy Drews. But I was glad they'd covered Ross up, out of modesty if not protection from the elements. Who would have guessed a professional stripper was shy to be naked in public in front of me?

Then who should come and place a cool hand on my forehead but Cozy Dinette?

"Help!" I called out. With everything I knew now she'd certainly kill me. "Help!" I screamed.

"*Shhhhhhh!*" went Cozy. "Calm down. I'm a good guy."

"You are?"

"Didn't you know?"

"But you were dead."

Cozy's grin luminesced in the whirling storm around us. She leaned close to my ear and murmured, "Bulletproof bustier."

"Bulletproof!"

"Jeez, Boston, pipe down. Are you trying to blow my cover?"

"You're a cop?"

"I guess you're not as smart as I thought," she said, "or else it's still the best-kept secret on the Keys."

"No wonder you were always around."

"Someone had to look out for you, Boston."

"Next thing you'll be telling me Ross is a cop too."

"I'll let you find out for yourself."

28

Lieutenant Sanfuentes came to see me in the emergency room at the local hospital. My wound was easily patched up. He told me he had a bit of bad news though.

"Not Ross?" I said.

"No," he replied. "He's fine, but your guest house closed up on account of the hurricane. Unless you want to stay here in the hospital, you're going to need a place to sleep tonight. If you want, you can camp out at the station, in one of the cells."

"What about Ross?" I said.

"What about him?" said Sanfuentes, now brusque.

"Can he stay with me?"

Sanfuentes wavered. "I'm not running a brothel."

"He works for you, doesn't he?"

The cop hesitated, then said quietly, "You wanna do me a favor, Stan, you'll forgot all about that. We got a small town here, and it's really hard to keep my good help under cover."

There were those words again—*good help*. Branco had said it about me, and Sanfuentes was saying it about Ross. Two straight cops and two gay helpers. A pretty good ratio.

I asked him, "Did the others know Ross was working for you? Is that why they captured him and tortured him?"

"They might have suspected," said Sanfuentes, "but my guess is they wanted to find out how much *you* knew."

"Then why didn't they just come after me?"

"Maybe they would have, but it turned out they didn't have to." He smirked. "They had irresistible bait."

He finally agreed to let Ross and me stay at the station together, on the condition there wasn't any hanky-panky. Hanky-panky? Hell, after what we'd been through I just wanted to have tantric sex with the guy.

Sanfuentes then excused himself to pay a solemn call on Attorney Nancy L. Drew, elsewhere in the hospital.

"The morgue?" I said.

"Not at all," replied the cop. "She only played dead, just like you."

Imagine that? Nancy Drew and I had used the same survival tactic.

Sanfuentes said, "Good thing she's alive. She promised to defend Laura Hope for killing her husband."

"Laura killed Josh?"

"Yeah," said the cop. "I owe you an apology on that one."

"What about Edsel and the countess?"

"Too bad about them," he said. "We got a crew out there trying to recover the bodies." Then he put his paw of a hand on my shoulder and said, "You better rest up for later."

By "later" I guess the lieutenant meant that night in a jail cell with Ross. I told Ross I knew he worked for Sanfuentes, but he denied it. Then I asked him again if all the affection between us was just another part of his job. Ross, a professional to the end, protested, "But darlin', I love ya'!" Too bad it sounded like a stock line. Still, it was the first time I didn't give him money for sex.

Next day life was back to normal, or as normal as it could be in Key West, off-season, after a major hurricane. Electric power and cellular phone service had been restored, and I miraculously did not catch a cold for all the time I'd spent in wet clothes the previous day. What more could anyone want?

Nancy L. Drew confessed her creation of Mindful Lotus, a "property systems development corporation" solely for the sale and distribution of Peter Willits's estate. "All perfectly legal," she claimed. And apparently it was, being just the simple transfer of massive property holdings from Peter Willits to his mother to her church to a corporation named Mindful Lotus, every step precipitated by Nancy Drew and her vast legal network. Still, her estimable reputation was a bit tarnished when the courts decided to reverse their original decision to award Peter Willits's estate to his mother. All the original legatees in Peter's will finally got what they rightly deserved, even the dead ones. I wondered who would receive the late Countess Rulalenska's central air-conditioning system.

For her part, the Countess Rulalenska had had no involvement with Mindful Lotus. All she'd wanted was her tour boats. She had no interest in the complexities of modern corporate practice, favoring instead the simpler methods of old-world entrepreneurs like the Borgias and the Macbeths. And through Lieutenant Sanfuentes's indirect line to FBI files, I learned the countess's regal origins: Before coming to Key West she'd been a garment maker in Australia, where her family had found exile after being banished from their native Transylvania. Transylvania, Louisiana, that is. The countess had invented every aspect of her life, including her limp accent. And she hadn't even gone to acting school.

Laura Hope confessed to killing Joshua Aytem. She had followed him to that desolate area near the power plant where he wrecked my Alfa. After his destructive spree, Joshua had passed out in the pink car. Laura had begun to help him, but then found Edsel's gun in the glove compartment. So she took advantage of the opportunity to liberate herself from a bad marriage. Her attorney, the great Nancy L. Drew, entered a plea of insanity, based on the evidence that only a crazy person would undergo a sex change. In a backhanded victory for transsexuals everywhere, the insanity plea was rejected.

The late Edsel Shamb had intended to convert the Gulf Coast Playhouse to a Hollywood sound stage for his future sitcoms and feature-length films. He'd used his contract money to start construction, and he'd got the building permit from the same judge who'd rigged Augusta's contest, all thanks to a conditional clause inserted especially for Edsel in the incorporation documents for Mindful Lotus by Nancy L. Drew, for an extravagant fee, of course. "All perfectly legal," she said again. But in a will made just after Peter Willits had promised the playhouse jointly to Edsel and Ken, Edsel had generously bequeathed his share of the playhouse to Ken, and Ken did the same for him. And though Edsel's vision had become distorted and megalomanic by his imminent Hollywood success and by the secret organization founded by Nancy L. Drew, he never changed his will. And so, with Peter Willits's estate back to its original distribution, Ken Kimble now owned the playhouse outright.

In a public statement Ken Kimble "witnessed and owned" his naïve trust for the Countess Anastasia Rulalenska and Edsel Shamb. Moments after healing, he began the less naïve process of filing a huge lawsuit against Mindful Lotus and its CEO for damages to the Gulf Coast Playhouse and to the coral shelf under Key West, all in the name of historical preservation and the sanctity of Gaia. With the settlement money he intended to rebuild the theater with state-of-the-art equipment. He did not engage Nancy L. Drew as his attorney because he was taking her to the cleaners.

Alas, Miss Drew, all perfectly legal.

Jeri Tiker, fed up with painting geckos, parrots, and tropical fish, sold her inherited property and moved to New York, which is where an artist of her talent and temperament belonged anyway. To thank me for helping prove her innocence, she gave me *Dinner of Uncertainty*. She did make one change to the work: She finally resolved that the unidentified person was Nancy L. Drew, as seen from behind. But Jeri painted her own face there instead, as a kind of self-portrait just for me. I also bought two other works that tickled my fancy.

And finally, I offered to finance Ross's dream to rehabilitate the Twin Palms into an upscale male brothel, but he flatly refused. "I don't want your money, darlin'," he said. "I make plenty myself, between the Tulle Box and my other work."

"But you have no security," I argued.

"Who does?" said Ross.

I tried another tack. "Hustling is dangerous."

Ross grinned. "But darlin', I like danger." Then he put his arm around my shoulder and told me it was no use, that we could never be partners.

"What's wrong?" I said. "I'm not dangerous enough?"

"It's not that," he replied. "Sex with you, sex with someone I really like, is the best. But I just don't want to settle down with one fella. You understand, don't you, darlin'?"

After mulling it awhile, I had to confess that I really didn't want to settle down either. It was probably the most honest moment in my entire sexual life.

So I rented a big boring sedan and drove back to Boston alone. I wasn't sure what to do about the wrecked Alfa. I could have replaced it with the insurance settlement from Joshua's attack on it. But that car had sentimental value. The answer came when I stopped overnight at Dania Beach, just north of Fort Lauderdale. There I met an expatriate Alfa Romeo mechanic who was eager and willing to bring the roadster back to life. He'd worked for Mario Andretti, and he assured me that the Alfa would be better than new after his divine ministerings.

"Like handmade," he said.

He'd even arrange its proper transport from Key West to Dania, and from there up to Boston.

What else was I going to do with the money?

I never did read Edsel Shamb's book. By the time I left Key West I still hadn't got past page ten. I guess I needed something more escapist, with lots of sex and money.

Maybe I'd write it myself.